VIVIE'S SECRET

TERRY LEE CARUTHERS

D1301721

Black Rose Writing | Texas

ISBN: 978-1-68433-527-5
PUBLISHED BY BLACK ROSE WRITING
www.blackrosewriting.com

Printed in the United States of America
Suggested Retail Price (SRP) $18.95

Vivie's Secret is printed in Calluna

*As a planet-friendly publisher, Black Rose Writing does its best to eliminate unnecessary waste to reduce paper usage and energy costs, while never compromising the reading experience. As a result, the final word count vs. page count may not meet common expectations.

DEDICATION

Vivie's Secret is dedicated to all those devoted rescuers and colony caretakers who give so tirelessly of their time, money, and effort to protect those felines living abandoned, strayed, and feral in our society as well as to the veterinary professionals who assist them in their work. This includes people like Kara Disbrow and Teresa Norwood as well as the veterinarians mentioned within this work: Dr. Robert 'Bob' Black, Dr. Benny Ferrell and Dr. Bill Martin of Central Veterinary Hospital and their caring staff during my own 'feral-cat years' (1996-2007) and those of Vivie's (c. 1993-2004). Thank you for all you do.

VIVIE'S SECRET

PROLOGUE

"Come quick. She's asking for you." I hung up the phone and grabbed my keys.

Cursing each red light and traffic delay, I rushed to the hospital—my breath coming in short, rapid gasps. "C'mon. C'mon," I muttered in the elevator as if words could speed the lumbering machine's ascent.

When it reached the eighth floor, I bolted out the door and almost knocked down two women waiting to board. "Sorry. Excuse me," I tossed over my shoulder while I raced down the hall, dodging slow-moving staff with their equipment, food trolleys, and carts.

I stopped outside the door of 864 East and stood there a moment, catching my breath before reaching over and pumping the wall dispenser. The sanitizer pooled in my palm. Its sharp scent of alcohol flared my nostrils as I rubbed the cool gel over my hands.

The mechanical, tinny notes of "She'll Be Coming 'Round the Mountain" filled the air. I glanced up. A code light flashed down the hall. Uh-oh! 860's 'escaped.' Over the last few weeks, the bed alarms that notified the nurses' station of patients ignoring safety protocols had become a source of humor on bleak days. It was almost like a maniacal form of 'Musical Chairs.'

"Excuse me." A nurse slipped from Vivie's room, pushing a small cart. As she removed the light-blue paper smock and peeled the rubber gloves from her hands, our eyes met. She gave a subtle shake of her head. I nodded.

Steeling myself, I stepped into the austere room. For a moment I stood there looking down at my friend. There she lay, this shell of a once vivacious woman, slowly withering away like an unwatered cut flower.

Outside the door, "She'll Be Coming 'Round the Mountain" sounded again. Piercing blue eyes stared back into mine. "Someone's 'escaped,'" she whispered. A slight smile curved her lips.

"Second one since I got here."

Vivie shook her head. A cough racked her slender form.

"Sip of water?"

She nodded.

I leaned over and held the straw to her lips. She sipped, taking less than a baby bird.

"You came."

My eyes stung with tears. I could not let her see me cry. I well knew her feelings about that! Only cry in the bathtub, so tears flow down the drain. Blinking them back, I reached out, squeezed her hand, and managed a smile. "Did you have any doubt, Vivie?"

Another chorus of "She'll Be Coming 'Round the Mountain" drifted down the hall.

Vivie's eyes locked with mine. "There's something I need you to do." Her faint whisper was filled with urgency. "Something very important."

CHAPTER 1

Knoxville, Tennessee, June 24, 2004, 4:00 p.m.

Vivie was dead. She died earlier today, but before she passed she tasked me with a favor. That's why I was here.

I jiggled the key in the stubborn lock. My persistence was rewarded with the dull metallic clack of the bolt's release. Easing the door open, I slipped inside and closed it behind me. In the dusky room, my hand fumbled against the wall. Soft fur rubbed against my ankles as my fingers located the elusive switch and light flooded the room. Cats lounged on the furniture and milled about the bare hardwood floor, their upturned faces mouthing silent meows.

I stood for a moment, taking stock of the home—a residence I had visited briefly once before. The clutter wasn't that of a hoarder's house. It was that of a home well-lived in by someone with a passion for learning, for music, for art—and cats.

Under the picture window, a floral-patterned brocade sofa sat against the wall. Coordinating throw pillows and a tabby-cat-imaged blanket covered its cushions. Across the back of the sofa lounged a three-legged Abyssian mix, gazing out the window. Her tail twitched back and forth in agitation. A pair of forest green damask armchairs flanked the windows. In one, a battle-scarred tuxedoed tom dozed. In the other, a one-eyed Persian yawned. Her pink tongue darted out to lick away the imperceptible dust mote that must have landed on her smoky gray coat. Stacks of magazines perched precariously on both maple end tables and covered the matching coffee table's surface.

Floor-to-ceiling fiberboard bookcases lined the other walls. Packed to overflowing, their shelves bowed under the weight of the heavy tomes. A quick scan of their contents revealed a variety of subjects—computer programming, mathematics, French, religion, travel, music, art, the classics, and cats.

Faint music played in the adjacent room. Peering inside, the soft glow of a radio dial stared back. When I turned on the light, three furry bodies scurried out the far door. An old stereo sat on the cherry credenza, its station tuned to National Public Radio. Strains of Vivaldi's *Four Seasons* flowed from its speakers. Classical music albums and CDs surrounded the stereo, obscuring the credenza's surface. Above it hung a reproduction of Everett Shinn's *Alley Cat.*

In the center of the room sat a 1950s formica-topped chrome dinette set, the seats and backs of the chairs covered in red vinyl. Three of them, and all but a one-foot-square space of its tabletop, were heaped with books and papers. A three-tier, wrought iron stand sat against the wall near a sliding glass door. Its assortment of potted plants lay shriveled and dead from the three weeks of neglect.

As I headed toward the far door and into the kitchen, several of the cats found their voices. They wended about my ankles and clamored to be fed. I laughed for the first time that day, actually the first time in weeks. "Oh, you rascals! I know full well that Chel was here earlier, and you have been fed! Don't pretend that you're starving."

I walked over to the large plastic bin. Unscrewing its lid, I reached down and pulled out several packets of kitty treats, then headed downstairs to the ferals' room. About ten cages lined the open space. Inside each one resided a cat in the process of socialization training. When I eased a long-handled brush inside of each cage, I was greeted with the occasional hiss or growl and once a paw swipe. As the bristles stroked their coats, a couple emitted deep, throaty purrs. After each interaction, I deposited the reward of a handful of dried kibble in their food bowls, then watched them cautiously slink forward and begin to eat.

Back upstairs, I distributed treats to the free-roaming cats. Tears pricked my eyes as I watched them gobble the kibble bits. Did they know? Did they have any idea—any clue—of the upheaval that was about to take place?

Shaking off the momentary melancholia, I headed toward the bedroom. Faded pink cabbage rose wallpaper lined the short hallway. On the right was a 1940s era blue-and-white tiled bathroom. Two spindle chrome legs supported the front of the wall-mounted basin. Above, a small medicine cabinet protruded from the wall. A diagonal crack marred the lower left corner of its mirror. From behind the bathtub's floral shower curtain came the steady drip, drip, drip of a worn faucet. A blue-and-white striped towel lay draped across the frayed wicker hamper.

With a deep sigh, I made my way into the darkened bedroom and turned on the light. The now familiar sight of more books and magazines greeted me. A single bed sat against the wall. Soft depressions marked the sage-colored, tufted chenille bedspread, evidence of the cats' preferred sleeping spots. Above the bed hung an oval gold-filigree framed print of Robert Ferruzzi's *Madonna of the Streets*. An ornate hand-carved mahogany dressing table with an oval mirror and a sage green cushioned stool occupied one corner of the room, its surface heaped with t-shirts and faded blue jeans. A worn pair of tennis shoes lay in the middle of the floor.

In the other corner stood an equally ornate mahogany armoire. I threaded my way over to it, reaching up and caressing its satiny surface. While gorgeous, both the dressing table and the armoire seemed out of place in this house whose furnishings trended toward items purchased at second-hand shops, bargain basements, or garage sales.

I took a deep breath, knowing it was time to do what I had been tasked with. Squatting down beside the armoire, my butt grazed a stack of magazines. The pile tipped and cascaded across the floor with a soft 'shush' like skis slicing through fresh snow. As I reached to pick them up, a cobby-bodied black cat with a pink collar butted against me. "Carmen!" I scooped her up and buried my face in her silky fur. Tears spilled down my cheeks and made soft divots in her ebony coat. She turned and nipped my chin, bringing me back to reality.

Setting Carmen and my grief aside, I wiped my tears and snotty nose on my sleeve. As the small cat jumped up on Vivie's bed and began to knead, I maneuvered my way past the magazines until I could reach behind the armoire. My fingers stretched and groped about the tight space. The package had to be here. She said it was. I was about to give up when the tips of my fingers grazed a strand of knotted twine. If I could just grasp it, I could pull it out. There! No. "Damn!" I could not get a grip.

I massaged the cramp in my shoulder, then got up and looked around the house. There had to be something I could use to maneuver the package from behind the armoire. While I rummaged about, several of the cats followed, reminding me of the Pied Piper. "No. No more treats tonight," I responded to their persistent meows.

In the corner of the kitchen, I found a broom. As I reached for it, the cats scattered. No doubt they had been subjected to the wrath of other brooms during their existence on the streets. Just the thought sickened me, but I couldn't dwell on that now.

Back in the bedroom, Carmen's large yellow eyes observed me from Vivie's pillow. Turning the broom upside down, I maneuvered its handle behind the armoire and eased the tip down to the floor. As I slowly drew it forward, the handle met with resistance.

Gradually, I bumped and bumped the object until a butcher-paper-wrapped corner was visible. Extracting the broom, I stooped and pulled the dust-covered, cobweb-laden packet out into the light.

Grabbing one of Vivie's t-shirts, I wiped the tattered package clean, then carried it over to the bed and sat down. When I flipped the packet over to untie the twine, a spiral notebook slipped out. As Carmen purred her way into my lap, I opened its cover and began to read.

CHAPTER 2

Budapest, Hungary, November 4, 1956, 5:18 a.m.

Another rumble rattled the house. Csaky stood at the window. Her vivid cornflower-blue eyes searched the dark sky. "All this thunder, but no lightning and not a drop of rain." She took a sip of coffee.

Her husband looked up from the newspaper. "It's not thunder."

"You mean—"

"Attention! Attention!" An announcer interrupted the Free Radio Kossuth broadcast. Seconds later the grim voice of the President of the Council of Ministers of the Hungarian People's Republic filled the room. "At daybreak Soviet forces started an attack against Budapest with the intent to overthrow the legal Hungarian democratic Government." Imre Nagy continued, "Our troops are fighting. The Government is in its place. I notify the people of our country and the entire world of this fact."

As the radio resumed its regular programming, a look of concern passed between Csaky and Lofo. She placed a hand on her husband's arm. "What does this mean? Are we in danger?"

Lofo covered her hand with his. "I don't know, my sweet. We'll have to wait and see what develops." He reached up and caressed her cheek. "While I make some calls, why don't you make preparations in case we need to depart."

She nodded and left the room.

Two and a half hours later, Lofo gazed out the window toward Pest. Smoke enveloped the suburb while thunderous booms continued to reverberate in the distance. He closed his eyes and let the radio's soft music transport him back to happier times.

Csaky poked her head into the room. "I can't find the blue carryall. Did you by chance move it from the back closet?"

Before he could reply, the regular broadcast was interrupted again. "This is the Association of Hungarian Writers speaking to all writers, scientists, all writers' associations, academies, and scientific unions of the world."

They turned and stared at the radio as the disembodied voice continued. "We turn to the leaders of intellectual life in all countries. Our time is limited. You know all the facts. There is no need to expand on them. Help Hungary! Help the Hungarian writers, scientists, workers, peasants, and intelligentsia. Help! Help! Help!"

Lofo ran a hand through his hair and sighed. He looked over at his wife. "Tell the children we must make ready to leave. I'll gather our documents."

Less than thirty minutes later, chaos reigned in the household. While the family prepared to depart, the radio blared into the empty room, "S.O.S.! S.O.S.! S.O.S.!"

In the study, the twelve-year-old girl ignored the frenzied activity. She brushed back her curly auburn hair and turned the page of her book. Norsk lay curled in her lap. Soft, throaty purrs rumbled from the black Norwegian Forest cat. The slender girl undraped her gangly legs from the arm of the over-sized, chintz-covered chair and tucked them up under her. Norsk resettled in her lap and continued to purr.

"Vivie!"

She startled at her father's shout.

"What are you doing? Your mother told you to pack a bag. Now, hurry! We must leave here shortly."

"But, Poppa—"

"Now, Vivie! Your mother is helping Mae."

She sighed and placed a marker in her book, then scooped up her cat. "Okay. I'll get Norsk's carrier."

"No, Vivie. The cat stays behind."

Her eyes narrowed as Norsk rubbed against her chin. "But, Poppa—"

"No, Vivie! Norsk stays. Put her down and get your bag."

Tears pricked her eyes. "But, Poppa, Norsk won't—"

"Now, Vivie!" Lofo grasped her arm. "No more arguments. We don't have time for—"

Cracks of gunfire sounded from the street. Norsk's claws sank into Vivie's flesh as she launched herself across the room and fled. The young girl cried out more from fear than from the long, deep, crimson scratches the cat left on her forearms.

As the blood began to well, Lofo yanked Vivie from the room. They careened down the hallway toward the foyer, the girl's heart jackhammering in her chest.

Lofo shouted, "Csaky! Mae!"

"Here we are, darling." His wife descended the staircase wearing a slate gray turtleneck sweater with black wool slacks. Two carryalls were draped over her arm. "C'mon, Mae," she urged.

The eight-year-old lagged behind her mother with a doll tucked under her arm. At the next burst of gunfire, she squealed and bolted down the steps.

"Let's go!" Lofo insisted. As they shrugged into their coats, he snatched up his leather satchel. "Everybody out through the back. Hurry!"

"Vivie! Get the shopping net," Csaky called out.

She grabbed the mesh food bag and followed.

At the rear door, her father stopped and cautiously peered out. Nothing stirred in the dormant fall garden. "Quiet now."

As they slipped through the backyard and past the garage, Mae asked, "Poppa? Why aren't we taking the car?"

"Hush, Mae," her mother responded. "No questions."

Easing out the rear gate, they crossed into the vacant back lot and made their way over to the adjacent street. Vivie glanced up and down it. Not a car was in sight. Even the sidewalks were deserted. Stately homes sat back from the narrow tree-lined road, their windows empty like the eyes of that American comic strip character Orphan Annie.

At the rat-a-tat-tat-tat-tat of machine gun fire, Vivie jumped and stifled a scream. Mae shrieked and clapped her hands over her ears. Csaky grabbed the girls and yanked them to the ground.

Lofo frowned at the staccato fire. "It's okay," he said. "The shots are coming from the direction of Gellert Hill. They seem to be firing toward Pest. Let's move on. Quickly now."

As they approached the intersection, a distant monotonous hum filled the air. Lofo held up his hand and motioned for them to stop. They faded into the trees and waited. Over the next few minutes, the sound increased to a low steady roar. Then up ahead, a convoy of smoke-belching Soviet tanks, army trucks, and armored infantry carriers appeared, thundering down the boulevard toward Pest.

"More tanks, Poppa?" Vivie shouted over the din.

"Yes," he replied.

"But...why?"

"The Soviets intend to quell the students' rebellion before it becomes a state-wide revolt. Remember? We talked about this."

She nodded, recalling the October demonstrations: the destruction of the Stalin statue on Dozsa-Gyorgy Street, the student demands, the riots, the killings, her parents' whispered concerns that the Russians might link Lofo's political science courses to the student uprising. Now, here they were fleeing. If the Russians found him, it could mean death—for them all. Vivie shuddered.

As the last tank roared past, Lofo turned. "I think we'll be safer avoiding the main roads."

Csaky nodded and pulled Mae closer.

For the next hour, they surreptitiously navigated the Buda suburb—keeping to side streets, creeping through backyards, scaling garden walls, hiding in shrubbery—while the Soviet convoys continued to rumble into the city. Explosions and artillery fire echoed across the Danube River.

As the choking acrid smoke drifted across the water and infiltrated the Buda suburb, Mae whined, "My eyes itch, and my throat hurts."

"I know, dear," her mother comforted. "Ours sting and ache, too. Try not to think about it."

Two streets later, they crossed behind a house with a large ornate fountain in the back garden. Trees and lilac bushes lined the perimeter walls. Lofo motioned them into the dense hedges at the back of the property. He reached into his satchel and pulled out a piece of paper, tore off the lower portion so it formed a square, and then folded it diagonally.

Vivie frowned.

"What are you doing, Poppa?" Mae whispered.

"Wait and see." After a few more folds, Lofo held up his creation.

"Oh! A paper cup. Look, Mama! Vivie! Poppa made a cup from a piece of paper."

Csaky's eyes twinkled. "Shh! Yes, he did."

Vivie smiled.

"Now, wait here," her father instructed. Keeping low, he crossed over to the fountain and filled the makeshift cup. Hastening back into the shrubbery, he held it out to Mae. "Have a sip and then pass it to Vivie and your mother."

"Thank you, Poppa."

As Vivie rubbed her eyes and waited, Lofo returned to the fountain.

"Here, Vivie," he said a moment later.

She looked up at the damp handkerchief in his hand. "Thank you." Vivie took it and pressed it against her eyes. Once the burning sensation eased, she passed the cloth on to Mae.

As Lofo returned from his third trip, car doors slammed in the distance. Voices murmured. A dog barked. "I guess we need to move on," he whispered.

Vivie looked out and gasped.

CHAPTER 3

Vivie grabbed her father's arm and pointed.

A Soviet officer wearing a gray greatcoat with gold epaulettes strolled out the back door. His hand rested on the Tokarev pistol that hung from his Sam Browne duty belt. Standing on the portico, he lit a large cigar and blew the smoke up into the air.

An East European Shepherd darted past him and out into the yard. The black-and-tan dog trotted over to the fir tree and lifted his leg. After relieving himself, his rear paws raked across the short grass. He bounded over to the fountain and noisily lapped up the water. The canine then lowered his head and began to nose about the ground.

Lofo's hand closed over Mae's mouth. "Quiet. Not a sound. Understand?" he whispered, looking directly at her.

The child nodded.

Csaky gathered up the carryalls and satchel, then flattened herself against the garden wall. "C'mon, Vivie," she murmured.

Vivie remained crouched down, observing the large shepherd. His nose continued to cast back and forth across the grass. Then he stopped and raised his head, his medium-sized, pricked ears pivoting forward.

A second later, raised voices sounded from inside the house. The Russian soldier lowered his cigar and turned toward the partially open door.

As her family eased toward the back gate, Vivie slowly rose and followed. Her hands nervously twisted the handles of the shopping net while she eyed the shepherd.

He pulled back his upper lip and tasted the air. With a low 'ruff,' the dog put his nose to the ground, tracking their scent trails.

Vivie's breath quickened. She glanced over at her father struggling with the gate's rusted cab latch. "Hurry, Poppa, hurry," Vivie whispered to herself, her heart racing.

The shepherd neared the hedge, his rapid sniffs filling Vivie's ears. She looked down for something—anything—she could use to distract him. An idea began to form. Vivie glanced back at her parents, then at the approaching dog. She would have to work fast.

A moment later, the canine's loud bark split the air. As the gate swung open, Vivie rushed to follow her parents.

"Vivie! Where's Vivie?"

The panicked tone in her mother's hoarse whisper spurred her forward. "Here I am." She darted out and closed the gate behind her. Vivie drew back at the kaleidoscope of emotions that raced across her father's face—fear, relief, anger.

He grabbed her by the arm and snapped, "C'mon." She winced and stumbled along beside him. His grasp eased as he reached over and snatched Mae from her mother's arms. "Let's go!" Lofo urged. Csaky followed.

For twenty minutes they fled through overgrown fields and woods, distancing themselves from the house and its occupants—not daring to look back. Vivie's ears strained for the telltale bark of pursuit, but only the crunch of grass and dead leaves met her ears.

When they finally stopped to catch their breath, Mae complained, "Mama? I'm hungry."

Vivie's stomach rumbled in agreement. She should have finished breakfast instead of sneaking into Poppa's study to read.

Csaky glanced down at her watch. "Lofo? It's well past lunch time. Can't we stop for a moment and let the girls have a snack?"

He turned and looked back across the field where a clamour of rooks circled on the wind drafts and swooped downward, taking advantage of the displaced prey. Tall weeds gently swayed in the light breeze. From a distance came the faint thud of weapons' fire. "Not here." Lofo shook his head. "But soon. I'd like to put a little more distance between us and them."

She nodded.

Fifteen minutes later, Lofo pointed. "Let's head for those bushes over there. They should offer us some cover."

The four crowded into the brush and sat down. "Vivie, please hand me the shopping net." Csaky rummaged through it, a confused look filling her face. "That's odd. I could have sworn I packed a slab of paprika bacon."

Vivie hung her head. "You did," she said softly.

Lofo's eyes narrowed.

"Well, where is it?" her mother asked.

She drew in a deep breath, then slowly exhaled. "I gave it to the dog."

"You did *what?*" her father exclaimed.

"The dog!" Mae shook her head and rolled her eyes. "That's crazy."

"Mae! Enough," her mother scolded. "Hush and eat your cheese. Vivie? Explain."

She frowned at her sister and continued. "Well...I thought if the dog had something to eat, it wouldn't come after us...and it'd give us time to get away."

Csaky and Lofo's eyes met. Her mother's lilting laughter broke the tension. "Oh, you clever, clever girl!" She reached over and hugged Vivie, her shoulder-length hair brushing against the girl's cheek.

The light fragrance of Chanel No. 5 filled Vivie's nostrils. She inhaled deeply and sighed. Mama's hair. Her scent. For a split second, Vivie was transported back in time. It was evening. She nestled in her mother's lap, enveloped in the bouquet of her perfume. Mama's auburn tresses gleamed in the firelight and tickled Vivie's cheek as she reached to turn the pages of the storybook.

"You *know* she gets that from my side of the family."

Her father's remark returned her to the present.

Csaky raised an eyebrow. "You wish!"

Lofo shook his head and laughed as she tossed him an apple.

Vivie smiled. Her parents' teasing lightened the mood.

"All kidding aside, Vivie," her father said. "I'm proud of you. That was smart thinking."

A warmth washed over her at his praise. "Thank you, Poppa."

"One thing is for sure, we won't have to worry about him tracking us any time soon!"

"Why's that, Poppa?" Mae asked.

"Because that spiced bacon will make him one sick dog!"

After their break, they resumed their trek. A kilometer later, Vivie squinted into the late afternoon sun and pointed. "Look, Poppa!"

Up ahead, men, women, and children of all ages plodded along the roadway like zombies. Some carried small suitcases, others satchels. Many were burdened with multiple layers of clothing. Blanket-filled bundles hung from their shoulders. Men pushed bicycles and wheelbarrows loaded with belongings. Women pushed strollers and prams. Children tagged along behind their parents. The older ones tended to the young, holding hands or walking with arms flung across the shoulders of siblings, cousins, and friends. The seemingly endless procession of misery stretched as far as the eye could see. Like Vivie's family, all appeared to be fleeing Budapest. At Lofo's urging, they moved forward and fell in step with them.

A short time later, Mae whined, "Aren't we there yet?"

"Not yet." Csaky shifted the carryalls and draped her arm across her young daughter's shoulders.

"But we've been walking *forever*, and I'm tired."

Csaky sighed. Drawing Mae near, she gave her a quick one-armed hug. "Not forever, dear. Don't exaggerate."

Vivie half listened as her mother attempted to placate the eight-year-old. Her blue eyes roamed the bucolic countryside. Trees stood, row upon row, in distant orchards—their limbs bare of fruit and leaves. Haystacks and cattle dotted the fields and pastures. Everything appeared so peaceful and serene. A stark contrast to the chaotic bombardment from the military advancing on the city.

She studied the people walking amongst them. Children wore a frightened, guarded countenance—a haunted look in their eyes at the uncertainty of what lay ahead. Adults grimaced, their faces etched with frowns and worry-creased foreheads. Some bore solemn expressions with tear-stained cheeks, their eyes wide with fear. Others sported pinched mouths and thinned lips, eyes narrowed in determination. They were a largely silent crowd—no bantering, no laughter. Only muffled movements, grunts, and sighs. The occasional cry of an infant. Despite their varied backgrounds, they shared a singular purpose—fleeing the oppressive Soviet regime that gripped their homeland.

As Lofo squatted to talk to Mae, the hum of a motor vehicle drifted forward, accompanied by the honk of its horn. Vivie glanced back as the crowd parted, allowing a white van to pass. When it drew near, the vehicle jerked to a stop, and the window rolled down. A tawny-haired head emerged. "Dr. Degirdro!"

Vivie froze. *The Russians! They've found us!*

CHAPTER 4

Vivie trembled, not daring to breathe, as her father rose and walked over to the van. She glanced at her mother and whispered, "Who's that?"

"I've no idea."

Her heart raced as she strained to hear the hushed conversation, but discerned nothing. Then a moment later, Poppa turned and motioned them near. Vivie's eyes narrowed at his smile.

"Csaky?" Lofo said as they approached. "This is Andrew Covington, and that's Martin Smith." He pointed to a dark-haired fellow in the passenger seat. "They're foreign correspondents with the *Manchester Guardian*. I met them a few weeks ago at the university." Following introductions, Lofo continued, "Good news! They're going to give us a ride to the border."

"Yippee!" Mae jumped up and down at the news, tossing her doll into the air.

A sense of relief washed over Vivie as Martin rose and slid open the van's panel door. Climbing inside, they settled in amongst the photographic equipment. Vivie sank down on the makeshift seat, relaxing in the van's warmth. Her eyes scanned the vehicle's cluttered interior. As their breath fogged the windows, Andrew set the defroster on high, then eased the van through the crowd.

Seconds later, Martin made his way to the back and opened a small trunk. He reached inside and withdrew two cameras, handing one to Lofo and the other to Csaky. "Hang these around your neck," the man instructed.

Mae clapped her hands. "I want one, too!"

"Hush, Mae. What's this for?" Csaky asked.

"Subterfuge." Martin continued to rummage about the back of the van. "In the event we should be stopped at a checkpoint, we'll tell the guards you're our photographers."

"Checkpoints?" Lofo scowled. "Then the Soviets are prepared to stop any refugees?"

"Not that *we've* encountered," Andrew responded. "At least not yet. Of course, it's probably because we avoid the main roads as much as possible...to circumvent *that* type of delay." Momentarily taking his eyes from the roadway, he turned his head toward them, wiggled his eyebrows, and grinned.

"If that's the case, then why this?" Csaky held up the camera.

"Look out!" Vivie cried as an old man lurched into the path of the van.

Andrew jerked around and slammed on the brakes, narrowly missing the elderly gentleman. As the van's contents shifted forward, Martin fought to maintain his balance. Vivie and her family were thrown to the floorboard where boxes rained down upon them.

With a sheepish expression, Andrew turned. "Sorry about that. Is everyone okay?"

Before anyone else could respond, Mae stood up with her hands on her hips. "Someone needs to learn how to drive!"

Vivie's mouth gaped open.

"Mae!" a reddened Csaky scolded. "Mind your manners! Apologize right now, young lady!"

She hung her head and mumbled, "I'm sorry."

"That's okay," Andrew said. "I shouldn't have taken my eyes off the road, especially in these crowded conditions." He turned back around and cautiously guided the van along the roadway. As Lofo and Martin restacked the boxes and cartons, Vivie helped with the smaller items while her mother had a stern talk with Mae.

"Csaky," Martin said with things back in place. "In answer to your earlier question, regarding the cameras? We've just learned to always be prepared." He opened another cardboard box and searched through it. "Aha!" Martin held up a small plastic bag and pulled two badges from it. He handed one to Csaky and the other to Lofo. "Clip these on."

As her father held his up, Vivie read, 'PRESS' in bold lettering.

"But what about the children?" Csaky asked.

"Hmm. There is that." Martin studied the van's interior as they rocked and bumped along the roadway. A gleam appeared in his eyes. "Mae? Do you like to play hide and seek?"

Vivie's sister clapped her hands. "I *love* to play hide and seek!" she shrilled.

"Come over here and see if you can fit inside this."

As Mae clambered over the equipment and into a trunk, Csaky's eyes widened with alarm. "Lofo—"

He placed his hand on her arm. "It's okay, my sweet."

Once Mae was curled up inside, Martin closed the lid. "Perfect!" He then opened the trunk and lifted her out. "Now, listen," Martin instructed. "If we come across a checkpoint, I'll say 'hide.' You need to hop into the trunk, close the lid, and be quiet until your mother tells you to come out. Understand?"

Mae nodded. "I'm *really* good at hiding. Aren't I, Mama?"

"Yes, dear. You are." Csaky smiled.

"Now," Martin turned toward Vivie. "We must find something to do about you." He moved about the side of the van, pulling and pushing at the crates and boxes until he had created a narrow space between them. "There! Should we approach a checkpoint, you slide right in here," Martin pointed. "Then, Lofo will shove these boxes across the end, and they'll never know you're behind them. Understand?"

"Yes, sir."

"Good girl." He patted her on the shoulder, then returned to his seat.

Vivie glanced back at the contrived 'hideaway,' wondering if she would have to use it. A shiver crept up her spine at the thought. With a subtle shake of her head, she pushed the idea away, then faced forward and concentrated on the roadway.

"Andrew?" Lofo asked as they cleared the crowd and picked up speed. "With all that's going on in Budapest, why are you leaving?"

"Our assignment editor cabled. We're being pulled and sent to Egypt to cover the Suez Canal developments."

"Oh, yes. I read something about that," Csaky said.

Andrew nodded. "We were supposed to have left yesterday, but...things didn't go as planned."

"Much to our good fortune," Lofo responded. "We certainly appreciate this."

"Glad to help out."

Vivie looked over at Mae, asleep in her mother's lap—her doll tucked up under her arm. As the conversation continued, she tuned it out. Vivie's throat tightened as her thoughts turned to Norsk. A tear trickled down her cheek. With a jagged sigh, she quickly brushed it away.

Her mother held out a tissue. "It's going to be all right, Vivie," she whispered, squeezing her arm. "Everything's going to be fine. You'll see."

Not without Norsk, she thought, staring out the front window. Several minutes later, Vivie's eyes grew as heavy as her heart. Lulled by the hum of conversation and the warmth and motion of the van, she nodded off.

· · · · ·

As the vehicle slowed, Vivie's eyes opened. She stretched and yawned, looking about. A frown etched Poppa's face, Mama was biting her lips, and Andrew and Martin leaned forward in their seats. Conversation had ceased. The four now stared intently out the front window.

Vivie followed their gaze. Up ahead, a small contingent of Russian soldiers with machine guns blocked the roadway. A tank and a couple of jeeps sat nearby. Her stomach gave a sickening lurch.

"What do you think?" Martin half whispered, as the van crept forward.

"I think we're screwed," Andrew responded. "We didn't factor machine guns and tanks into this equation."

Csaky made the sign of the cross and began to pray.

Lofo shook Mae awake. "It's time to play hide and seek."

She rubbed her eyes and mumbled, "Where's Dodo?"

"Dodo?" Martin turned.

"Her doll," Csaky responded. "Here she is, Mae. Now get into the trunk and be quiet as a mouse."

"Okay, Mama," she yawned.

As Csaky guided Mae into the trunk and closed the lid, Vivie laid down and scooted into her hiding place. Lofo then shoved a stack of boxes across the opening. A minute later, the van came to a stop.

"Permits!" a Russian voice barked out.

The soft rustle of documents filled the van as Andrew and Martin handed over their press credentials and passports. Through a small space between the boxes, Vivie peered out at her parents huddled behind a carton in the dim interior, the cameras dangling from their necks.

A moment later the voice ordered, "Exit the van. We must search inside."

Vivie's eyes widened, her blood pounding in her ears as her father pulled her mother near.

The van shifted as Andrew and Martin obeyed the directive.

At the Russian's muffled command of "Open the door," Vivie bit her lip, fighting back tears. When the panel door slid open, she blinked and squinted in the sliver of sunlight that now spilled into the interior. Vivie craned her neck, silently gasping, "I can see out!"

A loud voice summoned, "Borsky! Come!"

The Russian soldier placed a hand on Martin's shoulder. "You wait," he ordered, then waddled out of Vivie's sight.

From her peephole, trees, grass, and a couple of soldiers with machine guns were visible. She gently pushed against the boxes, trying to enlarge the small gap.

"Vivie! Stop that," her father hissed.

A second later, Andrew shifted position, blocking her view. "Irgum-burgum!" she muttered in frustration, her mouth tightening.

In the distance, voices sharpened—increasing in volume and intensity, talking over one another. Vivie strained to hear the debate, catching only snippets of it. The Borsky fellow seemed to want their van seized! The correspondents arrested! As he argued his point, Vivie's heart fluttered like a trapped dove's. With a trembling hand, she clutched at the rosary beads in her pocket and began to pray.

As the debate continued, time slogged by. Vivie held her clenched fist tightly against her lips, an urge to scream raging inside her.

"You can go now."

Vivie's head snapped up at the shouted words, her breath whooshing out. A wave of dizziness left her limp as a wet dish rag.

"Whew! That was close." Andrew climbed into the van.

"A little too close," Martin responded, closing the panel door. "Let's get the hell out of here."

As the engine roared to life and the van shifted into gear, sobs of relief wracked Vivie's young frame. They were safe...at least for now.

CHAPTER 5

Thirty minutes later, the setting sun silhouetted a giant oak tree by the roadside. Two large elongated objects hung from its massive naked limbs. Drawing near, Andrew stopped the van and got out. Martin and Lofo followed. Vivie leaned forward as the three men approached the tree. The flashes of Andrew's camera lit the dim surroundings, highlighting two blackened and burned corpses dangling by their feet.

"Mama!" Vivie gasped.

"What? What?" Mae tried to peer around her.

Csaky pulled the child back and turned her head away from the window. "Mae, take Dodo and go to the back of the van."

"I *never* get to see anything!" she pouted.

As Mae complained, Martin turned and heaved his stomach's contents out into the weedy grass, then wiped his mouth on his coat sleeve. He straightened, pulled out a small notebook and pen, and began to write. Lofo stood a short distance away, his head bowed and his hands in his pockets.

"Vivie?"

"Ma'am?"

"You need to get away from the window, too. Go back and sit with Mae."

"Yes, Mama."

As Vivie passed her mother, Csaky crossed herself and bowed her head.

Mae looked up from braiding her doll's hair. "Vivie? Tell me a story."

"Okay. I'll tell you 'The Enchanted Cat.'"

"Vivie?"

"Yes, Mama?"

"I don't think that's an appropriate story at this moment. Please tell something else."

"Yes, ma'am." She turned to her sister. "How about 'That's Not True?'"

Mae clapped her hands. "Yes! It's one of my favorites."

"Once upon a time, there was a princess…" As she related the familiar tale, Vivie kept glancing toward the front of the van, wondering what was taking so long. She looked over at her mother.

Csaky sat hunched over and continued to pray.

Mae laughed and clapped her hands when Vivie reached the part about the pig.

"'That's not true!' yelled the king—" She hesitated as the three men climbed back into the van.

"Finish it!" Mae demanded.

"Oh, you know the rest."

"Finish it!"

"All right," Vivie sighed. "So, the king allowed the peasant to marry his daughter, the princess, and they lived happily ever after. The end."

"Yea!"

"Now, you tell the story to Dodo."

As Mae began to repeat the tale, Vivie eased closer to the front of the van and eavesdropped on the whispered conversation.

"Who were those poor, unfortunate souls?" Csaky asked. "Refugees?"

"No," Lofo responded. "AVH officers. Hungarian secret police."

Vivie gulped.

"Are you sure?"

Lofo nodded. "Both had portraits of Stalin impaled in their chests."

"Impaled?" Csaky gasped and crossed herself.

Vivie shuddered.

A grim silence filled the van as they drove on.

Nearing a village, Andrew glanced down at the fuel gauge. "We should get some petrol while we're here."

"Good luck with that!" Martin pointed as they approached a row of scorched tanks and artillery pieces, surrounded by discarded jerrycans.

Inside the village, freedom fighters wandered the streets and stood in small groups. Confiscated Soviet machine guns and rifles hung from their shoulders or were casually cradled in their arms. A few carried mutilated Hungarian flags, the Soviet star removed. They seemed to glare with suspicion at the passing van.

Vivie leaned forward. On the corner stood a young girl, not much older than herself. Her shoulder-length brunette curls were topped by a black fur beret. The strap of a machine gun hung from the shoulder of her blue quilted coat. She grasped the weapon in her hands, appearing very brave—almost brazen in her defiance. A sullen expression marked her young face. Vivie's gaze remained fixated on the young girl as they passed.

Andrew steered the van over to the curb and parked in front of a small tavern. "I need to cable our editor that we're headed to Győr. On the way back, I'll check inside there"—he nodded toward the pub—"to see if the ladies can have a quick bathroom break before we head on." He looked over at Martin. "You try and find some petrol while Lofo guards the van."

"Will do." The man gave a mock salute, then rose and moved to the back of the vehicle. He hurriedly dug through several of the boxes, his brow furrowed in concentration. Then a grin split his face. "Yes!" He pulled out two bottles of brandy and exited the van.

Csaky gasped. "Did you see that? Are they going off to celebrate?" She turned and gripped her husband's arm. "Lofo, how well do you know these men? Could they be turning us over to the AVH?"

Vivie tensed, holding her breath as she awaited her father's response.

"No, my sweet." Lofo patted Csaky's hand. "Andrew and Martin are good men. You saw how they reacted at the checkpoint. They'll not betray us." He nodded toward the street. "And from what we've seen, I gather the AVH officers have fled. Most likely Martin's using the brandy for barter."

With a soft sigh, Vivie slumped back against her makeshift seat.

When Andrew returned, he ushered Csaky, Mae, and Vivie into the tavern. As they entered, Mae scrunched up her nose and whispered, "Mama, it stinks in here."

"Mind your manners, Mae," she whispered back.

Vivie sneezed as the harsh, vile odor of Hungarian cigarettes assaulted her nostrils. She rubbed her eyes and gazed out across the dimly lit room. Small wooden tables and straight-backed chairs filled the low-ceilinged space. The bar's wood-paneled walls were lined with the mounted heads of a variety of antlered animals. Their vacant, glassy eyes stared out at the room's boisterous occupants.

Several swarthy, robust men sat at the bar. Submachine guns hung from their shoulders, and cigarettes dangled from their lips. They toasted their recent victory over the AVH and hoisted their drinks.

Broken glass crunched underfoot, and the sharp scent of booze wafted upwards as Vivie followed her mother and sister through the bar and down the narrow hall. Ahead lay two wooden doors lettered in faded white script. The one marked 'Stallions' was decorated with a rearing horse. A mare with a long-flowing mane adorned the door marked 'Fillies.'

Csaky pushed it open and paused. She closed her eyes and shuddered. Mae stood with her fingers pinched over her nose. Vivie glanced past them. Water puddled on the floor from a blocked toilet. Despite the partially open window, a stench of stale urine permeated the air. Csaky shook her head, a look of disdain crossing her face as she muttered, "This will *not* do." She turned. "Mae? Vivie? Stand perfectly still. Do *not* touch a thing. Understand?"

"Yes, ma'am," they chorused.

Their mother headed back down the narrow hallway.

Vivie's head tilted at the faint scrambling coming from behind the door marked 'Stallions.' Warmth flooded her face at the deep grunt that followed.

Mae looked up at her, her brow furrowed. "What's that, Vivie?" she whispered, grasping her sister's hand.

"I don't—" She hesitated when a man appeared in the hallway and weaved toward them. Mae pressed against her as they stepped aside.

"S'cuse, me," he mumbled, stumbling past. With the nose of his machine gun, he pushed open the men's room door. As it swung shut, the small hallway was awash with the stench of urine and feces.

"Phew!" Mae clasped a hand over her nose.

Before Vivie could respond, a shout rang out from inside, followed by sounds of a scuffle. She and Mae screamed and ducked as a spray of machine gun fire peppered the air and ripped through the doorway just above their heads. With her pulse racing and the tiny hairs on the back of her neck erect, Vivie snatched Mae by the arm and fled back down the hall. Her sister's shrieks rang in her ears as they fought their way through the phalanx of men charging toward the gunfire.

"Mama! Mama!" Mae wailed as Vivie bobbed and weaved, maneuvering them forward.

A second later, someone grabbed Vivie in a vise-like grip and yanked her aside. She struggled to lash out with her free hand, only to find herself looking up at her father. As Vivie collapsed in relief, Lofo shoved her and Mae into Csaky's shaking arms.

Vivie gaped up at her mother's ashen face. In it was the reflection of her own fear. "Oh, Mama," she sobbed, her voice cracking.

She tried to slow her breathing as her mother's trembling hands quickly roamed her limbs—seeming to take inventory to assure herself that Vivie was not injured. After doing the same with Mae, Csaky crossed herself in prayer. Vivie bowed her head and prayed, too, thankful that she and Mae were safe.

"Let's go," Lofo said a minute later.

She glanced up at her father just as Andrew stepped out from the hallway.

"It's over," he reassured them. "Seems an AVH officer had crawled through the window of the men's room, then had holed up in one of the stalls. One of the rebels surprised him."

Vivie's heart skipped, realizing that was the grunt Mae had questioned earlier. Her stomach turned at the thought of danger so near.

"So, we're safe?" Csaky managed to stammer out.

"For now," Andrew nodded. "But just to be sure, let's get the—" His eyes drifted to the girls. "Heck out of here," he corrected.

Outside, the five of them rushed past Martin. He carried a jerrycan of fuel in one hand and a white sack in the other. "Hey, I got us some sandwiches."

Andrew turned back and grabbed the bag from him. "Hustle up and get that petrol in the tank. I want to get out of here."

"What's the rush?"

"Don't ask," he said, shoving the sack of sandwiches into Vivie's shaking hands.

CHAPTER 6

At dusk, the van's headlights illuminated the broad, straight avenues of Győr. A gray sooty pall hung in the air. Burned-out trams and trucks littered the roadway like a child's discarded toys. While almost two weeks had passed since the rebels had clashed with the AVH's armed forces in the city, quicklime outlines still marked the streets like crime tape where the dead had fallen and lain. The shops were shuttered—whether from the October massacre or the fall of night they were unsure. A hush fell over the van's occupants.

Up ahead a lone man stood, his cigarette a pinpoint glow in the murky night. Andrew stopped the van. "Wait here." He opened the door and got out. In the beam of the headlights, he made his way over to the stranger.

"Are we there yet?" Mae's question appeared to cut the tension.

Her father chuckled. "No, Mae. Not yet."

"It'll be a few more hours until we get to the border," Martin said.

The child sighed, "Did you hear that, Dodo?" She sat back and talked quietly to her doll.

Vivie half listened as Martin and her parents discussed their upcoming border crossing. She observed Andrew and the stranger who was now pointing down the street. The correspondent nodded, then headed off.

Several minutes passed before Andrew reappeared, a paper grasped in his hand.

"Where'd you go off to?" Martin asked.

"The telegraph office. I'm afraid I've got some bad news."

Martin frowned. "What is it?"

"Seems we're headed back to Budapest."

Vivie gasped.

Andrew continued. "Sorry, Lofo, but it looks like this is as far as we can carry you."

"That's understandable, Andrew." He nodded. "We appreciate that you've gotten us this far. It would have taken us over a week to cover this distance on foot." Lofo turned to his family. "Gather your things and say your goodbyes."

"Uh, Lofo?"

"Yes, Andrew?"

"May I speak with you outside the van for a moment?"

"Sure."

What's that about? Vivie wondered, as she shouldered the shopping net.

A moment later her father returned. In the van's overhead light, she noted the grim set of his jaw. He pulled Csaky aside and whispered in her ear. She paled.

Martin rose and shook Lofo's hand. "Good luck, my friend! May God be with you."

"Thank you for your kindness," Csaky said.

"Our pleasure." He handed her the paper sack. "Here, take the rest of the sandwiches."

She rested her hand on his outstretched arm. "How thoughtful."

"Mae?" Lofo squatted down beside her. "We're going to play a little game. Okay?"

"Okay, Poppa." She nodded her head of curly, brown hair.

He reached into his pocket and withdrew his handkerchief. "Now, Mae, I'm going to tie this around your eyes."

Vivie's brow furrowed.

"Like a blindfold, Poppa? Like when we play blind man's bluff?"

"Yes. Like when we play blind man's bluff. Only this time there's no peeking. Do you understand?"

She sighed. "Yes, Poppa."

"I mean it, Mae. Absolutely no peeking...at all. This is very serious. Okay?"

"Yes, Poppa."

Lofo tied his handkerchief over Mae's eyes. Then, for good measure, he looped his wool scarf about her head.

"Hey!" she squeaked. "No fair!"

"Yes, fair, Mae. Trust me."

Lofo picked her up, then nodded for Andrew to open the van's panel door. He turned to Vivie. "Remember this...keep your eyes focused in the center of our backs. Don't look anywhere else. I don't want you to see what's out there. Understand?"

"Yes, Poppa."

"And no talking."

Vivie and her family slipped out into the empty street. Overhead, the slender crescent moon dipped in the night sky. They tiptoed across the cobblestones, their shoes crunching in the broken glass, shell casings, and bits of rubble. The air hung heavy with a stench of death and charred bodies—mixed with diesel fumes, brick dust, and cordite.

"Something stinks!" Mae whispered.

"Hush," Lofo commanded.

Forced into silence, sleep soon claimed her as they navigated through the darkened city. The night was quiet, except for the echo of their footsteps. To Vivie, each crunch resounded like the crash of cymbals. She cringed with every step, her heart pounding with fear that the noise would alert the Russians to their presence.

Despite the late hour, a few beams of light escaped the confines of the occasional window shade or drape and lit small patches of the vacant streets. As Vivie trudged behind her family, her foot landed on a rubbery-like object. Catching herself, she looked back at the cobblestones. Her eyes widened in horror. Choking back a scream, Vivie managed to cover her mouth and not cry out. A shriveled, dismembered hand lay on the ground—teeming with maggots, its blood blackened.

A wave of nausea washed over her. Vivie's stomach churned. She gagged, vomit gathering at the back of her throat. A moment later the contents of her stomach splattered out onto the ancient cobblestones and mixed with the charred assortment of identity cards, photographs, books, and papers that littered the street—remnants of the recent uprising.

Csaky pulled Vivie's hair back from her face as she continued to heave. "Too much excitement, today."

Vivie took a tissue from her mother, wiping her eyes and mouth.

"Are you okay?" Mama peered at her with concern.

She nodded, unable to respond, the acidic taste of vomit stinging the back of her throat. Vivie gulped and tried to swallow it away.

Lofo shifted Mae's head on his shoulder. She let out a soft sigh. "Let's move on now," he urged. "I want to be well away from here by daybreak."

Csaky reached over and brushed at Vivie's unruly curls. "Feeling better?"

She managed another nod and thought, *Not really.*

Her mother smiled and gave her a quick hug, then turned to Lofo. "I think we're ready. Aren't we, Vivie?"

"Yes, Mama," she squeaked out. As they moved on, her mind continued to dwell on the nightmarish image. Shadows drifted across her parents' backs. Occasionally, one resembled the outline of that horrid severed hand.

Vivie could not stand it. Poppa had said to keep her eyes on their backs. He did not want her to see what was out there. A lot of good *that* did! She shuddered.

Her peripheral vision caught a movement to her right. Vivie glanced over and watched the slender rat dash ahead and dart around a corner. When they passed, she strained to see down the darkened alleyway.

Disobeying her father's instructions, Vivie's eyes now roamed Győr's shadowy streets. They resembled the World War II pictures in her history book. Piles of rubble were all that remained of some structures. Many of the streets were damaged, their large cobblestone blocks pried loose. The pale moonlight illuminated 'RUSZKIK HAZA!' daubed in garish lettering on bullet-riddled building walls and broken shop front windows. "Russians Out!" she read. In some areas, hand-lettered pieces of cardboard and small bunches of withered flowers memorialized the dead, bringing tears to Vivie's eyes.

Farther on, a flattened black object lay on the cobblestones. As she drew near, realization hit. It was a black cat. The imprint of tank treads marred the long-haired feline's corpse. Vivie sucked in her breath as panic gripped her heart. Norsk! For a split second, she could not breathe. Tears flooded her eyes as she choked back a sob.

Then Vivie sighted the dead cat's blood-stained, dirty-white ruff. She heaved a deep sigh of relief. Not Norsk.

How ridiculous, Vivie thought, shaking her head. Her beloved cat was in Budapest, not here in Győr. But...what about her? Would Norsk experience a similar fate? Vivie averted her eyes and shuddered, then hastened to catch up with her family.

CHAPTER 7

Vivie stumbled but managed to remain upright. Her leaden legs grew weightier with every step. She clenched her jaw, silencing her groans at the dull ache in her back and hips. Despite a few brief breaks, they had walked all night, leaving Győr five kilometers behind. She inhaled deeply, seeking to rid her lungs of the stench of death and destruction. Vivie wished she could free herself of the horrific images just as easily.

Lofo carried an exhausted Mae. Her head lightly flopped up and down on his shoulder. As Dodo slipped from her grasp and fell to the ground, Csaky stepped forward and picked up the treasured doll.

A second later, a drop of moisture struck Vivie's cheek, then another. She shook her head. *Great! Now, I get to be wet as well as tired!*

Up ahead, her father stopped. He looked to the right and then the left as though surveying their surroundings.

What was there to see? Vivie stared at the ubiquitous countryside. More orchards, more cattle, more pastures. If she did not know better, she would have thought they were still outside of Budapest!

Her father veered off into the field. "Follow me." Ten minutes later, he stopped and handed Mae to Csaky. Then Lofo walked up to a hayrick, squatted down, and began to dig. After several minutes, he stood up and dusted his hands. "There. We'll rest here for a bit."

Vivie peered around him, her eyes widening. Lofo had carved out a small cavern-like space in the side of the haystack. He took Mae from Csaky and tucked her inside, then turned. "Vivie?" She crawled into the hollow space. Her mother followed.

Instead of joining them, Lofo began to cover over the opening.

"Aren't you coming inside?" Csaky asked.

"I will, my sweet," he responded. "But first, I want to look around."

"Be careful."

"Always."

Vivie nestled down into the hay. As she warmed, her eyes gradually drifted shut.

•   •   •   •   •

The murmur of voices awakened Vivie. She yawned and stretched.

"Good afternoon, sleepyhead." Her mother smiled. "Are you hungry?"

"Yes, Mama." As her stomach rumbled, Vivie took the wizened apple and studied it.

"I know it's not much," Lofo apologized, "but it's all I—"

"But, Poppa, did you forget?" Mae held up the shopping net and grinned. "We've got food in here!"

"I know, Mae," he answered, "but we need to ration that until we get to Austria. We don't know how long it will be until we cross the border."

"Or how long it will take us to find food once we're there," Csaky added.

Vivie bit into the tough peel. She chewed and swallowed the dry mealy flesh. The tartness set her teeth on edge but eased the bite of hunger in her belly.

Mae looked at her apple and squinched up her face. "It's too ugly to eat."

"Ugly or not," Lofo responded. "If you're hungry enough, you'll eat almost anything and be thankful for it."

Mae sighed. She took a bite of the apple and grimaced, then leaned over and spat it out. "Yuck! Tastes nasty." Mae shrugged and looked at Dodo. "Guess I'm not hungry enough," she told the doll.

After finishing her apple, Vivie peered out into the gray wet afternoon.

"When the rain lets up, we'll be on our way," Lofo said.

Thirty minutes later, Vivie and her family headed out. As they traversed the damp roadway, the landscape's pastures and orchards transitioned into stands of dense forest. Chestnut, beech, oak, and birch trees filled the expanse. Vivie's eyes scanned the woodlands. Squirrels skittered and scurried across the naked branches. A few birds flitted and twittered in the trees. Overhead, a white-tailed eagle soared, alert for unsuspecting prey.

Mae busied herself collecting stray acorn caps and carrying on a conversation with her doll.

Vivie paused, her breath quickening. "Hush, Mae. I hear something."

Lofo turned. "What is it, Vivie?"

"I'm not sure, Poppa."

Csaky frowned. "I hear it, too." She reached down and clasped Mae's hand.

The back of Vivie's neck prickled as she turned, straining to see down the roadway.

As the faint droning hum drew near, she and her family instinctively moved to the edge of the forest, ready to seek refuge.

Then a crow of laughter burst from Lofo. "Listen closely," he urged.

Voices lifted in a sing-song chant approached, their muffled words now clear:

> *By all the gods of Hungary*
> *We hereby swear,*
> *That we the yoke of slavery*
> *No more shall wear.*

Vivie turned to her father. "Sandor Petöfi's poem."

"Correct." He grinned. "And what's its significance?"

"Honestly, Lofo?" Csaky rolled her eyes. "A history lesson? Now?"

He leaned over and brushed a kiss across her cheek. "Every situation provides a learning experience, my sweet."

She shook her head and sighed, extracting a piece of hay from Mae's curls.

"Vivie?" Lofo looked at her. ". . . the significance?"

"It was supposed to have inspired the 1848 Revolution."

"Fine thing," Csaky muttered. "Teaching our children subversive material that..." She glanced down at Mae.

"That what?" the little girl inquired, Dodo cradled in her arms.

"Never you mind, little miss." Csaky leaned over and kissed the top of her head.

The new group of refugees called out greetings upon their approach. Several recognized Lofo, having attended his classes at the university.

Vivie studied them. They were so different from the downtrodden refugees outside of Budapest. A joyous excitement gleamed in their eyes, and a sense of purpose enlivened their step. Laughter and banter filled the air. They were boastful, almost prideful about rejecting the Russians' communist fraud in favor of freedom. Many spoke of their dreams and the bright future that lay ahead. They appeared so hopeful.

Her worries seemed to wane amidst the camaraderie and gaiety of the young refugees. Their enthusiasm invigorated Vivie's tired steps. With the celebratory atmosphere, the remainder of the afternoon passed quickly into twilight and the group moved into the forest to make camp for the night. Fires were lit, and food was shared.

While nibbling on a hunk of bread, Vivie glanced about the encampment. In the flickering firelight, Mae played tea party with Dodo. Her collection of acorn caps served as tea cups, holding minuscule drops of water from the nearby stream. Mama sat alone in the shadows, a pensive look on her face. By the fireside, Poppa talked with a few of his students. There was a tension in his face—a wariness that was not present earlier in the day.

"Mae? Vivie?" her mother summoned. "Time for bed." She had fashioned them a pallet from their rain slickers, padded with leaves. "Sweet dreams, my loves." Csaky kissed their foreheads and tucked Lofo's heavy coat around them.

As Mae snuggled near, her warm breath caressed Vivie's cheek, reminding her of Norsk. At bedtime, the cat had always nestled against her neck. The feline's rumbling purrs soothed Vivie and helped her drift off to sleep, unlike Mae's light snores. *Where are you tonight, Norsk?* Vivie wondered, her throat tightening. A tear strayed across her cheek. She sniffed and stared up at the twinkling stars. Wispy clouds wafted across the sliver of moon. An owl hooted in the distance.

Once the camp settled and the night sounds stilled, the soft murmur of Lofo's fireside conversation drifted over Vivie. Her eyes narrowed at the strain in her father's voice. Something had changed in the last couple of hours. But what? While puzzling this, her eyes grew heavy and she drifted off to sleep.

Sometime later, a soft rustling interrupted Vivie's slumber. She opened her eyes. Shadows wavered in the dying firelight. A short distance away sat the huddled silhouettes of her parents. Vivie glared at Mae, her sister's snores making it difficult to hear their whispered exchange.

"This is too dangerous," Poppa said.

"Lofo—" Mama's voice dropped.

Vivie held her breath, trying to hear, but her response was unintelligible.

"You'd think they'd have some common sense," her father replied.

"You forget the recklessness that comes with youth, Lofo—"

"Irgum-burgum!" Vivie softly growled as Mae's snort drowned out the rest of their mother's response.

"It's more than that," Poppa continued. "It's almost suicidal. Campfires in this terrain at night? It's like a beacon to the communists, telegraphing: 'Here we are! Come get us!'"

Vivie stiffened and softly gasped.

"Lofo," Mama's voice softened as Mae shifted, her snores ceasing. "Nothing can be done at the moment. Please, my darling, just try and get some rest."

"I can't, my sweet. I don't want to chance being caught off guard."

So, *that* was Poppa's concern! The Russians finding them. Memories of Győr flooded her thoughts—the death, the destruction, the severed hand. Now determined to watch too, she lay still, straining to hear over the camp movements. Vivie squinted out into the darkness. Sleep beckoned, but she valiantly fought off the drowsiness—shaking her head, blinking and widening her eyes. But eventually, despite Vivie's efforts, the warmth radiating off of her sister and the day's exhaustion won out. Her soft snores soon joined those of Mae's.

The next morning, Vivie awakened as the camp began to stir. She stretched and groaned at the ache of her muscles and the weighty pressure in her head. It was as though an elephant had tromped all over her and was now sitting on her face. But Vivie did not complain. She just slipped off into the woods to find a secluded spot to pee.

After a light breakfast, Vivie and her family set out again with the small caravan. The day passed much as the afternoon before. When the refugees began to move into the woods at sunset, her family continued on down the road.

"Hey! Dr. Degirdro!" one of Lofo's students shouted. "Where're you going?"

"We have relatives nearby," he responded. "We're going to bed down with them for the night. Probably stay a couple of days...to give the children a rest."

Relatives? Vivie thought, as a few more students gathered around.

Farewells and best wishes were exchanged, then the Degirdros were on their way. A kilometer later, Vivie asked, "Poppa? What relatives were you talking about back there? After Nagamama and Nagypa died, I thought you said there were only the four of us left?"

He stopped and turned toward her. "You're right, Vivie."

"Mama?" Mae danced up and down in the twilight. "I *have* to go!"

Taking her by the hand, Csaky led her into the shadowy roadside brush.

"I lied, Vivie." Lofo sighed and shook his head. "I needed an excuse for us to separate from the group."

"But...why, Poppa? I thought those students were your friends?"

"They are, Vivie, but things were too dangerous. These are troubling times." He frowned. "And well, sometimes well-intentioned people, even intelligent people, get carried away by their emotions and can make poor decisions, creating situations that negatively impact or hurt others."

She nodded as he continued.

"You'll better understand when you're older that sometimes, in order to achieve a greater good—like security or safety for the people you love, it is necessary to lie."

"I understand, Poppa."

He leaned over and hugged her.

"Vivie? Do you need a bathroom break?" Csaky asked, returning with Mae.

"No, ma'am. I'm fine."

"All right, then," Lofo said. "Let's move on."

"Nooooo," Mae whined. "I'm tired." She rubbed her eyes, tears spilling down her cheeks.

"Hush now, Mae. I'll carry you." He picked her up, and they set off down the road.

Forty-five minutes later the last rays of the setting sun vanished below the horizon, engulfing them in darkness. "Lofo?"

"Yes, my sweet?"

"Don't you think it's time we stopped for the night?"

Vivie perked up at her mother's words, awaiting her father's response. She was more than ready to stretch out on the cold, hard ground and rest her weary limbs.

"Not yet," he responded as Mae shifted restlessly in his arms.

Vivie's shoulders drooped and her pace slowed. She silently groaned at her father's reply.

"But why?" Csaky asked. "The children are exhausted, and I can barely put one foot in front of the other at this point."

He stopped and sighed. "Well...I guess we could take a short break. Here, take Mae." Rummaging through his satchel, Lofo pulled out a flashlight, then a black sheet of paper. He wrapped it around the light's head.

"What are you doing?" Vivie asked.

"I'm concentrating the flashlight's beam."

"But...why?"

"To make it more like a spotlight...so its beam can't be seen from a distance."

She nodded.

Using the converted light, her father led them a short way into the woods.

Vivie's head rose as soft rustlings accompanied their passage. Just night creatures fleeing their approach, much like her family eluding the Soviets. She shook her head at the irony.

"We'll rest here," Lofo said, a few minutes later. He took the carryalls from Csaky and laid them on the ground, then lay Mae atop one. "Here, Vivie. Stretch out on the other and rest."

Numb with exhaustion, she just nodded and laid down as her parents sat on a nearby log.

"I don't understand why we can't stay here for the night, Lofo," her mother asked.

"Because, my sweet, we're safer traveling at dark."

"How so?"

"It will be easier to spot and avoid checkpoints as we near Kapuvár. We'll be able to see their lights...their campfires from a distance."

An hour later they resumed their trek.

CHAPTER 8

"Norsk!" The cat repeatedly dunked her paw in the water dish, then daintily lapped at the moisture droplets clinging to her paw pad. Vivie reached for her, only to grasp air. With an anguished cry, she fought her way out from the fog of sleep.

As the splash of water continued, Vivie lay there a moment, disoriented by the muted daylight seeping into the lean-to. Over the past week, her family had drifted into a routine. By dawn, they scavenged to supplement their dwindling food supply, then sheltered and slept the day away. Nightfall found them traveling by the light of the waxing moon. Each day bled into the next.

Wide awake, Vivie frowned at the rhythmic splashing. She sat up and glanced around, looking for Mama and Poppa.

Mae grunted in her sleep and burrowed deeper under Csaky's coat.

Outside the makeshift shelter, snow blanketed the landscape. Vivie rose and stepped out into the gray daylight. Tiny snowflakes drifted and swirled, landing on her nose and eyelashes. Memories of previous snowfalls came to mind. Sledding, snowball fights, making snow angels, building snowmen. How she would snuggle down afterwards in Poppa's study with a book and a cup of cocoa—and Norsk. Her heart ached at the recollection. How she missed her.

With a heavy sigh, she pushed all thoughts of the beloved cat away and concentrated on the distant splashing. Pulling her coat collar tighter, Vivie followed the sound.

Her mother knelt at the edge of the creek, a cake of soap in her reddened hands, scrubbing a pair of Mae's pants. A sheltered fire flamed nearby. Damp garments draped the nearby bushes and rocks.

"Mama?"

Csaky jumped. "Vivie!" Her damp hand pressed against her bosom. "You startled me."

"I'm sorry."

"That's okay. What are you doing up?"

"I heard the splashing. Where's Poppa?"

"He's gone into the village on some business."

"The village?" Vivie studied their surroundings. "Where are we?"

"Just outside of Kapuvár."

"Why didn't all of us go?"

"You and Mae needed the rest. And I needed to wash our clothes, so we'll be ready for the train trip."

"Train trip?" Vivie exclaimed.

"Yes. Your father's gone to try and hire a guide who can secure our passage to Balf. Maybe even as far as Sopron."

"Oh, Mama!" Vivie clasped her hands. "A train trip! I can hardly wait. Why I'll—"

"Now, Vivie, don't get excited." Csaky rinsed out the pants and began wringing them dry. "For one thing, there is no guarantee that your father can find a guide. And for another, train travel is difficult with the current unrest. Not how it was when you traveled with Nagamama. So back to bed with you, young lady."

"Okay, Mama."

In the lean-to, her mind wandered back to the train trip she had taken with her grandparents. Vivie remembered the luxurious passenger coach where they sat and watched the landscape stream past. Her mouth watered just thinking about the dining car's sumptuous food selections. Then there was the gift shop at the station where she stumbled across the Agatha Christie mystery, *Murder on the Orient Express*. Excited that the book shared the same name as their train, she had shown it to Nagypa. When he bought it for her, Nagamama complained the novel was inappropriate for a girl her age, but he had disagreed. Oh, how Vivie loved reading the Hercule Poirot adventure and trying to solve the murder before the famed detective. She yawned and thought about her grandparents. It had been a year since the accident. Vivie still missed them so much. While reminiscing about their times together, she drifted off to sleep.

. . . . .

"Vivie? Mae? Wake up."

Vivie stretched and looked up at her mother. "What time is it?"

"About 3:00 p.m. Mae, wake up. C'mon now. I need you both to wash up and change into clean clothes."

"SNOW!" her sister shouted when she looked outside. "Mama! Vivie! It's snowing!"

"Yes, dear. We know. Now, hurry, so we'll be ready when Poppa gets back."

Vivie sucked in her breath when she rubbed the ice-cold rag against her skin. Her teeth chattered as she hurriedly dried herself, donned clean clothes, and then huddled next to the sparse warmth of the small fire.

"I don't see why we had to wash," Mae grumbled. "We're just going to get dirty again."

"Because it's what civilized people do," Vivie responded.

"And what is it that civilized people do?"

"Poppa!" Mae jumped up and ran to Lofo, throwing her arms about his waist.

As he extracted himself from her grasp, Csaky appeared with the last of the damp clothes. "Well?" she asked, draping them by the fire.

Vivie noticed the look of concern on her face.

Lofo smiled and nodded. "Yes. I've found a guide to arrange our passage. We'll leave tomorrow evening on the train for Balf."

Csaky crossed herself and bowed her head.

"And," Lofo continued, "I bought a few things while I was in town."

"Cheese! Bread!" Mae exclaimed as she peered into the sack. "And bacon!" She glowered at her sister. "I hope you don't give it to another dog."

Vivie rolled her eyes.

"Practically a feast," Csaky said, ignoring Mae's remark.

That evening, instead of packing up and moving on, Vivie and her family remained secluded in their camp. Lofo let the fire die down so it would not be seen from a distance. "Well, girls," he said. "I've got a surprise for you."

Mae's eyes danced. "A surprise? What is it, Poppa? What is it?"

"You girls have been so good on the journey, I thought you deserved a treat." He reached into his coat pocket and withdrew a small bakery sack.

Vivie's mouth watered in anticipation.

Lofo opened the bag and handed both of them a fat swirled pastry.

"Cocoa snails!" Mae shrieked. "My favorite!"

"Shhh!" Csaky cautioned. "Keep your voice down, Mae."

"Thank you, Poppa." Vivie held the snail-shaped pastry to her nose and inhaled its aromatic scents of cinnamon and chocolate. When she bit into the soft yeasty dough, the confection melted in her mouth. Little explosions of cinnamon and chocolate danced across her tongue. She closed her eyes, savoring each bite.

"How are they?" Lofo asked.

Mae's response was unintelligible, her mouth crammed full of the pastry.

"Delicious!" Vivie remarked, as she licked the remnants of the cinnamony chocolate from her fingers.

•　　　•　　　•　　　•　　　•

Vivie held her mother's hand and pressed against her back as the family threaded their way through the crowded train depot and out onto the platform. Station lights illuminated the night, casting garish shadows on the refugees who stood packed like canned sardines. The stench of soured, unwashed bodies assaulted her nostrils. Vivie squinched up her face and glanced at Mae, waiting for an outburst from her sister. But she kept silent in Lofo's arms. No doubt Poppa had told her to be quiet.

They followed the tall angular guide as he slipped through the crowd like a cockroach, using his cane to prod his way through the masses. Vivie winced at the tightening of Csaky's grasp as they fought their way toward the passenger car. A few minutes later, they were aboard. Vivie sighed with relief, glancing about. The train was not as opulent as the *Orient Express.* It was darker, dingier. They crowded into the small compartment. The dimly lit space had an odd musky odor—like wet dog.

As the train lurched forward, there was a knock at the door. "Tickets?" The conductor stepped inside.

Vivie studied the beads of sweat dotting her father's brow.

The guide stood and grasped the conductor's hand, holding it a moment too long.

Her mouth dropped open as she glimpsed the folded money that changed hands. A smuggler! Their 'guide' was a smuggler!

With the conductor's departure, a smug smile crossed his face. "See? Piece of cake!" His raucous laugh startled Mae, the locomotive's whistle muffling her cry as the train chugged on down the track.

Fifteen minutes later, the brakes creaked, and the train slowed. Vivie's stomach clenched at the expression on her parents' faces.

CHAPTER 9

At the staccato pop of gunfire, Vivie froze, hardly daring to breathe. Mae's screams filled the compartment. Their guide leapt to his feet and smashed the overhead bulb with his cane. Minuscule shards of glass rained down upon them. Vivie flinched, the sting of the slivers pricking her face.

"Hush her and follow me!" the smuggler growled, as Mae's screams of terror became a keening wail. Yanking open the compartment door, the guide stormed out shouting in Russian, "Back to your rooms! Nothing to see here!" He shoved aside passengers that got in his way and smashed lights along the corridor, engulfing the car in darkness. Amid the curses, shrieks, and cries of men, women, and children, gunfire continued to echo from the front of the train.

Vivie cringed, her heart thudding in her chest like the machine gun fire that day in Buda. Their train compartment was only about five meters from the exit, but it seemed more like a hundred as she slogged her way through the confused and frightened passengers.

At the end of the train car, their guide jerked open the door. "Jump!" he whispered, shoving Vivie toward the opening. She tripped, pitching forward as a carryall on her mother's back bounced up and smacked her in the face. Microbursts of light exploded behind her eyes. The world seemed to spin. Nausea clogged her throat. For a split second, Vivie was stunned.

"Hurry!" the man hissed.

She shook her head, trying to clear her sight. Despite the pain, Vivie's fear drove her forward, her breath coming in short, ragged gasps. She stumbled and rolled down the steep snow-covered incline, scrambling into the line of fir trees with her family.

Footsteps pounded along the track's verge. In the faint moonlight, soldiers shouted, "HALT!" A shot rang out, followed by a muffled cry. Vivie stifled a scream as the smuggler slumped and fell to the ground. Tears pricked her eyes. The man just lay there, not moving.

Time seemed to stand still in the dense snow-encased foliage. Vivie pressed her aching face into a small icy drift. Its cold momentarily numbed and soothed her swelling nose. She trembled and huddled against her father as more shots rang out into the night.

At the sound of voices, Vivie peeked out. Two soldiers walked over to the guide's prone form and dragged it away, leaving behind a blackened patch of snow. A queasiness washed over her at the realization the dark spot was the man's blood. She slipped her hand into her pocket and fingered her rosary beads as a silent prayer crossed her lips.

After what seemed an interminable amount of time, steam burst from the engine, and the locomotive slowly pulled away. Vivie and her family remained secluded in the firs, watching the train disappear into the night.

When silence filled the black space, air whooshed from Vivie's lungs. She had no idea she had been holding her breath.

Mae began to sob.

"There, there," her mother comforted, rubbing the child's back. "You were so brave. Everything's going to be fine."

I'm not so sure, Vivie thought, glancing back at the blood-stained snow.

Lofo slowly rose and helped Csaky to her feet. While her mother coaxed Mae up from the snow, Vivie helped her father gather their things. She picked up the food bag. "Where are we, Poppa?"

"I'd say just outside of Fertőd."

She nodded, remembering her trip there with Nagamama to see Esterháza, the grand palace.

"Let's get moving," her father urged.

Vivie pushed aside her memories and fell in step behind her parents. Slipping and sliding in the snow, they made their way down to the foot of the slope, then proceeded west—parallel to the train tracks.

Cold winds moaned through the bare tree branches. When they died down, an eerie silence filled the air. Moonbeams reflected off the snow pack, creating an odd bluish glow that gave their surroundings a surreal appearance. Any minute Vivie expected a Russian soldier to emerge from the woodland shadows with a machine gun, ready to arrest them or shoot them dead. She shivered at the thought.

The family's narrow escape invigorated their pace. By dawn, they had reached the marshlands. Hoarfrost covered the frozen expanse. Reeds snapped and crackled in the wind. A misty fog enshrouded them as they threaded their way through the rushes and cattails.

As the sky lightened and the fog dissipated, Mae exclaimed, "Oooh! Look at Vivie's purple face!"

Csaky pivoted and gasped, "VIVIE! What happened?" She reached out and grasped the girl's chin, turning it to the right and then the left.

"It's nothing," she replied. "I just got hit in the face by one of the carryalls when we jumped down from the train."

"Oh! My love. I'm so sorry."

"It's okay, Mama. It doesn't hurt now."

Lofo peered over Csaky's shoulder. "You've got two fine shiners there, my girl. Like you went a couple of rounds in the ring with Rocky Marciano."

"Lofo!" Csaky cut her eyes at him.

Mae shrugged. "I don't know about Rocky Marshmallow, but if she had a tail, she could be a raccoon!"

Vivie sighed and rolled her eyes.

Csaky kissed her forehead, then wrapped an arm about her shoulders as they continued their trek.

Passing through a grove of alders, Mae leaned close and whispered, "Vivie?"

"What?"

"Do you know what these trees remind me of?"

"Witches brooms?" she responded, voicing her thoughts.

The child shook her head. "No. Chicken legs."

"Chicken legs?" Vivie frowned.

Mae nodded. "Like in my picture book, *Baba Yaga*."

Vivie studied the alders' vein-like trunks and splayed roots, then smiled. "Yeah, they do, don't they?" She glanced up, almost expecting to see the old hag's hovel tottering above them.

Under the warmth of the sun's rays, the snow began to melt. As they walked, the ice-covered swamp popped and cracked under their weight.

"It sounds like popcorn popping," Mae said, riding atop her father's shoulders.

By mid-day, each step gave way, plunging Vivie's feet into the slush of the reedy marsh. The wet saturated her loafers and soaked into her socks. As she walked, trickles of moisture squished between her toes. Nothing worse than cold, wet feet. All she wanted at the moment was to be home in bed—warm and dry, with Norsk curled at her side. Realization hit that she had not thought of her beloved cat in a couple of days. Guilt washed over Vivie, and her steps grew a little heavier.

A few hours later, the marshland was behind them. Vivie was relieved to see the end of it, but even happier for the warmth of their evening fire when they finally stopped for the night. As Lofo dried their shoes by the fireside, Csaky exchanged their wet socks for dry and rubbed their chaffed feet.

After a quick bite to eat, the family lay huddled together for warmth near the campfire. Vivie yawned. The long day's journey coupled with the previous evening's stress and trauma took their toll. Despite the hard ground and the cold, exhaustion grasped hold, and Vivie was asleep the moment her eyes closed.

• • • • •

"Time to get up, Vivie." Csaky gently shook her shoulder.

It seemed as though she had just fallen asleep, and yet here was her mother waking her. Vivie stretched and rubbed her eyes. Before she knew it, they were on the road again. Her shoes were stiff and tight and still a bit damp, but better than the day before.

A second day of walking, and then another. By the close of the third day, the lights of Balf appeared on the horizon.

CHAPTER 10

Vivie's teeth chattered. A watery trickle tickled her left nostril. As it started to drip, she brushed a cold, stiffened finger under her reddened nose and sniffed. The fingers on her left hand ached in the frigid air. Somewhere along the way, she had lost one of her mittens. Probably when they fled the train. Vivie had not told her parents. They had more important things to worry about.

Snowflakes floated about, eddying at her feet. Sleet pellets stung her face. She pulled her coat collar a little tighter, tucked her head down, and hunched her shoulders against the brisk wind. Would she ever be warm again?

It had been two days since they had left Balf. They had stayed just long enough for Lofo to restock their meager supplies and attempt to locate another smuggler, but word of the train raid outside of Kapuvár had sent them into hiding.

"Mama," Mae whined, "I'm cold."

"Yes, dear. We all are."

"We need to get out of this wind." Lofo studied their surroundings.

A short time later, they found refuge in an abandoned barn.

I wish we could build a fire, Vivie thought as she huddled with Mae in the stale straw.

Once the winds died down, they were back on the road to Sopron. The sun now shone and Vivie turned her face up to the sky, drinking in its warm rays.

"Oh, look!" Mae pointed. "It's like a fairyland."

Vivie gazed across the ice-covered vineyards. Water droplets danced and dripped off the vines, sparkling in the sunlight.

"Isn't it beautiful?" her sister whispered. "It looks like it's raining diamonds."

"Yes, it does."

"What if those really were diamonds?" Mae asked. "And they were all ours. What would you buy?"

Vivie shrugged. "I don't know." Yes, she did. She would try and buy their old life back. Then they could be home, and she could be with Norsk. Her throat tightened.

"I know what I'd buy," her sister said. "I'd buy an ice cream parlor, so I could eat *all* the ice cream I wanted."

"You'll need to use some of that money to see a doctor," her father cautioned, "because you'll end up with quite a tummy ache."

She huffed and rolled her eyes, then continued. "I'd buy a new dollhouse, some clothes for Dodo, and..."

Vivie shook her head as her sister rattled off her litany of purchases while they continued down the roadway.

In the distance, church bells pealed. Csaky grabbed her husband's arm. "Lofo? Please, let's attend noon Mass."

Vivie leaned forward to hear her father's response.

"I'm sorry, my sweet. I don't think we'll make it into the village in time."

Csaky nodded.

●   ●   ●   ●   ●

Outside of Sopron, a Hungarian flag with the Soviet emblem intact was prominently displayed across a burned-out tank, indicative of the city's Russian occupation.

Lofo paused. "Perhaps it would be best if you wait for me here. Let me go ahead alone and check things out."

Vivie sucked in her breath, chewing her bottom lip.

"And if you don't return? What then?" Csaky shook her head. "No, Lofo. We'll all go. We're in this together."

"But—"

"Lofo!"

"She's right, Poppa," Vivie nodded.

"Well...okay," he sighed.

Vivie's heart skipped as they entered the village.

"Stay close," her father ordered.

She reached over and clasped Mae's hand, her breath coming in shallow, rapid gasps. Vivie's eyes darted from side to side, taking everything in. For the most part, they appeared to pass through the town unnoticed. A few people nodded to them. *They seem friendly enough,* Vivie thought as her breath began to ease.

After safely traversing a series of streets, they made their way into a square. Bells pealed again. A small group of people began to make their way toward a church. "Lofo? What's going on? Why are they heading there?"

"You know as much as I do, my sweet."

"Well...ask someone."

Lofo walked over and stopped a stooped gray-haired woman. She clasped the handle of her wooden cane in one hand. Rosary beads dangled between the fingers of the other as she nodded and pointed toward the ornate structure.

"Well?" Csaky asked upon his return.

"A special Mass is being offered for the students and faculty who fled the city to avoid the Soviets."

"Please, Lofo? May we attend?"

"Please, Poppa?" Vivie echoed. While she loved the religious service, Vivie had an ulterior motive—the opportunity to rest and escape the cold.

Her father stood for a moment, scanning the square. At the end of one street, a small contingent of Russian soldiers surveyed the crowd. He nodded. "Sounds like a good idea."

They merged into the stream of worshippers crossing the plaza toward the neo-Gothic-styled church that dominated one end of the square. As they passed a large stone fountain, Vivie gazed up at the statue of the Virgin Mary standing at its center. In her arms she clasped her infant son, his hands outstretched to the world.

Inside the church, Vivie's family crowded into the last pew. "Mae, sit in your father's lap to make room," Csaky said, as an old man shuffled inside.

Vivie settled back onto the wooden bench. She sighed, relieved to be safe and warm. Vivie studied the people sitting around them. Most were older, her grandparents' age. There were only a couple of young families with children.

Her eyes roamed the sanctuary. Below the main altar stood the communion table, prepared for the special Mass. Above it was a sizeable, intricately carved altarpiece—its panels detailing the life of the Virgin Mary. A tall marble statue of her dominated its center.

As the service began, a hush fell over the sanctuary. Vivie had always enjoyed the ritual of the ceremony, despite the cloying scent of incense. Over the years she had learned to ease her breathing, keeping a damp handkerchief on hand to cover her nose and mouth.

For Vivie, there was a comfort and familiarity about the small church. As she relaxed, her eyes grew heavy. At a poke in her side, Vivie jerked upright. "Sorry," she whispered at her mother's frown.

Vivie's gaze drifted to a smaller sculpture of the Virgin Mary on a pedestal to the right of the altar. A similar statue of Jesus graced the left. Something appeared to be moving about its base. Vivie squinted. A mouse! She drew in her breath, leaning forward to get a better view.

"Vivie Gabrielle," Csaky whispered.

She knew that tone well. Vivie sat back and immediately bowed her head.

Following the service, Lofo excused himself. "I want to speak with the priest for a moment."

Csaky nodded and ushered the girls out into the vestibule where a few worshippers lingered.

A moment later, Mae was laughing and talking with two other little girls. She made friends so easily.

To the left of the entryway, shadows appeared to dance against the far wall. Vivie wandered toward them. In a small alcove, she spied a bank of prayer candles, their flames flickering in the drafts of air from the vestibule. Vivie stood there a moment, gazing at the image of the saint hanging on the wall. She glanced back at her mother. Csaky had stooped down to talk to Mae.

Vivie reached over and lit a candle for Norsk. She knew some people would be appalled, thinking that praying for a cat was sacrilegious. But not her. Vivie believed in praying for those she loved. And to her, Norsk was family—just like Mama, Poppa, and Mae!

As she crossed herself and started to pray, a movement to the left caught her eye. A gray tabby trotted down the corridor. Vivie started after it, momentarily losing sight of the cat when it turned the corner. She followed, scanning the empty hallway. Then up ahead, Vivie glimpsed its slender tail slipping through a doorway. She approached and peered inside.

"Yes?" A quavery voice queried.

"Excuse me, Sister." Vivie nodded to the old woman sitting in an oversize chair, the tabby kneading in her lap. "I was just following the cat."

"Tobias?" The last rays of sunlight shone through the window, creating a soft halo about the old nun's coif. "Yes, he's a fine mouser. Aren't you, boy?" Her gnarled fingers stroked the feline's striped fur. He arched his back and emitted a rumbling purr.

Vivie took a tentative step forward. "May I pet him?"

"Yes, child. Tobias loves attention."

She slowly approached and squatted down. The feline leaned toward her and bumped his head against hers, just as Norsk always had. Tears filled her eyes as she reached out and scratched the old tom between the ears.

Tobias tilted his head back and closed his eyes.

"Seems you know cats."

"Yes, ma'am." Vivie swiped at an escaped tear. "I have..." Her head drooped, and her voice caught. "I...had one." A ragged sigh escaped her.

The nun's wrinkled hand reached out and clasped Vivie's. "Tell me, child."

For the next several minutes, she talked about Norsk. The cat's likes, dislikes, the times they shared, how she had had to leave her behind, and her worry over the beloved feline's unknown fate. Vivie wept, her tears dropping and glistening on the nun's black tunic. Then, she confessed about lighting the prayer candle for Norsk. "And...and...I didn't even have any money to put in the donation box," she sobbed.

"There, there, child," the old woman comforted. She shook her head. "I know it seems a burden of worry, but we can make it better."

Vivie raised her head and sniffed. "H-how?"

Tobias stretched and pawed at her hand until her fingers again scratched between his ears.

"We will ask for the intercession of Saint Gertrude of Nivelles."

"Who is she?"

"Saint Gertrude? Why she is the patron saint of cats, child."

As they left the church that evening, Vivie's heart was a tad lighter, knowing that Saint Gertrude would watch over Norsk.

• • • • •

Lofo led them down the street to a small stone building, where he stopped and knocked. The door opened a crack. Vivie strained to hear the whispered exchange, but the murmurs were too faint. A second later, they were ushered inside.

She glanced about the austere room. The faces of other weary travelers—young and old—stared back, most with indifference to the new arrivals. A fire flamed in the fireplace, warming the space. Curled on the hearth lay a tri-colored hound, his tail lazily thumping against the stones.

Csaky made her way to an unoccupied corner and sat down. Mae joined her.

As Vivie started to follow, her father asked, "How about taking a stroll with me?"

"Okay, Poppa." She turned and followed him out the door. A few minutes later, Vivie asked, "Where are we going?"

"Just looking around. Trying to evaluate the best place to cross the border." He glanced down at her. "With you along, hopefully I won't attract any attention."

They traversed the moonlit streets in silence. Vivie scrutinized the shadows, alert for any movement. Up ahead, a stray cat crossed the intersection. Two kittens scampered behind. "Poppa!" Vivie grabbed her father's arm.

"I see." His hand covered hers. "Cute, aren't they?"

She nodded, unable to speak.

A few steps later her father said, "Vivie? I know you miss Norsk."

Again, she nodded. Vivie blinked, fighting back tears.

Lofo stopped and turned toward her. "You understand now why she couldn't come with us?"

"Yes, Poppa." Her words came out as a whisper. She stared down at the cobblestones.

His index finger slipped under her chin, raising her head. Lofo gazed into her eyes. "I promise you, Vivie, as soon as we get settled, I'll buy you another Norsk."

A pain seared through Vivie's heart as though she had been stabbed. Her eyes widened with hurt. He did not understand. Norsk could not be replaced. She was not an object like a broken pencil, a worn-out pair of shoes, or a lost mitten. A wave of guilt washed over her as she glanced down at her newly-mittened hands.

"A new cat, just like Norsk. Won't that be nice? Something to look forward to."

Vivie wanted to scream at him, 'No. It *won't* be the same.' Instead, she softly responded, "Yes, Poppa." Vivie chewed the inside of her lip.

As they resumed their walk, he clasped her hand. "You can name this one Norsk, too." Lofo glanced at her. "Get it, Vivie? Norsk *Two*, as in the number."

She cringed inside, her stomach giving a twist. *No, Poppa,* Vivie thought. *There will never be another Norsk.* "I get it," she replied. "That's really bad."

He chuckled. "Yes, it is."

Another companionable silence fell between them. Vivie studied the houses lining the street. The windows of some homes were dark. Others were lit. A silhouetted cat sat in one, licking its paw.

"Vivie?"

"Yes, Poppa?"

"I have a question I'd like to ask you."

"What?"

He raised her hand. "Where did you get these mittens?"

Vivie stopped. Her face warmed. With everything they were going through, she did not think he would notice. Especially since they resembled her others.

He turned and raised an eyebrow. "Well?"

"Sister Agnes. She gave them to me." As they continued their walk, Vivie related the time she had spent with the elderly nun and her cat.

When they neared the western edge of the village, he held up his hand and motioned for her to stop. They moved into the shadows of a nearby building. In the moonlight, Vivie stared out across the distant field at the chevaux-de-frise. The large, wooden-spiked, knife-rest barriers lined the acreage as though a child had taken a fat brown crayon and drawn giant asterisks across the expanse. Strands of barbed wire were strung between them like telephone cables, making the spiked uprights look like beads on a gigantic necklace.

To the right stood a machine gun watchtower, extending several hundred meters into the air and accessed by a progression of ladder-like steps. At the top sat a small building bounded by a fenced porch where the silhouettes of two Hungarian border guards could be seen. The hum of their murmured conversation droned in the night air.

Lofo glowered. "Well, we definitely can't cross here."

"What will we do, Poppa?"

"I don't know, Vivie, but somehow we'll find a way."

CHAPTER 11

Vivie's eyes narrowed as the flashlight's concealed beam briefly strayed across the bridge. It was just as the guide described it—a washed out structure with abutments jutting from both sides of the bank. Across the river's expanse lay a narrow tree trunk. Above it hung a length of cord for balance.

Her father frowned. He extended his foot and tested the log's stability. "Okay. I'll lead." Lofo looked at Csaky. "We'll put Mae between us. Vivie? You'll follow your mother."

She nodded.

"Are you sure this is safe?" Csaky asked.

"We have no choice." He reached down and grasped Mae's hand. "Now, let your mother hold your other hand."

"I can't, Poppa. I've got to carry Dodo."

Vivie rolled her eyes.

"Let Poppa tuck her in his coat," Csaky said.

"No, Dodo is scared of the water. She wants to stay with me."

"Mae, we don't have time to argue. Give me your doll."

"No, Poppa. I'll tuck her into my coat."

"Fine." He hooked the handle of the satchel over his right thumb and grasped the cord. Mae took hold of her father's left hand and her mother's right.

After securing the straps of the carryalls, Csaky grabbed onto the rope. "Okay. I'm ready." The three of them then eased out onto the log.

Vivie took a deep, shaky breath, then reached for the cord and followed, her arms and legs trembling. As she moved farther out over the water, her body centered. The food bag lightly bumped against her back as though encouraging her. Vivie's fear ebbed away with each step. Gaining confidence, she let go and held her arms out for balance like a tightrope walker at the circus. Occasionally, she reached up for the security of the rope that softly vibrated with her parents' movements.

"Halfway there," her father stated. An owl hooted in response. When they neared the shore, Lofo said, "We need to stop a moment."

"What's wrong?" Csaky asked.

"There's a broken limb. We'll need to maneuver around it."

"How difficult will it be?"

"Not bad. Just a little tricky. Mae, I need to let go of your hand for a minute. You need to stand very still."

"Okay, Poppa." She reached up and patted her doll. "Hear that, Dodo?"

He tossed the satchel onto the bank and eased his way around the limb.

Vivie glanced up. Puffy clouds drifted across the sky like globs of marshmallow cream. A pinkish-orange moon slowly rose amidst them. Etched against the night sky, the naked tree limbs resembled the gnarled hands of witches grasping for the glowing, peach-like orb. She looked down at its reflection on the shimmering water. Ice fragments glistened at the river's edge.

A shriek rang out, accompanied by a splash. Vivie's eyes riveted on her sister struggling in the freezing water, Dodo floating downstream. She stiffened, her mouth gaping open.

"Mae!" Csaky jumped in after her.

"Mama!" Vivie gasped, her chest tightening as Csaky vanished into the river. Seconds later, the carryalls bobbed to the surface, drifting along after Dodo.

Mae flailed and shrieked in the current, fighting to keep her head above the water.

Panic gripped Vivie's heart. Her eyes raked the river for any sign of her mother. She struggled to breathe, her stomach cramping.

Shedding his overcoat, Lofo rushed back across the log just as Csaky's head surfaced a few meters from Mae's.

"Wait, Poppa!" Vivie choked out amid tears. "Look!"

Treading water, Csaky reached over and grasped the collar of Mae's coat. She swam toward the bank with her in tow as Lofo hastened to help them ashore.

Vivie's knees jellied. She grasped onto the cord and wobbled her way across the log, her breath coming in short, panicked gasps.

From the far bank, whistles shrilled. Shouts filled the air, and footsteps pounded. Dogs barked.

"Vivie, help your mother and sister hide," Lofo urged. "Quickly now!"

Her heart thudded as though it would burst from her chest as she helped Mae and Csaky up the steep incline and settled them into the brush. Then, she turned to go back.

"Vivie, stay here!" her mother hissed.

She glanced down. Her father had grabbed a stout tree limb and was trying to lever the log off the bank. "But I want to help Poppa."

"He can handle this himself. You'd only be in his way."

Vivie bit her lip, blinking back tears. Her mother's words stung. While trying to ignore the pang of disappointment, she startled as a gunfire-like 'crack' rang out. Vivie looked back down at her father. Lofo tossed the broken limb aside, then stooped down and struggled to dislodge the stubborn log.

In the distance, voices, footfalls, and barking drew near. Lights bobbed up and down.

Mae continued to emit shivery sobs. She would give them away if Mama could not quieten her.

Oh, Poppa! Hurry! Vivie thought, fingering the rosary beads in her coat pocket.

Lofo sat down on the muddy bank and frantically kicked at the trunk's end. With a thrust of both legs, the tree finally gave way—rolling and splashing down into the water.

Vivie held her breath as the soldiers approached. Her eyes wavered between their lights and Poppa scrambling up the embankment. Vivie's breath whooshed out as he dropped into the bushes just as a small group of Russian soldiers assembled on the far bank.

The East European Shepherds barked and strained against their leashes. Flashlights panned across the water and into the brush, then downstream. A beam of light played across the bank and momentarily landed upon them. "Look there!"

They've found us! Vivie thought, her eyes darting to her parents. But Lofo and Csaky stared down river. She followed their gaze.

Flashlight beams illuminated the floating log. A little farther downstream bobbed the lost doll and carryalls, tangled with other debris and trapped by the current against the distant bank. Vivie sighed in relief.

The soldiers' conversation drifted across the river.

"Drowned?"

"Looks like it."

"Where's Oleg? He was supposed to be on guard in this sector."

Vivie's head snapped back at the mention of their guide.

"Don't know. Maybe he went off to take a piss."

"Must have been a long one. We've been here at least ten minutes."

Laughter burst out into the night.

"Most likely he found himself a warm bed with a local."

"Ha! We should all be so lucky."

"C'mon. Let's head back."

"But what about Oleg?"

"Fuck him. I'm cold."

Vivie's mouth gaped open at the exchange.

The soldiers and their dogs turned and headed back across the field.

After several minutes, Lofo sighed, "They're gone."

Csaky held Mae close, rocking her in her lap. "It's okay, baby. Everything's okay."

The child's body shuddered. Tears cascaded down her cheeks.

"Mae? You want me to tell you a story?" Vivie offered.

Her sister failed to respond.

"We need to move on," Lofo urged. He leaned over and picked up Mae, then headed toward the roadway. Vivie helped her mother up, grabbed the leather satchel, and followed.

Moonglow basked the roadway, lighting their path. Mae's sobs filled the night air, eventually dissolving into soft hiccups. Vivie craned her neck, trying to get a glimpse of her sister.

"W-we've got to get Mae out of those w-wet clothes," Csaky shivered. "She'll catch pneumonia...or w-worse hypothermia."

"The same holds true for you," Lofo commented.

"M-m-me? I'll b-b-be f-f-fine." Her teeth chattered.

"Mae can wear my coat," Vivie volunteered.

"Don't be ridiculous," Csaky snapped. "Then, we'll have you to w-worry about as w-well!"

Vivie's head reared back at her mother's harsh tone. She was only trying to help.

"Csaky, she does have a point."

"A point?" Csaky shrieked. "What do you mean, Lofo? She's just a child herself!"

The twelve-year-old's shoulders sagged. Her head drooped. She stared down at the ground as they continued walking.

Lofo turned toward his wife. "Hear me out, my sweet—"

Csaky stopped. "My sweet! My sweet!" She stamped her foot. "*Don't* attempt to placate me! Damn it, Lofo, I'm sick of this. It's almost cost us one of our children. We *never* should have left Budapest!"

Vivie gulped.

"You don't mean that, Csaky."

"Don't *mean* it? How do *you* know? Yes, Lofo, maybe *I* do. If we were still at home, we'd be—"

Vivie tried not to listen, but there was no place for her to go. Nothing for her to do. This was awful. What was wrong with Mama? Why was she saying these things? Her parents had argued in the past, but never like this. Harsh words were never spoken. It was all her fault. If she had not tried to help, this never would have happened. Vivie swallowed and blinked back tears.

"Where are you going, Lofo? Lofo?" Csaky screamed out as he strode off into the woods. "Where are you going with my child?"

He did not answer. Instead, he said, "Vivie? Come with me."

She hesitated, torn between going with her father and remaining with her mother—despite the hurtful things she had said.

Lofo turned back. "Please, Vivie? I need your help...with Mae."

The girl glanced at her mother scowling in the moonlight. "Yes, Poppa."

As they moved farther into the woods, Mama's footsteps crunched behind them.

When they reached a sheltered ravine, her father stooped and laid her sister on the ground. "Vivie? Undress Mae and put your coat on her while I gather some wood."

"Yes, sir."

A short while later, Vivie sat near the campfire helping her father dry Mae's clothes. She glanced at her sister, still shivering despite the warmth of Vivie's coat and the fire. Her mother sat huddled a few meters away. No one had spoken since the argument, other than to attend to Mae. This was so awkward. She did not even know what to say to try and make things better.

Above, the peach-colored moon had paled to a powdery white. A wealth of stars filled the sky. Frost glazed the woods. An owl screeched somewhere in the night, and the fire's yellow-orange flames flickered and popped nearby.

At a soft rustling off to her left, Vivie's neck tightened. She squinted, focusing on the shopping net. It appeared to be undulating. Was it really moving? Or just a trick cast by the fire's light? Vivie continued to stare. "Poppa, look," she whispered, pointing.

As he rose and started toward it, a masked, furry face emerged.

"Oh, Mae! Look!" Vivie exclaimed. "It's a raccoon!"

The ring-tailed bandit waddled into the thicket with an apple.

Mae ignored her and continued staring into the fire.

Lofo picked up the mesh sack and moved it closer to them. "Just in case he has some friends."

Vivie nodded and smiled.

He walked over to Csaky and handed her his coat. "Here. Change into this and let me dry your clothes."

She silently reached for it, then slipped into the brush. A moment later Csaky returned and handed her wet garments to Lofo. He spread them out by the fire with Mae's.

Still, no one spoke. The tension hung between them like a stretched rubber band.

"I'm sorry," Vivie burst out. "I'm sorry for starting all of this." Tears spilled down her cheeks.

"No, Vivie. I'm sorry. It was my fault." Csaky rose and sat beside her, wrapping Vivie in her arms. "I never should have said those things. You were only trying to help."

She sniffed and swiped at her tears.

"I was scared, Vivie." Her mother continued. "We almost lost Mae. And all because of her attachment to that doll."

"She does...I mean...she did love it."

"Yes, she did," her mother nodded. "And jumping into the river after it, almost cost her her life. I'm sorry. I never meant to hurt you." She glanced over at Lofo. "Or your father. I love you both very much. And Mae. It's just that sometimes when you're frightened, you say things you don't mean."

"I understand, Mama."

"Now, hand me the shopping net, and let's see what that raccoon didn't eat!"

"That was Vivie's apple that he absconded with." Lofo rose and sat down next to Csaky.

"Yes, Poppa." Vivie's head dipped in agreement. "I wasn't responsible for the food bag like I should have been."

"You know, I was only teasing, Vivie."

"But, Poppa, I *should* have been more mindful—"

His hand reached across Csaky and clasped hers. "Vivie, we all could have been more mindful over the last few weeks. Okay? Now, let's have a bite to eat and settle in for the night."

She smiled at the love shining in his eyes. "Okay, Poppa."

CHAPTER 12

Vivie awakened to the sound of a harsh cough. Mae. Her mother was right about her getting sick. But when she rolled over and looked, the cough came from her mother.

"C'mon, sleepy head," her father urged. "We need to get back on the road."

"How much farther to Austria, Poppa?"

"We crossed the border at the river. Now, we need to find a refugee center."

Vivie's fear of capture eased away as they returned to the road, then continued westward. She glanced over at her sister, her eyes widening in surprise. The eight-year-old plodded along with her thumb in her mouth. "Mama?"

Csaky coughed. "Yes, Vi-vie?"

She tried again with a little more emphasis. "*Mama?*"

"I said, '*Yes?*' Vivie." Csaky stopped and turned toward her.

Vivie nodded at Mae and raised her eyebrows.

"I know," her mother choked out. "Just leave her be."

She shrugged. Maybe she could distract her. "Hey, Mae? You want me to tell you a story?"

Her sister ignored her.

"I know. I'll tell you 'The Hedgehog.' You always liked that one." Even though Mae made no response, Vivie began the tale. "Once upon a time, there was a shopkeeper, a king, and a poor man..."

She finished just as they topped a small rise. "Look, Poppa!" Vivie pointed. Below lay a crossroads swarming with activity. A small crowd of refugees, their meager belongings in tow, milled about the staging area. All seemed haggard and worn, their clothes tattered. Arm-banded workers directed them aboard vehicles, their sides draped with Red Cross banners.

Energized by the sight, Vivie and her family made their way down to the rescue workers. A short time later, they, too, boarded one of the buses. Outside Vivie's window the passing landscape rose and fell gently on one side of the road, while on the other it lay steep and barren. Snow-covered craggy peaks loomed in the distance.

As they neared a small village, Vivie returned the waves of the Austrian people. Five kilometers later they stopped at another staging area, teeming with refugees. Red Cross ambulances, buses, and police cars lined the roadway. Large tents housing army field kitchens, medical facilities, and clothing centers abounded.

Exiting the bus, Vivie noticed a tall brunette woman among the crowd, her hair matted and tangled. A smudge marred the cheek of her wan, pinched face. Underneath her fur-collared coat, she wore a thin evening dress, now muddied and stained. Tottering about in high heels, the woman ranted in rapid French about her capture by the Russians. "They held us in a bunker. Some were shot," she sobbed hysterically. "I escaped. I escaped."

That poor woman, Vivie thought as a short heavy-set aid worker approached with a clipboard. Her horn-rimmed glasses dangled around her neck on a slender silver chain. With an expert flick of her wrist, the frame unfolded, and she popped the cat eye glasses onto her face. Flipping a page on the clipboard, she extracted a pencil from her hair bun and began interrogating them. "Names?"

"Lofo and Csaky Degridro," Lofo said. He nodded. "This is Vivie, and that's Mae."

The woman peered over her glasses at the two girls.

"Ages?"

"Vivie's twelve, and Mae's eight."

"Yours?"

Lofo's face reddened. "Well, of *course* they're my children!" he answered, an edge to his voice.

Csaky placed a hand on his arm.

"No, sir." The woman's pert, freckled nose wrinkled. "You misunderstand. *Your* age."

"Oh." His voice softened. "Thirty-six."

"And yours, ma'am?"

"Thirty-four."

After her father finished answering the woman's questions and completed some forms, they received their refugee classification and were directed to the medical facilities. At the women's tent, Vivie studied the women and children in the queue. Ahead of them stood the high-heeled woman, still ranting about her escape.

Vivie jumped as a shriek split the air. She glanced back near the end of the line where a frail woman clutched at a small boy. Her wails of "He's dead! He's dead!" filled the air. Vivie's hand flew to her mouth as a medic rushed over and checked the boy's pulse. Tears filled her eyes.

Csaky's hand came to rest on her shoulder. "Don't stare."

"Yes, Mama." Vivie turned back around and faced the tent, wiping her cheeks.

A moment later, the medic pushed past them, carrying the boy's limp body. Another aid worker followed with an arm around the bereft woman.

"Hey!" the high-heeled woman shouted. "He's dead. Why are you taking them ahead of us? We were here first!"

Vivie gasped as mothers clasped their children near and gave the loud-mouthed woman a wide berth.

"Manners, Vivie," her mother hoarsely whispered. "No matter your birth or station in life, manners define you."

"Yes, ma'am."

Inside the tent, the doctor turned to Csaky, "Other than being a little malnourished, your girls seem fine. Get some food in them. They'll fatten up in no time."

What an odd thing to say, Vivie thought, helping Mae button her coat. It was like the witch in "Hansel and Gretel!"

"I'm more concerned about that cough of yours," the doctor continued. "Wouldn't do for you to come down with pneumonia." He handed Csaky a slip of paper. "I've written you a scrip for some cough medicine."

"Thank you," she choked out.

•　　　•　　　•　　　•　　　•

When they exited the Red Cross tent, a young woman limped over and directed them to one of the army kitchens. A moment later, Lofo joined them. Following their meal, they headed over to one of the clothing tents.

"Look, Mae. Here's a purple-and-red plaid scarf. Your favorite colors." Vivie held it out to her.

She glowered and turned her head away.

Vivie shrugged and tossed it back onto the pile, wondering if her sister was ever going to show interest in anything again.

"Look what I found, Mae." Lofo walked over with a Raggedy Ann doll.

As he tried to hand it to her, Mae slapped it from him and screamed, "It's not Dodo! I want Dodo!"

Vivie stiffened as eyes turned in their direction. Her face flooded with warmth.

Csaky squatted down and grasped Mae by the shoulders. "Enough!" she said in a firm tone. "Dodo's gone. Now...pick up the doll. And if you don't want it, lay it over there in the toy bin."

Mae shut her eyes and turned her head away.

"I'll get it," Vivie offered.

"No." Csaky coughed. "This is Mae's responsibility."

She watched her sister's face redden and her body vibrate with rage at her mother's words.

"*Now*, Mae!"

Grudgingly, the little girl bent down and picked up the cloth doll, then stomped over and crammed it back into the bin.

Mae was being a brat. That was not like her. Not like her at all! Vivie looked up at Mama and Poppa, her teeth worrying her lip at the concern etched across their faces.

•   •   •   •   •

Despite the chill, perspiration trickled from under Vivie's arms as Lofo gave her a hug and a kiss, then boarded the waiting bus. Her heart ached at the thought of being apart from him. It reminded Vivie of the World War II concentration camps in her history book, where women and children were separated from the men. She glanced over at her mother.

Csaky prompted, "Mae? Wave goodbye to Poppa," but she only turned and buried her face into her mother's waist. "C'mon, Vivie. Let's head over to the school."

As the bus drove off Vivie glanced back, wondering how her mother could be so calm. Her mind whirled as they headed toward the brick building. "Mama?"

"Yes?"

"Aren't you worried about where they're taking Poppa?"

Csaky frowned. "Worried? Why? Should I be?"

Vivie's head swam. Her body swayed.

"Are you okay, Vivie?" Her mother's hand reached out and cupped her forehead. "You're not looking well at all. Come over and sit here on this bench. Do you feel like you're going to be sick?"

Mae trailed after them.

Vivie shook her head. "I'm..." She drew in a breath and slowly exhaled; her words then gushed out. "I'm worried about what's going to happen to Poppa." Tears welled in her eyes and spilled down her cheeks.

"Why, Vivie! What's brought this on? You're trembling."

When her mother's arms reached out and enfolded her, she released a jagged sigh. Mama then leaned back and took her chin in hand. She looked into Vivie's eyes. "Your Poppa's going to be fine."

"Are you sure?"

"Yes. Whatever made you think otherwise?"

"They sent him away from us. Like they did to those families in World War II in the concentration camps."

Csaky's brows raised. "Is *that* what you've been thinking, Vivie?"

She nodded.

Despite her age and size, Mama pulled her close, rocking Vivie in her arms. Her mother's hand stroked her back. "Vivie, your father's staying in the men's barracks, a few streets over."

Tension slowly eased from her body as her mother continued. "Once he's settled in, we'll see him. And as soon as arrangements can be made, we'll be moving on."

Vivie heaved a deep sigh.

"Feel better now?"

"Yes, Mama." She wiped away her tears.

Csaky brushed back Vivie's curls, then stood. She reached down and clasped Mae's hand. "Well, let's go see about our living quarters. Okay?"

Vivie nodded.

Inside the school, a kind-faced woman ushered them down the hall. "I know it's not much," she apologized, "but there are just so many of you. We've been a little overwhelmed trying to accommodate everyone."

Csaky smiled and placed her hand on the woman's arm. "It is much appreciated. And better than most of the conditions we've experienced over the last few weeks."

"I cannot even begin to imagine. You poor soul. And with children as well." The woman shook her head. "Just settle in where you can find a place and..."

While her mother conversed with the Red Cross volunteer, Vivie studied the school gymnasium. It was filled with straw beds—some occupied, some not. A couple of little boys ran between the makeshift aisles playing tag. "Look, Mae." She pointed to the middle of the gym. "There are some girls over there you can play with."

The child again burrowed her face into her mother's waist.

•   •   •   •   •

Mae lay asleep on a straw bed, her thumb hanging from her slack mouth and a line of drool trickling down her chin.

"Mama? Is she okay?"

"I think so, Vivie. She's had a bad shock. It's going to take time for her to process it."

She nodded. "Mama?"

"Yes?"

"Will we ever go back home?"

Csaky sighed and looked out across the gym. "Only time will tell, Vivie."

"But what will happen to our house and all our things?"

"I don't know, dear." She reached over and caressed Vivie's cheek. A sad smile crossed her face. "Don't fret about it, Vivie. Everything we had can be replaced."

Not everything, she thought as Norsk padded through her mind. The one thing Vivie knew for sure was that nothing would or ever could take the place of her beloved cat.

As a silence fell between them, Vivie watched the little boys dart about the space, their mothers trying to get them to settle down for the night.

"Vivie?"

She looked over at her mother.

"There's something we need to talk about."

Her breath caught at her mother's tone.

Mama's voice dropped to a whisper. "I wanted to caution you that under *no* circumstances are you to tell *anyone* about us."

Vivie leaned forward.

"Even though we've escaped Hungary—" Csaky's harsh cough echoed through the gym. "There are still going to be people out there looking for us because of who we are. Some of whom may wish to do us harm."

She gulped, her eyes widening.

Csaky reached over and drew Vivie near. "I don't mean to frighten you."

But you are, Vivie thought as she leaned into her mother's embrace.

"As long as no one knows who we are, we're safe. Do you understand, Vivie?"

"I think so, Mama," she strangled out.

"You're *never* to tell *anyone.* It's to be kept secret." Her mother clasped her hand. "So, promise me, Vivie. Promise me you will *always* keep our secret."

"I promise, Mama," she hoarsely whispered. "No one will ever know."

CHAPTER 13

Vivie stood on the train platform with her family, awaiting their transfer to the refugee camp at Traiskirchen. When they boarded, memories of their failed trip from Kapuvár flooded her thoughts. She purposely chose a forward-facing seat by the window, wanting to be alert in the event anything happened.

Her father took the seat next to hers while Csaky and Mae settled across from them. Tension hung heavy in the air like an overfilled water balloon.

Vivie studied her sister. She remained listless and apathetic, startling at the train's whistle.

"It's okay, Mae," Csaky soothed, pulling her close.

Seconds after the train began to move, a conductor approached. His gold watch fob strained across his belly. "Tickets?" he asked in German.

Vivie's sharp intake of breath slowly eased out as her father produced a gray transit card.

The conductor glanced at it and nodded. "Ah, Traiskirchen! You're refugees!" His arm swept outwards. "Welcome to Austria."

"Thank you." Lofo pocketed the returned card.

"Where in Hungary are you from?"

"Budapest."

"So many bad things there." The conductor shook his head. "You are fortunate to have escaped."

"Indeed."

As the train accelerated, Vivie tried to relax. She thumbed through the well-worn magazine from the refugee camp, having read it so many times she almost had the stories memorized. At the moment the magazine held no interest. Setting it aside, she peered out at the bleak December landscape, her thoughts wandering back over the last few weeks: to their journey, their home—and her Norsk.

•   •   •   •   •

"We're here."

Vivie startled at her father's words. "Traiskirchen?"

"No, Vivie. Vienna." He gathered their few belongings. "We have to change trains, remember?"

"Oh, yes."

As they prepared to disembark, the conductor passed them and nodded. "There's been a delay on your connection."

Vivie stiffened.

A frown appeared on her father's face. "A delay?"

"Just a short one," the conductor reassured. "Another train was blocking the track. You've got about a fifteen to twenty-minute wait." He nodded toward Csaky. "You might like to step outside the station and let the children get a glimpse of the Christmas markets."

"Thank you. That would be a nice"—she coughed—"diversion for them."

"Here!" He handed a coin to Lofo. "Buy them some gingerbread. My treat."

"Oh, but no—" Csaky choked out. She took the coin and tried to return it.

"Please," he entreated, refusing to take it back.

"You are too kind," she rasped. "Thank him, girls."

As they stepped down from the train car, the conductor gave them a wave. "I wish you and your family well in your new life."

"Thank you," Lofo called after him.

Outside the train station, Vivie grinned. "Look, Mae! Isn't it wonderful? Almost like home!"

Vienna was decorated like a Christmas wonderland. Lights and decorations adorned the city, its shop and café windows filled with seasonal displays and toys. The streets were lined with rows of booths and stalls stocked with colorful ornaments and enticing foods. Vivie inhaled. The tantalizing aromas of gingerbread, pretzels, sausages, strudel, and roasted chestnuts mingled and wafted through the air. Her mouth watered.

Lofo returned from one of the stalls. "Here." He held out a piece of gingerbread to Vivie.

"Thank you, Poppa." She bit into it. "Mmm. Still warm."

"Mae?" he asked.

The child buried her face into Csaky's waist.

"Well, all right then," her father said. "More for the rest of us."

●　　　●　　　●　　　●　　　●

Vivie settled into the seat of the southbound train, her mouth all tingly numb with the taste of ginger and cloves. As they streamed along the tracks for Traiskirchen, Vienna's beautifully decorated tree came to mind. Funny, she had not even thought about Christmas. The Christ Child likely would not be bringing a tree or gifts this year. And no szaloncukors. She sighed. That could be a good thing. Mae had eaten so many of the chocolate-covered fondants last year that she had vomited all over Mama's party dress. Well, at least that would not happen this year.

Her thoughts drifted to Norsk, remembering how the cat liked to pounce in the piles of wrapping paper, batting at bows and nesting in the empty boxes. She missed her so much. Vivie brushed away an escaped tear and sent up a prayer to Saint Gertrude.

●　　　●　　　●　　　●　　　●

On the station's platform, a young man approached them. "Hello. You must be the Degirdros," he stated in a voice smooth and rich as syrup.

Vivie's eyes narrowed at the stranger. She stepped closer to her father.

"Yes," Lofo said, shaking his outstretched hand. "Yes, we are. And you must be Theodolf Berlinger. Sorry we're late."

"That's all right."

As he talked with her parents, Vivie realized he was from the refugee camp. Breathing a sigh of relief, she glanced about.

Several young women were standing off to the side, tittering behind their hands and pointing to the young man. "Isn't he just divine?"

"So dreamy."

"I think I'm going to swoon."

A woman eyed him as she passed, almost bumping into a post.

Vivie bit her lip and managed not to laugh. She continued to eavesdrop on their conversation.

Theodolf ran a hand through his wavy hair.

"Doesn't he look like Tab Hunter?"

"Who?"

"Tab Hunter! The American movie star, silly."

"Look at that sandy blond hair. That tan. I think it *is* Tab Hunter!"

Vivie thought back to the photographs in the movie magazines left behind by her mother's friend Alice and shrugged. She did not see it.

"This way," Theodolf said, directing them to the van.

•　　•　　•　　•　　•

As the young man showed them into the main office at the refugee camp, a skinny brunette entered the room. "Theodolf?"

"Yes, ma'am?"

"We're short-handed right now. Would you mind showing the family to their quarters and around the camp?"

"Certainly," he replied. "Right this way, Dr. Degirdro."

Outside, Csaky coughed, "Such—a large facility."

"Yes, ma'am. It used to be a cadet training school." As he led them to their housing, he pointed out various structures along the way.

Vivie scrutinized her surroundings, taking it all in.

"That building over there, Dr. Degirdro?"

Lofo nodded.

"That's where they process the asylum requests. I'll walk you back over as I leave."

"Thank you."

"Well, here we are." Theodolf climbed the concrete steps and pulled open the wooden door. "Be thankful you're here now, rather than a few weeks ago." He ushered them inside. "In November, there was no heat or electricity. And most of the windows were broken."

They followed him down the hallway and up a set of stairs to the second floor. "Here's your new home," Theodolf said, stepping inside the small room. A pair of bunk beds filled the closet-like space, along with a small table and a couple of wooden upright chairs. Overhead, a single light bulb hung from the ceiling.

Vivie's nostrils flared at the scent of fresh paint.

"This is really very nice," Lofo remarked. "Much better than we've had in the past."

"Yes," Csaky agreed. "And at least here, we can be together as a family." Her cough rang out in the sparsely furnished room.

Lofo's arm encircled her waist, displacing Mae.

The child stepped back, lip poked out.

Theodolf went to the window and pointed to a small building off to the right. "A couple of volunteers have started a makeshift school over there. I'm sure they would welcome Vivie and Mae for classes."

"That's wonderful." Csaky smiled. "Maybe get us back to some degree of normalcy." She glanced over at Mae.

"Oh, one other thing before I leave," Theodolf said. "I'm sorry, but the facilities are a little scarce around here. We've got some showers over in the old gymnasium, and there are latrines at the back of the building near the fence."

"No need to apologize," Lofo replied. "We understand."

"Well, if you don't need anything else, I'll walk you over to the processing center."

"Poppa?" Vivie asked. "May I come, too?"

"Certainly."

Upon bidding Theodolf goodbye, Lofo and Vivie entered the asylum office and got in line. Twelve people were ahead of them, all exuding a sense of hopelessness—both in posture and face.

She peeked around them at the interviewers, who looked as though they would rather be anywhere else but here. No one seemed happy, not even those who had been processed and were heading out the door.

Finally, it was their turn.

"I have a letter here..." Lofo dug into the satchel and produced it. "This is from a US banker, vouching for me and my family. William O. McNabb with New York's National Bank has agreed to be our sponsor. He's one of their international representatives."

The official took the proferred document and glanced at it, then handed it back. "Dr. Degirdro," the man said, "we will make you an appointment to meet with the United States immigration officers when they come out, but you must understand there is up to a three-month wait while they evaluate these applications."

Vivie chewed her lip, glancing up at her father as the official continued.

"And it could be longer. From what we've experienced, they're very thorough in their interview process and...hmm...how to say this....Ah! Selective in whom they accept. Unlike other countries who merely seem to ask for a show of hands." He waved in a dismissive gesture. "However, since the US appears to have a preference for those with academic degrees, then your wait could possibly be less than many of the others....That is, if they do accept you. We will notify you when your appointment is scheduled. Is this agreeable?"

"Not really," he responded. "But I guess I don't have any other choice."

"No, you don't."

"C'mon, Vivie."

•   •   •   •   •

On the way to the latrine that night, a movement to the right caught Vivie's attention. In the moonlight, the shadowy form of a cat traveled the edge of the fence line. The skinny stray, intent on some apparent prey, eased forward, slinking across the ground on silent paws despite the dead leaves. It stopped, then crouched down. A second later its butt wriggled, and the cat pounced! A high-pitched squeal from its prey signaled a successful catch.

The feline, apparently hearing her sharp intake of breath, turned its head. Their eyes met. The limp form of a small rat hung from the predator's jaws. A second later, the cat turned and darted away.

Was this the type of life that Norsk was leading? Vivie could not help but wonder. Lying in bed that night, her thoughts drifted back to the scrawny stray. There must be something she could do to help. Inspiration hit about the time her eyes drifted shut.

The next day in the mess hall, Vivie surreptitiously slid bits of food from her plate into a napkin, then slipped the small packet into her pocket. At dusk, she excused herself and headed toward the latrines. By the fence, she left the food scraps for the lone stray, but before she parted whispered, "I'll be back tomorrow."

Sneaking out to feed the cat two weeks later, Vivie had the distinct impression she was being followed. As the unease crept over her, the hairs on the back of her neck stood on end. She glanced over her shoulder, but no one was there. Still, she could not shed the feeling that she was being watched.

The yellow glow of two eyes peered from under the fence. "Aha!" Vivie whispered, "I guess it's *you* that's watching me. Ready to eat, kitty?" She stooped down and held out a piece of boiled fish. The stray watched her but would not approach. "Hmm," Vivie said. "Don't really blame you. It's not that appetizing, but as Poppa says, 'If you're hungry enough, you'll eat anything.'" A sad smile crossed her lips. "Well, here you go." Vivie laid the food on the ground and walked a short distance away. Then she turned back and watched the cat slink forward, bolting down the scraps.

"So, *that's* what you've been up to!"

Vivie jumped, her hand flying to her chest. She spun around. Theodolf stood behind her, his arms crossed. "It's you!" she stammered out.

"Sorry, Vivie. I didn't mean to startle you."

Catching her breath, she managed, "T-that's all right."

"So, how long have you been feeding the stray?"

"For a couple of days, now. Actually—" She hung her head. "Ever since we arrived. How did you know?"

"I didn't know for sure." He glanced over at the cat. "But I had seen you slipping food off your plate and wondered. Then tonight, when I saw you sneaking about on my way back to the office, I decided to follow you."

She teared up. "Are you going to tell?"

"It all depends, Vivie."

"Depends?" She gulped. "Depends on what?"

"C'mon. It's getting late. I'll walk you back. We'll talk on the way."

"Okay."

"There's this woman...Ruth something-or-other in the United Kingdom. She's been doing some work with feral cats....Now, what was her last name?...Hmm. That is going to drive me crazy for the rest of the evening!" He glanced over at her. "Don't you hate it when that happens?"

Vivie nodded and thought, *He's not making any sense. Where is he going with this?*

"She talks about trapping the cats and—"

"Trapping the cats?" Vivie choked out, her stomach clinching.

"No, Vivie. Not trapping, trapping. Not like that at all."

Vivie's eyes hardened, her stomach still in a knot. "What do you mean?"

"She lures them into what they call a 'humane trap,' because all it does is safely close them inside."

Vivie scowled, still unsure about the process.

He continued. "Then, she takes them to a vet to be...uh...'fixed.'" His face darkened.

"I know about that," she reassured him. "Spaying and neutering."

"Oh! Well...uh...good. Then, she takes the cat back and releases it where she caught it, and someone comes and feeds it regularly."

Vivie nodded, absorbing his words. "Sounds okay....I guess." They were standing outside the building. "How did you find out about it?"

"I read an article that mentioned her work. What *is* her last name?" He shook his head and sighed.

"So..." Vivie asked. "What does that have to do with me feeding this cat?"

"Nothing right now, but that one stray can begin to multiply. Then, when the camp becomes overrun with cats, there'll be a big problem...and things will not necessarily be handled in a humane way."

"You mean..." She gulped. "They'll kill them?"

He nodded. "I'm afraid so, Vivie."

Tears filled her eyes. "That is so wrong! So heartless! So cruel!"

"I agree."

Her throat tightened. "So...what happens now?" She could barely get the words out.

"Well, first of all, you're going to start eating your food instead of sharing it with the cat."

"But...what will it eat?"

"Don't worry, Vivie. There's plenty of scraps left at the end of the day. I'll see that the cat is fed, and I'll trap it and get it fixed. Is it a deal?"

She stood a moment, thinking it over. "It's a deal," she nodded. "And you won't tell on me?"

"No, Vivie. I won't tell."

CHAPTER 14

Vivie and Theodolf watched the altered tabby eat.

"I thought you would be happy, Vivie," Theodolf turned and looked at her, nodding toward the ear-tipped cat.

"Oh, I am," she replied.

"Really? It doesn't seem like it."

"Oh, no. I am." She sighed. "It's just..." Her voice trailed off.

"Just what, Vivie?"

"Poppa."

"What about him?"

"I think he's getting very frustrated. Every day we go to the immigration clerks to see if we've been accepted to go to America with nothing to show for it. Bácsi Oswald is willing to sponsor us, but nobody in the asylum office will listen to Poppa, much less read his papers. All they say is that we have to go through 'the process.'"

"You have an uncle in America?"

"Well...he's not really my uncle. You know how it is. He and his wife are close friends with Mama and Poppa, so Mae and I've always called them Bácsi Oswald and Néni Alice."

Theodolf nodded.

They sat in silence as the cat washed her face.

"Maybe I can help, Vivie."

"Help? But how?"

"I've got an idea. I can't make any promises, but we'll see."

•   •   •   •   •

"Switzerland?" Lofo cocked his head.

"Yes, sir," Theodolf said. "My father is willing to sponsor you until you can reach Mr. McNabb."

Lofo shook his head. "Just our luck that Oswald has taken an extended holiday at this time."

Vivie's eyes darted between Theodolf and her father.

Csaky entered the room, a disheveled Mae in tow. "Fighting again. Honestly—" She caught sight of Theodolf.

He nodded. "Afternoon, ma'am."

"Good afternoon."

Lofo looked over at his wife. He put a hand on Theodolf's shoulder. "This young man has brought me a very interesting proposition."

"He has?" She coughed and cleared her throat.

"Well, if you will excuse me, now. I'll let you and your family discuss it."

"Thank you, Theodolf. We will."

As he left the room, Csaky frowned, "What was that all about?" She divested Mae of her torn jumper and led her over to the ewer and basin.

"Theodolf's father has offered to sponsor us in Switzerland."

"Switzerland?" she rasped, "but Alice and Oswald have sponsored us in America."

"And have taken an extended holiday and cannot be reached," Lofo concluded.

"So...what are you saying?"

"Theodolf has proposed that we accept his father's sponsorship for now. That will get us out of the refugee camp and into Switzerland. Then, from there we work at contacting Oswald and getting our sponsorship accepted in America."

"And his parents are willing to take on the responsibility for the four of us?"

"Apparently so. He says now that he and his brothers are grown, it's just his parents rattling about in a large farmhouse. Says his mother would love the company."

Vivie crossed her fingers, awaiting her mother's response.

•   •   •   •   •

"Come in! Come in! Welcome to our home!" Mrs. Berlinger ushered them inside the red brick house. "I'm Guta. Here, let me take your coats."

Vivie caught a whiff of cinnamon as the large-boned woman reached for hers.

Following introductions, Csaky remarked, "This is so kind of you. Opening your home to us."

"Yes," Lofo nodded. "We really appreciate it."

"Think nothing of it," Guta responded, waving her hand. "From what Theodolf has said, we are blessed to have you."

Before Vivie could consider the remark, her eyes lit upon the large black cat stretched out across the hearth. As she started toward it, a meaty hand closed around her arm.

"No child. Don't touch the cat."

She looked up into the black eyes of a grizzled old man. His bushy white eyebrows resembled a couple of hairy caterpillars, his mustache an over-used scrub brush.

"Don't touch the cat," he reiterated. "He's an evil bastard."

"Anders!" Guta nodded toward Vivie, then Mae. "Watch your language." She turned toward Csaky and Lofo. "I apologize for my husband."

"No worries," Lofo replied, his hand caressing Mae's head.

"Anders?" Guta nodded toward the couple. "These are Theodolf's friends, the Degirdros. And this is Mae and that's Vivie."

The eight-year-old clung to her mother as Lofo stepped forward and extended his hand. "Thank you so much for sponsoring us."

"Glad to do it," he nodded. "I hope you will be comfortable in our home. We look forward to the company."

"Come, then," Guta said. "Let me show you your rooms."

Vivie turned to follow. As she reached the doorway, she glanced back to see the feline observing her through slitted, green eyes. The girl walked over to where Anders had settled into his chair and was lighting his pipe. "Excuse me, sir?"

"Yes?" His left brow arched.

She nodded to the cat. "Why do you call him an 'evil bastard?'"

"Ha!" burst from the old man. "He's what you call a 'feral.' Would sooner scratch your eyes out than befriend you."

"I know about ferals."

His eyebrows raised. "Do you?"

"Well...not a lot," she admitted. "I know some."

Anders nodded. He pursed his lips, then puffed his pipe. His eyes narrowed as though taking her measure.

As smoke rings rose and encircled his head, Vivie gave a slight cough and stepped back.

The feline stood and stretched, then assumed a sphinx-like pose.

"That cat," Anders said, with a tilt of his head toward the animal, "was hit by a car down the lane one night. Broke his leg. Theodolf found him. Brute liked to tore him up. But he managed to get him home and..."

While he told the cat's tale, Vivie studied the now upright feline. She noted the slight outward bow to his left front leg. As Anders finished his account, Vivie asked, "Does he have a name?"

The old man chuckled. "We call him Satan."

"Satan?" Vivie's head drew back. "But why?"

"Because he was the devil himself to try to care for." Anders paused and took another puff of his pipe. He shrugged. "Name just stuck after that."

Vivie nodded. She turned and gave the cat a slow blink of her eyes. He slow blinked back.

When Anders rose and started toward the fireplace, Satan's ears flattened back against his head. His eyes dilated. The cat arched his back and hissed, before turning and fleeing the room.

"See what I mean?" The old man moved aside the fire screen and tossed a couple more logs on the fire. With the metal poker, he reached in and pushed them back against the grate.

"Vivie?" Csaky called from the hallway. "Come—" Her croupy cough broke off her words. "See —your—room."

•   •   •   •   •

"Are you sure they won't be a bother?" Csaky's brow raised as Lofo tried to usher her out the door.

"No bother at all," Guta replied. "I've raised a houseful of boys. Two little girls will be no trouble at all. You go see Dr. Whitfield about that cough and don't worry about us."

"C'mon, Csaky," Lofo urged. "The sooner we go, the sooner we'll get back. Mae's asleep, and Vivie will help look after her. Won't you?"

"Yes, Poppa."

Back in the main living area, Vivie browsed the contents of the bookcase.

"What do you want to do when you grow up, Vivie?" the old man asked.

She subconsciously flinched. It was the clichéd question that adults always seemed to ask when trying to make conversation. Her eyes strayed across the room to the cat, again stretched across the hearth. Vivie longed to scoop up the forbidden feline and bury her face deep into his dense fur. Instead, she answered, "To travel and see the world. Maybe teach."

Anders chuckled and shook his head. "Ambitious for one so young. Right, Guta?" He smacked the newspaper on his knee, turning to his wife. "Sounds like you when you were that age. Before I came along and swept you off your feet." Anders grinned and wiggled his eyebrows. "That's all well and good for now, Vivie. Until some young man comes along. Right, Guta? Then it will be marriage, cooking, and babies filling your head!" He chuckled.

Her face warmed.

"Vivie?"

She turned, puzzling at the rigid set of Guta's jaw.

"Come with me, please."

Vivie followed her down the hall.

"That's right. Take her into the kitchen. Start her off right," Anders called after them. "Show her how to make a man happy." He picked up his newspaper and opened it. "After all, the key to a man's heart is through his stomach."

"Stupid old man," Guta muttered.

Vivie's breath caught.

Inside the kitchen, the woman washed her hands, then strode over to the counter and retrieved a giant bowl and large tin. "Wash your hands and sit down, Vivie."

As she obeyed, Guta opened the tin, threw three fistfuls of flour onto the table's surface, then dumped the bowl's doughy contents onto the pile. "Dust your hands with the flour," she instructed when Vivie sat down.

After she did, Guta pinched off a hunk of dough and handed it to her, then began to knead the remaining lump. She nodded to Vivie. "Do the same."

"Yes, ma'am," the girl responded, duplicating her motions.

"Vivie?...I'm going to give you the best advice I never got."

She nodded as the wad of dough began to take on a satiny feel.

"Not so hard. You don't want to toughen it."

"Yes, ma'am."

"Don't compromise, Vivie." The old woman shook a doughy finger at her. "Don't let society or a man stand in the way of your dreams." Guta sighed. "Not everybody is meant to be married." She looked back at the doorway. "I had dreams, Vivie. Like you, I wanted to travel. I wanted to be a missionary. But..." A faraway look appeared in her eyes. She shook her head. "It was a different time, child. Women were expected to marry. To have children." A crease marred her forehead. "And if not...well," she sighed. "Things were said, and eyebrows were raised. So, I did what was expected."

A series of emotions played across the woman's face. "I came to love Anders. Pompous old goat that he is." A smile flitted across Guta's lips. "He can be an ass. But he has a sweet side as well. He was a good father. A good provider. And kind....Ahh, well, enough of that!" She gave a little shake like a dog flicking moisture from its coat. "The point is, Vivie, follow your dreams. Don't let others dissuade you, otherwise you will live a life filled with regret and what-ifs."

•   •   •   •   •

That night, Vivie settled into the feather bed. As she reflected on Guta's advice, sleep quickly engulfed her.

Norsk dashed through the streets. Brakes screeched. A car horn blared. There was a soft thud, followed by an instantaneous cry of pain. Then silence. Her beloved cat lay dead in a ditch, the feline's bloodstained mouth frozen in a grimace of pain. Her wide-open eyes now dull and sightless. Maggots, like those on the severed hand in Győr, infested her corpse.

Writhing and sweating, Vivie fought to waken from the nightmare. She gasped, her eyes flying open. Sitting up, tears streamed down her face. She crawled out of bed, trembling. "It was only a dream," Vivie mumbled to herself as she turned on the light. She walked over to the window and pulled back its curtain. Looking out into the moon-drenched night, she sent a prayer to Saint Gertrude.

A soft knock caused her to turn. "Come in."

Anders's bald head peeped around the door. "I saw the light. Are you okay, Vivie?"

"Yes, sir."

The old man stood a moment. His head gave a soft shake. "I think not so much. Come, Vivie. Let's go to the kitchen and have a snack."

She hesitated, not wanting to impose.

"Come on. Indulge an old man."

Vivie nodded, following him out the door and down the hall.

In the kitchen, Anders pulled a plate of turkey from the refrigerator and began assembling two sandwiches. "Vivie? In that upper cabinet to the right of the sink? Grab us a couple of plates and glasses. Then pour us some milk."

She obeyed.

At the table, Anders bit into his sandwich. A moment later, he asked. "Is it not good? Why you not eat?"

Vivie dipped her head. "It's fine. Thank you," she managed, then took a bite.

Anders got up and went to the cupboard. He brought back two napkins, handing one to her. "You know, Vivie? I can tell you are a 'thinker.'" He reached up and tapped the side of his head with his index finger. "Sometimes that is good." He shrugged. "Sometimes it is bad."

"Bad?" she puzzled. "How can thinking be bad?"

"Ahh!" he said, upon taking a drink of milk. "When it stimulates the imagination and causes unfounded fears."

Her eyes narrowed as she absorbed his words.

Anders pushed his empty plate back and patted his rotund belly. "Nightmares, Vivie."

"How did you know?" she whispered, warmth flooding her face.

"I heard you cry out."

Vivie dropped her head. "I'm so sorry that I woke you."

Anders softly chuckled. "No worry, dear. Old men are light sleepers. Up and down several times a night."

She nodded, thinking back to Nagypa's noisy movements through the house when he and Nagamama used to stay overnight.

"Well, I'm off to bed, Vivie." He rose and carried his dishes to the sink. "Take your time. I'll see you in the morning."

"Thank you," she called after him as he headed through the doorway.

Back in the bedroom, Vivie studied Theodolf's bookcase. She pulled a copy of *Treasure Island* from the shelf and curled up in bed to read. Before Vivie had finished the third page, her eyes drifted shut, and the book slipped from her hands softly thudding onto the area rug.

Sometime during the night, Vivie was conscious of a slight shift in the bed and a warm body snuggling next to hers. Mae. Sleep quickly reclaimed her.

•　　•　　•　　•　　•

Upon awakening the next morning, Vivie stretched and turned. A slight smile crossed her lips as her sister promptly responded, shifting and pressing back against Vivie, once again nestling near. When she reached over to give Mae a hug, Vivie's hand jerked back, and her eyes flew open. Two slitted green eyes met her wide-eyed stare. She drew in her breath, hardly believing what she was seeing. Satan, not Mae! Hesitantly, Vivie's fingers stretched out and stroked the cat's silky soft fur. Her heart soared with delight as the low rumble of a purr responded.

Moments later, a soft knock sounded at the door. "Vivie?" Guta's head appeared. "Are—Oh, my!" The old woman's eyes widened in surprise.

"It's Satan." Vivie smiled.

"Why...I can't believe my eyes." Guta's head disappeared. "Anders! Anders! You've got to come see."

A second later, the old man's bald head appeared.

Vivie grinned and glanced down at the purring cat. "Guess he's not such an 'evil bastard' after all."

The hoot of Anders's laugh echoed down the hall.

CHAPTER 15

Vivie glanced back at Satan, sitting midway up the staircase. Over the last few weeks, she had grown attached to him. Like Norsk, every morning Vivie awakened to find the feline curled at her side. She walked over and stroked his fur. He purred, rubbing against her arm. "I'm going to miss you," Vivie whispered.

Mae stood silently, looking out the window. Still not herself, she had shown some improvement over the last couple of weeks.

Lofo glanced at his watch. "We're going to be late if Anders doesn't get back here with the car."

"You've got the papers changing our sponsorship to Oswald?" Csaky coughed out.

He nodded and patted the leather satchel. "Right here."

"Here comes Bácsi Anders now," Mae announced as tires crunched on the snow-covered driveway.

At the bus station, Guta shoved a slip of paper into Csaky's hand. "Here's our telephone number and address. Make sure you stay in touch."

"We will," she reassured her, passing the note into Lofo's care.

"I'm going to miss you so much," Guta said. Her voice cracked with emotion.

"We'll miss you, too." Csaky gave her a hug. "Opening your home to us. Making us feel like family."

Guta embraced Vivie, whispering in her ear, "Promise me you'll remember what we talked about? Following your dreams and not compromising?"

"I promise, Néni Guta," Vivie whispered back.

The old woman's lips grazed her cheek, before she reached out for Mae.

As the bus left the station, Vivie glanced back at Anders comforting his weeping wife.

Csaky sniffed. "They are good people."

"Indeed," Lofo replied. He relaxed back into the seat. "For a minute there, I thought we were going to end up missing the bus."

"You know," Csaky said, "Anders would have insisted on driving us all the way."

"You're probably right."

Vivie gazed out at the snowy landscape. The last couple of weeks had flown by. Néni Guta and Bácsi Anders had treated the girls like grandchildren. When not sightseeing with them, Vivie had curled up and read by the fireplace with Satan purring in her lap. The cat had reformed— even deigning to befriend Anders, but the old man would not admit it. Vivie had entered the room and seen Satan curled in his lap one afternoon. The old man had coughed and quickly adjusted his newspaper to cover the feline. Vivie pretended she did not notice, grabbing a magazine from the table and heading out the door where she doubled over with laughter. For someone who had appeared so grizzled and gruff at their first encounter, Anders's actions proved there was a lovable teddy bear underneath his bluster. She thought he even had a tear in his eye last night when they had shared their final midnight snack.

"You're awfully quiet, Vivie."

She turned and looked at her father.

"Which cat do you think you'll miss the most, Satan or that stray?"

"Stray?" Vivie's head tilted. "What stray, Poppa?"

"The one you were feeding at Traiskirchen?"

Vivie gasped. "You know about her?" she stammered out.

"You're my daughter, Vivie. You think your mother and I don't know your heart and that you were slipping food to that stray?"

Her face warmed.

"You know you shouldn't do that," Csaky coughed. "It only serves to attract more."

Vivie shook her head. "Not if you do it right. Ruth Plant..." She explained the woman's concept to her parents adding, "So the cat then defends its territory, and no other strays intrude."

Lofo nodded. "Interesting. Where did you learn about this?"

"From Theodolf. He's studying to be a veterinarian."

"A bright young man," Csaky remarked.

•　　•　　•　　•　　•

A loud grinding pop and a clunk jarred Vivie awake. The bus gave a lurch, then ground to a halt.

"Sorry, folks," the driver called. "We seem to have developed some engine trouble."

"Great," Lofo muttered. "Of all times—"

"Calm down, dear." Csaky patted his arm.

"Calm down? We're going to miss the train."

"We have plenty of time."

They gathered outside the bus with the other passengers while the driver opened the hood. Several of the men crowded around, prodding and poking, while debating the mechanical failure. One fellow crawled under the bus. "There's your problem," he announced. "Transmission."

"C'mon," Lofo said. "Let's walk. Hopefully, we can hitch a ride with someone."

"Why don't we wait until they fix the bus?" Csaky asked.

"Because that will take too long. C'mon now. Let's get going." Lofo gathered their belongings and headed down the snow-covered roadway. Csaky and the girls followed.

Vivie glanced over at her sister. "Mae, you forgot your doll."

"No, I didn't," she replied. "I left it for the Holy Angel to take."

As they walked, Vivie thought back to the day Guta had bought the doll for Mae. The child had pitched a tantrum similar to the one at the refugee camp. After Vivie explained to the couple what had happened to the beloved Dodo, Anders had taken the child aside. He told her that the Holy Angel had taken her doll for some sad little girl in Heaven. His explanation had appeared to placate Mae, for afterwards she accepted the new doll without complaint.

•　　•　　•　　•　　•

Vivie's head rose as a rattly, black pickup truck approached from behind, slowing as it passed. Lofo waved, but it drove on before stopping a short distance ahead. A moment later, the truck slowly backed toward them. When it stopped, the driver got out and walked to the back of the vehicle. Two passengers peered from the cab's rear window.

"Hello," her father called out.

The man did not respond. He just stood by the back of the truck and stared as Lofo explained their dilemma. ". . . and we need a ride to the train station, if you could oblige."

After a brief hesitation, the man glanced back at the cab.

Vivie gave a soft sigh of relief at his companions' nods.

"Get in," the driver said, gruffly.

Calling words of thanks, Vivie and her family climbed into the truck bed. They had no sooner sat down than the vehicle roared off, the momentum slamming Vivie against the wheel hub. She winced as a jolt of pain shot through her hip.

They huddled together in the center of the bed, hunkering down to avoid the whipping winds. Vivie stretched out her legs and braced them against the side of the truck bed, attempting to keep from sliding about.

Mae gave a shriek as the vehicle rounded a curve and slewed about on the icy road. Still, the driver did not slow down. A moment later, the truck veered off the main road, then diverted onto a small lane.

As the snowy woods appeared to surround them, Lofo shook his head and muttered, "I don't think this is the right way."

"How can you say that?" Csaky questioned. "We've never been here before."

Knocking on the back window, he yelled, "Is this the way to the train station?"

"Shortcut," one of the men responded, then laughed.

"See?" Csaky said.

"I don't know..." A look of concern crossed Lofo's face.

The truck continued to hurtle down the narrow lane, naked limbs and vines slapping and snapping against its sides. As the vehicle careened onto an overgrown pathway and into the brush, daylight began to fade.

Vivie's heart raced as they appeared to plunge deeper and deeper into the forest.

Minutes later, the truck jerked to a stop in a small clearing.

"Not again," Mae sighed.

"Hush!" Csaky drew her near as the doors opened, and the three men spilled out.

"Fucking refugees," the driver spat. "Get out of truck."

Lofo frowned. "I don't understand." Bewilderment filled his face

Vivie's eyes darted between the man and her father.

"Get the hell out of truck!"

"C'mon." Lofo jumped down and helped Csaky climb from the truck bed. Vivie and Mae followed, moving off to the side with their mother.

"What a pretty one," the tall man said, a smarmy smile creeping across his face.

Csaky flinched under the scrutiny. She pulled Vivie and Mae closer, taking a step back.

The driver walked up and stuck his finger in Lofo's face. "Filthy bozgors. You come our country. Take jobs," he growled out through gritted teeth.

Lofo held up his hands and tried backing away but bumped into the man's friends. "No one's trying—"

"Shut up!"

"Please—"

"I said, 'Shut up!'" he spat out, then mumbled, "Damned bozgor."

Vivie gasped as the driver then backhanded her father. His two friends grabbed Lofo and held his arms while the man riffled through his pockets.

"Look!" the driver crowed. He held up their money, fanning it in the air.

"Please don't—"

"How many times I tell you? Shut up! Show him what happens when not listen, men."

"Poppa!" Vivie shrieked as they pummeled her father. When she tried to run to him, her mother grabbed her arm in a vise-like grip, jerking her back.

"No!" she hissed.

Vivie looked back at her. Mama held Mae's head firmly against her body, not allowing her to see the men beating their father.

"Come," she said softly, backing away.

"But—"

"Shh—"

At the scowl on her mother's face, Vivie ceased to argue.

Taking advantage of the twilight, they eased toward the safety of the heavy brush. From a snow-encased thicket, Vivie watched in horror as her father writhed in the snow under the beam of the truck's headlights.

"Nasty Hungarians," the driver muttered, snatching up Poppa's satchel and dumping its contents on the ground. In the failing light, he stooped and sorted through the papers. "This shit? I can't read." He hurled a handful of them to the side, then dug into the satchel's interior pocket. "But I know *these*!" The man held up their train tickets and refugee documents. "*I'll* teach you to come where not welcome." He reared back and landed a kick into her father's ribs.

Vivie cringed at his grunt of pain.

"We don't want you here!" the driver's tall friend growled out, then leaned over and spat on Poppa.

"Yes!" the third man said. "Go back your own country, bozgor!"

Then all three began to kick him.

Vivie averted her eyes, a wave of nausea washing over her. The thud of their vicious kicks and her father's cries hurtled her back to the day the cruel bullies attacked the old stray dog that wandered into the schoolyard. Its pitiful yelps had attracted her, but she had arrived too late. The schoolmaster had found her cradling the dead mutt in her arms, its blood staining her dress while she wept. *Please,* she entreated Saint Jude, *please don't let them kill Poppa!*

There was a snap and a sizzle, followed by the sharp scent of sulfur. Vivie's eyes flew open and instantly riveted on the match's bright flame. It flickered, then flared—igniting and engulfing the documents and tickets still grasped in the driver's hand. She gasped in horror as he tossed them onto Lofo. "NOOOO," Vivie screamed. "Don't burn Poppa!" Her mother's grip tightened.

"Vivie, hush," she hissed.

The tall man turned in their direction, squinting in the dusk. "Where's woman with children? I wanted her," he said, rubbing himself.

Understanding his intent, Vivie dizzied, her stomach pitching.

"Vivie," her mother whispered, "take Mae. Run and hide. Quickly now."

"But, Mama—"

"Don't argue!" she snapped. A wild look appeared in her mother's eyes as the crash of brush drew closer. "Go!"

Vivie grabbed her sister's hand, her heart pounding. "C'mon, Mae," she whispered. "Time to play hide and seek."

The little girl nodded, placed her finger against her lips, and followed.

At the ravine's edge, tears coursed down Vivie's cheeks as flames licked at her father's coat. She clutched Mae's head against her lips, whispering stories in one ear while covering the other—attempting to block out their mother's whimpering cries. Her free hand slipped into her coat pocket. Vivie clasped her rosary beads and sent up a silent prayer, again asking for the intercession of Saint Jude as she tried to keep Mae quiet.

"You through?" the driver yelled into the woods.

"With bozgor slut? Yeah," the tall man said. "Now, I want little one."

Bile rose in Vivie's throat. She gripped Mae closer, her eyes scrutinizing the ground in search of anything she could use as a weapon. They lit upon a short but sturdy tree branch just centimeters away. Vivie reached for it. She would protect her sister at all cost.

"Never mind her," the driver spat out. "We need to go. Throw bags into truck. There might be things we sell." He reared back and kicked Lofo in the head.

As the vehicle's tail lights disappeared into the falling darkness, Vivie stumbled from the woods and out into the clearing. She raced toward her father's smoldering form and fell to her knees. With her head in her hands, she wailed, "Oh, Poppa! Poppa!"

His strong hand closed about her wrist. "I'm okay, Vivie," he moaned. "I'm okay."

She blinked through her tears and looked down at her father's sooty face.

"You aren't burned?"

Poppa shook his head. "No," he groaned out. "When they weren't looking, I rolled into the snow to put out the flames." Her father grimaced, pain etching his face as he tried to rise. "Where's your mother?" he asked, cradling his head in his hands.

Vivie sucked in her breath, her eyes widening. "I don't know, Poppa," she managed to stammer out. Her hands shook as she reached to help him shed the smoldering coat. Vivie's eyes raked the fading light in search of her mother, eventually lighting on the empty satchel and the charred fragments of their refugee cards and Oswald's letter. Their papers destroyed. Mama missing. What had she done? Guilt washed over her. Vivie's stomach churned. A second later, she leaned over and vomited the remaining contents of her afternoon lunch out onto the snowy ground. As steam rose from its warmth, tears clouded Vivie's eyes and streamed down her cheeks.

Mae's voice broke through her misery. "Mama, what happened to your clothes?"

Vivie whipped around to see her mother buttoning her coat over her torn garments. She froze at the look of understanding that passed between her parents.

Lofo turned his head away, but not before Vivie saw the tears brimming in his eyes.

Csaky walked over and pulled Mae into her arms, clutching her near.

This is all my fault, Vivie thought as Mama led Mae over to a fallen log and sat down. *I should have kept my mouth shut like I was told.* Vivie knew she had hurt everyone, all because she had not minded Mama.

Poppa sat with his head in his hands, a trickle of blood oozing along his cheek. Mama continued to rock Mae in her lap, her lips pressed into the child's curls. Shock silenced their tongues. Everyone was lost in their own thoughts—their individual worlds.

Despite the proximity of her family, an overwhelming sense of abandonment washed over Vivie. Her thoughts turned to Norsk. The only one she could always count on to make her feel better—not so alone. But not now. She found no solace thinking about her tonight. More bereft than ever, Vivie sat off by herself with tears coursing down her cheeks.

CHAPTER 16

Vivie nibbled at the slice of stale bread. With her fingernail, she attempted to scrape the mold off its small piece of cheese. Looking out across the snowy landscape, she realized, *We're like feral cats—scavenging for our existence and hiding out.*

It had been two weeks since the attack. Without documentation, her bruised and battered father had become overly cautious—keeping to back-country roads and avoiding people. He slipped away at night and dug through refuse containers for their food. Some finds were better than others.

"Mae"—Csaky coughed—"Eat your bread."

"Tastes like cardboard," she complained, tossing the slice on the ground.

Vivie awaited her father's outburst, but he said nothing. Her brow furrowed as he turned away and gazed off into the distance.

"Very well," her mother rasped. She picked up the slice of bread and returned it to the sack. "We'll save it for later."

After finishing their meager meal, they set out again. As the hours passed, the snow continued to fall—deepening the drifts along the desolate country road. Fields to the left. Pastures to the right. A vast expanse of snow-covered nothingness surrounded them. Exhausted and cold, the four trudged on. Only the crunch of their sodden shoes cracking the icy surface broke the silence. Their puffs of breath lingered in the air like steam from a passing locomotive. Lofo and Csaky led the way. Mae lagged a short distance behind. Vivie brought up the rear.

One foot in front of the other. One foot in front of the other. One foot in front of the other, looped through Vivie's head. The refrain diverted her thoughts from the wet that penetrated her loafers and dampened her wool socks. From the sting of the raw blister on her left heel. From the bitter wind that knifed through her jacket and cut her to the bone as though she were naked. From the numbing ache of her fingers and toes. *One foot in front of the other. One foot in front of the other. One foot—*

Mae's screams shattered Vivie's reverie. The child lay prone on the ground and wailed, "I want to go home! I want to go home!" Her hands and feet flailed against the frozen ground, mimicking a two-year-old's tantrum.

Lofo walked back to the child and squatted beside her. Csaky remained where he left her. Vivie frowned. It was unlike her mother not to hasten to Mae's side.

The little girl's screams dissolved into tears. Sobs racked her small body. Her father patted and rubbed her back. "Mae, I know this is difficult for you to understand, but we no longer have a home. There's no place for us to go back to. The only choice we have is to move on and start over."

As he tried to reason with her, Csaky turned toward the pair. Lofo's satchel slipped from her hands and plopped down in the soft fresh snow. Vivie walked over and retrieved it. When she attempted to hand the leather case back to her mother, Csaky ignored her and stared straight ahead.

Vivie studied her in the fading light. Weariness radiated from her very soul. Her breathing appeared rapid and shallow. Dark, purple smudges underscored pink-rimmed eyes—their vivid cornflower blue now faded and flat. The mischievous twinkle gone, along with her lilting laugh. She looked so fragile. So frail. Like a delicate piece of fine porcelain that might crack or shatter at the slightest touch. Her peaches and cream complexion now held a ghostly pallor. Csaky's shiny auburn locks hung dull and limp. She was almost unrecognizable from the vibrant, beautiful woman Vivie knew and loved. Her heart ached at this change.

"But, Poppa," Vivie turned at Mae's shrill whine. "I don't want to continue on. I'm tired and cold, and my legs ache."

He took out his handkerchief and wiped her small face. "Come, Mae. I'll carry you for a bit. As soon as we find some shelter, we'll stop for the night. Okay?"

She sniffed and rose to her feet.

Lofo picked her up and nodded to Vivie. "Help your mother."

"Yes, Poppa." She took hold of Csaky's arm.

One more kilometer covered and then another. A short time later, Csaky began to cough. Lofo glanced back at her. "C'mon now. Let's pick up the pace. It won't be long until dark."

"One foot in front of the other, Mama." Vivie quietly urged her mother forward. As their pace intensified, so did her mother's hacking cough. When Csaky stumbled, Vivie yanked back on her arm and prevented her from falling.

Her mother patted her hand. "Thank you, az én kis cica."

'My little kitten.' Tears pricked Vivie's eyes at the endearment. Her throat tightened. Mama had not called her that in years.

When Csaky stumbled for the third time, Lofo stopped and put Mae down. "Okay. It's time for you to walk. I need to help Vivie with your mother."

They plodded down the road in the dimming light. Lofo supported one side of Csaky and Vivie the other. Mae followed, sucking her thumb. Csaky's raw, ragged cough echoed through the silent twilight.

At the crossroads, Lofo stopped. "I think we're nearing the outskirts of Filisur. Here, Vivie. Support your mother while I check the map."

She passed him the satchel and tucked an arm about Csaky's small waist. Her mother's head drooped. Vivie leaned in and rested her cheek against Csaky's forehead, immediately drawing back. "Poppa! Mama has a fever! Feel!"

Lofo's head snapped up from the map just as his wife's body sagged to the ground.

"Mama! Mama!" Mae shrieked and threw herself across her mother's prone form.

Lofo grabbed the child by her shoulders and pulled her away. Picking up Csaky's still body, he stepped off the roadway and waded into the white field.

As Mae wailed, Vivie snatched up the map and shoved it back into the leather case. Grabbing her sister's hand, she followed.

•   •   •   •   •

In the drafty barn loft, Lofo bathed Csaky's face and wrists in snow. From below rose the earthy scent of fresh manure. A pair of horses snorted, and a cow lowed. Hunger rumbled Vivie's belly as she gently rocked Mae in her lap and hummed "Evening Song."

When she reached the second verse, her father's tenor voice softly sang the words,

Oh my Lord, give me a place to sleep.
I am weary with wandering.
With walking around and hiding.
With living in a foreign land.

As the song concluded, Lofo nodded. "A very appropriate lullaby in this time...for us and our countrymen."

"Yes, Poppa."

Upon her groan, Lofo turned back to Csaky.

Mae looked up at Vivie and whispered, "Is Mama on her way to heaven? Is the Holy Angel coming...like the one in the song? Like the one that took Dodo?"

Vivie blinked back tears and pulled her sister closer. "Hush now and rest. Don't think such things." She reassured Mae, but deep down inside she could not help but wonder this herself.

When her sister drifted off to sleep, Vivie tucked her deep into the fresh straw. Then, she fumbled her way over to her father. He startled at her touch. "How is she, Poppa?"

"I can't really say, Vivie. Her fever appears to have subsided, but she's very weak."

Her mother's wheezy intake of breath was broken by a raw, raspy cough that jarred her body and rattled deep in her chest. Csaky moaned as though in pain.

"Go get some rest, Vivie." Lofo sighed. "We'll need to head out of here before dawn, so we won't be discovered."

"Yes, Poppa." Vivie made her way back over to her sister. Soft snores rumbled from the exhausted child. Digging deep into the straw, she snuggled next to Mae.

Minutes later, something brushed up against her back. *A rat!* Vivie's eyes flew open at the thought. In her mind, she could see the nasty, beady-eyed rodent. Its long, skinny, naked tail. Its squinched-up, wriggling nose. Its yellowed, sharp incisors and clawed feet. She shuddered.

As the animal continued to press against the small of her back, Vivie bit her cracked lips, stifling a scream. She stiffened, trying to remain relatively still so as not to awaken Mae. Then a moment later, the movement ceased, and the creature began to purr. A barn cat. Nothing more. Breath whooshed from Vivie's lungs. With a deep, ragged sigh, she pretended it was Norsk. Then snuggling down into the straw, Vivie drifted off to sleep.

•   •   •   •   •

At the creak of the barn door, Vivie bolted up in alarm. The pale light of dawn filtered in between the building's wooden boards. From across the loft, Lofo's panicked eyes met hers. He held his finger to his lips, closed his eyes, and pointed to Mae. The child continued to slumber.

From below, a cow voiced her need to be milked. As a tin pail clanked to the ground, Csaky's croupy cough echoed through the barn. Vivie and her father froze. Below, silence. A moment later, light footfalls crossed the floor and trod the ladder rungs. The soft glow of a lantern brightened the dim loft. Vivie placed her arm across Mae.

Behind the lantern stood a stocky ruddy-faced man bundled in a patched woolen jacket. His sparse head of hair was topped with a brown cap held in place by a gray wool scarf.

Mae sat up and rubbed her eyes. "Is that the Holy Angel, Vivie? Has he come for us?"

"Hush, Mae," she whispered.

A series of deep, raspy coughs erupted from Csaky. As Lofo turned back to her, the old man made his way into the loft and over to them. Memories of their recent attack assaulted Vivie. Her eyes darted about in search of something—anything—she could use as a weapon. Vivie's hand closed around the handle of the leather satchel. "Quiet, Mae," she whispered in her sister's ear, then slowly rose and crept forward.

In the lantern's glow, beads of sweat glistened on her mother's pale face. At Csaky's moan, the farmer motioned and said, "You bring, and come."

Lofo nodded.

Vivie took a step back and tried to slow her breathing. The leather satchel now hung at her side. A second later she moved forward and helped her father ease Csaky down the ladder. "C'mon, Mae," Vivie urged.

Across the farmyard, the man stood in the doorway with his wife. The short plump woman with black eyes as bright as a robin's led Lofo into a bedroom. Vivie and Mae followed.

They watched as she bundled their mother into bed. A moment later, the woman shooed them out into the main room. There, she heated some water on the hearth, then handed Vivie a towel and a hunk of soap. "You wash. Then eat."

She nodded. "Yes, ma'am."

Vivie helped Mae as the three of them washed their faces and hands. When they were done, the old woman directed, "Sit." While they gathered around the rough-hewn table in the center of the room, she dipped out a hearty rustic goulash. Vivie inhaled the rich aroma while the old woman cut each of them a slab of fresh black bread and slathered it with homemade butter, before carrying a cup of broth into Csaky.

Hunger silenced their tongues. As they devoured their first hot meal since leaving the Berlinger's, Vivie's eyes consumed the room—the handmade furniture, the butter churn, the spinning wheel. Everything spoke a simple, humble existence. A slight gasp escaped Vivie. At her father's glance, she nodded toward a shelf in the corner of the room. Amidst a small selection of books sat a miniature Hungarian flag. Lofo's eyes brightened. His hand reached over and patted hers.

Vivie sat back, sighing in satisfaction as the combined warmth of the cottage farmhouse, its reassurance of safety, and a full belly relaxed her. She glanced over at Mae. Her sister's eyes blinked long and slow, and her head began to nod. Moments later, spoon in hand, the child fell asleep at the table. As Vivie started to rise and tend to her, Lofo's hand touched her arm. "Leave her be."

A burst of cold air filled the room when the farmer returned from the barn with a pail of milk. He pulled up a chair and sat down at the table. "I'm Josef. And my wife is Maigret."

As Lofo introduced his family and told of their flight from Budapest, Vivie made herself useful clearing the table.

Maigret returned and whispered to her husband. He shook his head. The old woman took his chin in her hand. She firmly nodded and said, "Yes. Go now!" Josef arose, then donned his coat and cap before heading outside.

Vivie walked over to the window. When the farmer disappeared into the barn, she glanced back over at her father and Mae.

"You, come." Maigret motioned to Lofo. He rose and followed her into Mama's room.

A horse-drawn wagon rattled from the yard as Vivie wandered over to the bookshelf and studied the titles. She startled when a hand clasped hold of her arm. Maigret's black eyes bored into hers. "Come."

Vivie followed the old woman into another small bedroom, probably hers from the looks of it. Like Josef, Maigret took her chin in hand.

She shifted uncomfortably under the scrutiny.

"Yes," Maigret slowly nodded, continuing to eye her. "My mother, Magda, she had the sight. She passed it on to me. I see, you are the one."

Her breath caught.

"You!" She poked her finger at Vivie. "You are the strong one." Maigret motioned toward the main room. "The little one. She is weak." The old woman took her finger and tapped just above her ear. "Not right in the head."

"No!" Vivie's cheeks warmed. She shook her head. "You're wrong. There's nothing the matter with Mae. She's just tired. That's all."

The old woman shook her finger. "Not Maigret!" Her robin-bright eyes drilled into Vivie's. "I'm never wrong. Your father? He will be lost without the love of his life. Others will fill his heart, but none that flame so deep and true."

Vivie shuddered.

"But you, Vivie? Your name means one who is full of life. You have a good and caring heart." Maigret leaned closer and lowered her voice. "You also have a deep secret that you will guard until your death. But...that is many years from now."

She drew back at the woman's words. What did she know? More importantly, how did she know?

"Child, your mother...well, suffice it to say I sent Josef to try to find a priest." With a deep sigh, Maigret turned and left her.

Vivie's hands trembled as she wiped at the tears streaming down her cheeks, her greatest fear realized. After a couple of deep, jagged breaths, she straightened her shoulders and returned to the main room. A myriad of emotions hurtled through her head. She glanced over at Mae.

Her sister rocked back and forth in a straight-backed chair, humming last night's lullaby. At the rattle of the wagon, Mae stared at her. "The Holy Angel is coming. Did you know that, Vivie? The Holy Angel is coming soon."

Before she could respond, the front door opened, and Josef entered accompanied by a lanky, elderly man. "I could not find a priest but brought Dr. Korda."

As the physician removed his coat and hat, Mae fixated on him. "That's okay," she said. "The Holy Angel is coming." The two men frowned.

"Don't mind her," Vivie strangled out. "Mama is in here with Poppa." Her eyes locked onto Maigret's.

The old woman raised an eyebrow, then turned and followed the doctor.

Lofo emerged from the room and sat at the table next to Mae. Vivie joined them. Josef sat in the rocker by the fire. He picked up a piece of wood and pulled out his knife. As he whittled, soft paper-thin curls of wood drifted down and fell onto the floor. Minutes ticked by, seeming like hours in the silent room.

Vivie studied her father. A worry crease marred his noble brow. Lilac smudges underscored his haunted hazel eyes. His dark chestnut hair now sported streaks of gray. Shallow wrinkles etched his face, lines not present back in November. Instead of thirty-six, he looked more like fifty-six.

Her gaze then sought out Mae. The child picked at her cuticles, making them bleed. "Stop that!" Vivie scolded.

At the sound of footsteps, everyone but Mae turned. Lofo half rose as the doctor entered the room, followed by Maigret. "I'm sorry," he said. "There's nothing I can do. Too much fluid in her lungs. It's just a matter of time."

Lofo paled and bolted from the room.

Tears pricked Vivie's eyes. Her throat closed, and a knot formed in her stomach.

Mae began to hum.

By the hearth, Josef stilled his rocker. He looked down at the pile of wood shavings, then retrieved his coat and cap and walked out the front door.

•　　•　　•　　•　　•

The cloying scent of illness filled the small room. Csaky's croupy, harsh cough racked her willow-thin body. Her labored gasps dominated the air.

Mae huddled in the corner. Tears cascaded down her cheeks, and sobs shook her young frame.

Csaky wheezed. Her eyes opened, bright and luminous. She stretched out her hand and summoned, "Kis hiba. Come, kis hiba."

"Hear that, little bug?" Vivie walked over to her sister. "Mama's calling you." With her help, Mae rose and approached their mother.

In a hoarse whisper, Csaky said, "I love you, kis hiba."

Little bug. Vivie was Mama's 'little kitten,' and Mae was always her 'little bug.'

The child buried her face in her mother's frail neck and sobbed, "Mama! Don't l-leave m-me!"

Lofo knelt at the foot of the bed, his head in his hands.

Vivie stood stoically beside Dr. Korda. He picked up Csaky's wrist and checked her pulse. "I'm afraid it won't be long now." Her mother's chest rose and fell intermittently under the thin sheet. The inevitability of her mother's imminent death assaulted Vivie, shutting her down inside, as Csaky's gasps for air grew fewer and farther between. Then, with a small whoosh of breath, her mother was gone.

She glanced over at her father. Overwhelmed with grief and loss, he lay almost prostrate on the bare wooden floor. Great heaving sobs racked his body. Vivie looked back at Mae, draped over their mother's still form. She took a deep breath and slowly let it out, then turned to Dr. Korda, standing helplessly by her side. "Thank you, sir," Vivie strangled out.

He nodded and placed his hand on her shoulder. "I'm sorry, Vivie. I'm sorry I could not help her. I'll see what arrangements can be made for your mother's burial."

As he slipped from the room, Vivie stared down at the woman who had given her life. The one who carried her beneath her heart for nine months and birthed her into this world. Who had loved her, nurtured her, and imbued her with a love of learning. The sweet fragrant mother who kissed away her tears, bandaged her skinned knees, and cooled her fevered brow. Mama, who loved her unconditionally—even when Vivie broke her favorite vase.

As she continued to gaze down at her, Vivie silently gasped in the realization that in Mama's last moments she never had the opportunity to tell her she was sorry. To thank her mother for everything she had ever done. To tell her how much she loved her. Or to even simply say, "Goodbye."

As a stunned numbness washed over her, Vivie eased Mae to her feet only to have the child sink to the floor. Upon covering her mother's face with the sheet, Vivie looked back at her father. He was now huddled in the corner with his face buried in his hands.

With a heavy sigh, she reached into her pocket and pulled out her rosary beads. Then, Vivie clasped Mae's small damp hand. Drawing her sister near, she kissed the top of her head and whispered, "Come, Mae. Let's pray for Mama." Vivie knelt beside the bed and made the sign of the cross. "I believe in God, the Father Almighty. Creator of heaven and earth..." Seconds later, her father's husky, tenor voice joined in.

CHAPTER 17

Vivie helped Maigret bathe and prepare her mother's body for burial. When Lofo and Josef carried in the casket the old man had made, Maigret left the room. She returned with the most beautiful ecru-colored, woven blanket Vivie had ever seen. Her eyes teared up as the old woman used it to line her mother's coffin. Maigret touched Vivie's shoulder. "My gift to your mother." Overcome with emotion, words of appreciation would not come. Vivie simply nodded.

While the three adults transferred Csaky into the wooden box, she left the room and sought out Mae. Vivie found her sister by the hearth, staring into the yellow-orange flames. "Mae?" The child ignored her. "Mae?" She moved forward and touched her sister's shoulder. Still, no response. "Come, Mae. We have to get ready to say goodbye to Mama." Vivie took her sister's hand, and the child followed.

•   •   •   •   •

As the sun began its descent, a few snowflakes swirled in the faint breeze. Lofo, Vivie, and Mae stood huddled in the snow-covered graveyard beside Csaky's coffin. A young Protestant minister with his head bowed, recited a litany of foreign prayers.

This is not how it should be, Vivie thought, fingering her rosary beads. Her eyes scanned the church's small graveyard. Rooks perched atop several of the tombstones, their heads bowed like silent feathered mourners. A few meters away stood a tall granite marker, topped by a small winged child. Dark stains marred her solemn face like permanent inky tears. The angelic figure clutched a stone doll in her arms.

Lofo, more composed than earlier, looked down at the ground. He closed his eyes and sighed.

Mae stood silent with a vacant stare. As the minister continued, she bolted from the graveside and made a beeline for the winged child.

Vivie started after her.

"Leave her be," her father said.

Mae stood before the monument, gazing up at the angelic figure's stone doll. She appeared to be having a conversation with it. Vivie subtly shook her head, then closed her eyes. She took a deep breath and slowly let it out, tamping down the grief that welled inside her heart.

After the unfamiliar service, Vivie approached the minister. "Thank you, sir."

"You're most welcome, child." He shook her outstretched hand. "Your mother's in a better place."

Vivie bit her lip at his statement. She had heard adults espouse this before but was not convinced that it was necessarily true. "Sir, what do we owe you?" Vivie asked, knowing they could not pay.

His hand reached out and touched her arm. "There's no charge, my child."

Before she could thank him, the man flawlessly began speaking in her native tongue. Her eyes widened at his words.

"We had hoped for change in Hungary. Think of this as a small token of our support. Please excuse me, now."

As the young man turned to Lofo, Mae tugged at her arm.

"Do you see, Vivie?" she asked. "Do you see the Holy Angel with Dodo over there?"

"Mae, that isn't—"

"*Yes*, it *is*, Vivie. Look."

At the intensity in her sister's stare and the set of her jaw, Vivie sighed. "You're right, Mae." It was easier to concede the point than to try and reason with the eight-year-old.

•   •   •   •   •

Vivie replaced the dishes in the cupboard. A week had passed, and she still could not believe that her mother was gone. Maigret and Josef had tried to console her and her family, but the grief was still painfully raw, like an open wound. Would the hurt ever heal?

As if in response, Norsk came to mind. Even after two months, the mere thought of her beloved cat continued to evoke heartache. At least with Mama it was different. She *knew* where Csaky was.

Lofo emerged from the bedroom and reached for his coat.

"Where are you going, Poppa?"

"To the church."

"May I go, too?" She untied her apron.

"No, Vivie. I'm only going to meet up with Reverend Montcliff. Then we're going into Filisur to see an attorney."

"An attorney, Poppa? But...why?"

"He's going to help see about replacing our documents."

Her stomach flipped at the thought.

"You stay here and help look after Mae. I'll be back in a bit."

Vivie followed him outside where he climbed into the wagon with Josef. As they drove away, something soft brushed against her ankles. Vivie looked down at the barn cat. 'Griselda,' Maigret called this one. She scooped up the tortoiseshell and buried her face in her fur, the scent of hay filling her nostrils.

Back inside, Vivie sat by the fireside, the cat nestled in her lap. Norsk had once been her only solace, but she found Griselda to be a comforting substitute. Vivie gazed down at the feline, slowly stroking its back. "My problem is," she told her, "I've let everyone down." Vivie thought back to the day her mother died. Her throat tightened, remembering how Csaky had called for Mae, but not her. "Mama told Mae she loved her"—Vivie gulped—"but she didn't tell me." Guilt washed over her. "It was because I let her down. That day in the woods. If I had only minded." Hurt filled her very soul—knowing the pain, the suffering, and the humiliation she had caused her mother. She swallowed back a sob, quickly wiping away her tears as Maigret and Mae came through the door.

"Vivie!" Her sister raced into the room, the child's cheeks rosy from the cold. "Did you know eggs come from a chicken's butt?"

Maigret laughed. "No, Mae."

"Don't say 'butt,' Mae," Vivie corrected. She reached over and brushed back her sister's curls.

Aware of Maigret's eyes upon her, Vivie took her sister by the hand. "We need to get you washed up. Look at those smudges on your face. What will Ma—" Vivie froze, realizing what she almost said.

"Mae?" Maigret interrupted, "The chickens? See if they need more feed."

The child danced over to the door. "If they do, may I give them some?"

"Yes," the old woman said. After Mae dashed outside, Maigret turned to Vivie. "There's a dark aura about you, child. Something troubles you."

Vivie stilled at her words, wondering how she sensed these things. "I'm fine."

Maigret stood with her hands on her hips. "You're conflicted. That first day? I knew. Something's gnawing at your soul. You must conquer it. Else, it will eat you alive."

Vivie did not respond. Her forefinger slowly circled a spot of orange in the tortoiseshell's fur.

The old woman walked over and placed her hand on Vivie's shoulder. "Know I'm here for you, child. Willing to listen."

Still, she did not respond. *Please just go away and leave me be,* Vivie thought, continuing to trace the pattern of the cat's coat.

Maigret sighed. "Suit yourself."

When the old woman left the room, Vivie reached down and cuddled Griselda. She buried her face in the feline's fur. "If I couldn't talk about it with Mama," she whispered, tears filling her eyes, "how can I talk about it with her?"

•　　•　　•　　•　　•

The three barn cats clustered around Vivie, rubbing against her ankles. She squatted down and ran her hand along their sleek backs. "Bet you'll miss me," Vivie murmured. "There'll be no more extra treats." When she scooped up Griselda, the cat nuzzled against her chin. "Thanks for keeping my secrets." Vivie kissed the top of the feline's head. "I'm going to miss you," she whispered, a longing in her voice.

"Vivie, you and Mae come on," Lofo called. "It's time to head for the train station."

She turned to see Josef and her father standing by the wagon, Maigret on the porch. "Mae's not with me, Poppa."

"What do you mean? Didn't she come outside with you?"

"No, sir. The last time I saw her, she was pouting in the bedroom."

As Maigret stepped back inside, he followed.

Moments later, Lofo came out calling, "Mae? Mae! Mae, answer me," but there was no response. He ran toward the chicken coop while Josef headed toward the silo. A quick search of the barnyard and its outbuildings revealed nothing. Back on the porch, Lofo's strained voice muttered, "Where could she have gotten to?" Panic filled his eyes.

Vivie chewed her lip at the angst on her father's face—a combination of frustration, anger, and fear. Where *could* Mae be? Her eyes widened. "Poppa? I think I might know."

"Where?" he snapped.

She took a step back and gulped. "I think maybe she's gone to the church cemetery."

"The cemetery?"

"To see Dodo."

An exasperated sigh of disgust burst from him. "What nonsense are you talking, Vivie? That damned doll is long gone!"

"B-but, Poppa..."

While she tried to explain, Josef herded them into the waiting wagon.

●　　　●　　　●　　　●　　　●

As they pulled into the churchyard, Lofo leapt out at a run before Josef managed to rein in the horses. With the wagon at a standstill, Vivie clambered down and started after her father just as Reverend Montcliff stepped from the church. "Very fortuitous of you arriving when you did. Must be the Lord's—"

Before he could finish, Vivie darted past him in pursuit of her father. As she approached the winged monument, Mae wailed, "NO! I don't want to go! I don't want to leave Dodo." The child had managed to scale the base and stood atop its platform with her arms wrapped around the hands of the stone child and her doll.

Lofo was attempting to wrestle her sister away from the statue.

Reverend Montcliff slipped up beside Vivie. "What's going on?"

"Mae thinks that doll is the one she lost as we were escaping Hungary. She's obsessed with it."

The minister's brow raised.

They watched from a distance while Lofo attempted to now coax Mae down from the pedestal.

"Vivie?"

She turned and looked up at the minister.

"I have something for your family. I was on my way to the train station with it when you arrived." He pressed an envelope into her hands.

Her eyes narrowed.

"Enclosed are some funds that the congregation managed to raise for your travel."

"Oh, but no—"

"Yes, Vivie. There will be expenses associated with your travel to Le Havre. It's not much, but it will help."

"But, Poppa won't—"

"Vivie..." Reverend Montcliff's hand reached out and touched her shoulder. "There's a scripture, Proverbs 16:18, 'Pride goeth before destruction and a haughty spirit before a fall.' Do you understand what that means?"

"I think so," she answered softly. "Don't let pride stand in your way."

"That's right." He nodded. "Tuck this away and give it to your father when necessary."

"Thank you." Vivie slipped the envelope into her pocket as Lofo approached with a sobbing Mae.

•   •   •   •   •

Seated in the train car, Vivie observed the boarding passengers. Several averted their eyes upon passing. Others blatantly stared. A few whispered and frowned. One well-to-do, middle-aged couple hesitated a moment beside them. The man looked down at his tickets, then grasped his wife's elbow and steered her forward to the conductor, engaging him in what appeared to be a spirited discussion.

Mae sat across from Vivie, sucking her thumb. Dried tears streaked her face. She had thrown a tantrum upon leaving the churchyard, another upon their arrival at the station, and still another upon boarding the train.

Vivie had tried to cajole her with stories and Maigret's cookies to no avail. It was as though Mae had completely shut down. She responded to nothing.

Lofo sank into his seat with a heavy sigh. Vivie studied him. He seemed so defeated—as though all the fight had been sucked out of him. The creases on his forehead had deepened. His warm hazel eyes held an emptiness she had never seen before, similar to those of Mae's. He was quieter now, almost non-communicative at times. Again, like Mae.

This is all my fault.

Her sister began to rock forward and back, bouncing her head against her seat.

"Stop it, Mae," Lofo ordered.

As she continued, the man in the affected seat turned around and glared. Vivie's cheeks heated at his angry scowl. The portly man emitted a loud "hrumph," then rose and made his way to the front of the car.

"Mae, I said stop it."

Instead of responding to her father's command, she leapt up, catapulted herself over him and bolted down the aisle. When Lofo grabbed her, the child's shrieks echoed through the car. As he attempted to wrestle her back into the seat, passengers turned and stared.

The conductor approached, a stern look on his face. He stopped beside them. "Sir?" The man glared at Lofo. "We've had some complaints. If you can't control your child, we're going to have to ask your family to step off the train."

Vivie watched the flush of pink creep across her father's cheeks. *Oh, my,* she thought, *that must have been why those people acted the way they did.*

"I'm sorry, sir," Lofo responded. "She's recently lost her mother—my wife. She's having difficulty—"

"Sir, I don't care the reason," the conductor abruptly responded. "Just see that it doesn't happen again." He pivoted and headed back down the aisle as the train pulled out of the station.

Vivie's teeth worried her lip as she puzzled over her father's response. In any other instance he would have politely requested to speak to the conductor's supervisor to plead his case, not sit there like a scolded school boy.

She glanced at Mae. The child had collapsed against the seat, her struggle ceased. With a thumb popped into her mouth, Mae appeared to have retreated into herself. Seconds later, she was asleep, almost as though she was a mechanical toy whose switch had been flipped to the 'off' position.

Lofo heaved another deep sigh. He bent forward, his elbows on his knees and his hands rubbing his face. "I'll be so relieved when this is over," he murmured.

Vivie frowned, wondering what Poppa meant.

CHAPTER 18

Le Havre, France, February 1957

Vivie shivered behind the crates in the dusky alleyway, wishing Theodolf was there to trap and alter these feral cats. As she watched them battle over the food scraps she had set out, Vivie realized how much her life was like theirs. Hungry. Skinny. Scared. And without a real home.

"Vivie!" She startled at her father's harsh shout. The feral cats scattered and vanished into the dawn shadows. "Get in here." She brushed away a tear and pulled her tattered jacket closer, then turned and slowly headed toward the dilapidated shed.

Inside, Lofo stood by the table, shuffling through his papers.

"I'm sorry—"

"No need for apologies." He cut her off. "Just look after your sister. I need to step out for a bit." Lofo headed for the door.

Poppa had been coming and going a lot lately. He had become sullen and ill-tempered, easily angered. For that reason, Vivie tried her best to be invisible around him.

She walked over to the small cot and sat down beside Mae. Vivie placed her hand on her sister's forehead. A slight warmth met her touch. She picked up the small rag, dipped it in the basin, and began giving her sister a sponge bath. As she did, her thoughts slipped away to a better time—when Mae was well, when her mother was alive, when they had a home and food on the table. And when she had Norsk. The cat slipped into her thoughts at the oddest times. A scent, an object, a phrase—triggering memories of times spent with her beloved feline. Like that potato the other day. When it rolled off the table and onto the floor, Vivie recalled how Norsk liked to bat those wobbly vegetables about the kitchen. A slight smile curled her lips at the treasured memory.

She startled as the shed's door opened. Lofo stepped back inside, barely glancing at her. Lately, it was as though he could not stomach the sight of her. Poppa hated her. Vivie was sure of it. She knew he blamed her for her mother's death. *I don't fault him for feeling that way.* Vivie blinked back the tears. *He's right.* She took a deep breath and slowly let it out as she tended to Mae.

"Vivie?"

Her father's hands came to rest on her shoulders. Vivie's neck tightened. What had she done now? She turned to him. "Yes, Poppa?"

"There's something we need to talk about."

He looked so serious. Her hands clenched, their fingernails biting into her palms.

"Vivie, I've made—" A light tapping on the door interrupted him. He dropped his head and sighed. "I thought we'd have more time."

At the look of angst on his face, Vivie's eyes widened. "Oh, Poppa," she whispered. "Is it the Russian soldiers? Have they found us?"

He shook his head. "No, Vivie. It's Oswald and Alice. They are going to take you to America."

Tears filled her eyes as she processed his words. *I'm being sent away.* She gulped. *And Mae's staying here—with Poppa.* He had not included her sister in these plans. So, this is what it had come to. He had grown to hate her that much. She managed to choke out, "But I want to stay with Mae." *And you,* she thought, but did not say.

Her father looked down and subtly shook his head. "No, Vivie. Here." Lofo handed her his handkerchief. "Dry your eyes," he said, before heading toward the door.

She fingered the tattered piece of cloth, remembering that November day in the shrubs. Poppa had been proud of her then...but no more. How everything had changed! She wished she could turn back the clock.

"Oswald. Alice. Please, come in."

Vivie wiped away her tears as the statuesque blonde pushed past Lofo and into the one-room shack. She was stylishly dressed in a wool coat with a lush fox-fur collar. Atop her head sat a taupe, fur felt, brimmed hat accented with pheasant feathers. A coppery brown cut-velvet handbag with a brass clasp hung from her arm. Alice smiled and said, "Hello, Vivie," as she removed a pair of beige kid-leather gloves, revealing her well-manicured hands. Her diamond ring caught the morning light filtering in through the smudged glass of the small window.

The girl's gaze flitted from the fashionable woman to the dingy surroundings, finally landing on her own patched and stained dress. "Hello, Néni Alice," Vivie softly responded.

Csaky had met the Viennese woman at boarding school. Despite Alice being several years older, the two had become best friends. Vivie remembered Mama's stories about the mischievous adventures the two had shared. Then years later, Alice had written her mother about the 'long tall Texan' who had stolen her heart.

For Vivie, the phrase conjured thoughts of a lanky cowboy. But upon meeting the man, she had found Oswald was about as far removed from that image as he could get. In fact, Vivie had thought the stately, dignified man greatly resembled the 1930s British movie star Ronald Colman down to the pencil-style mustache.

After shaking hands with Lofo, Oswald removed his gray felt homberg. His hand drifted upwards, unconsciously smoothing his dark hair. It was perfectly coiffed in the current style, parted on the side and well-pomaded. He had a soft scent of citrus about him. Oswald looked about the tiny hovel. "Be it ever so humble, there's no place like home," he quoted.

Vivie's throat tightened. Many times she had heard Mama say that Bácsi Oswald would "spout poetry at the drop of a hat," often in the most bizarre circumstances. "Nothing wrong with that," her father usually responded. "Oswald is a man of culture and refinement. I would expect nothing less." Lofo greatly admired the older man. Upon meeting, the two had found they held common interests and took an immediate liking to each other as though they were old friends.

At Mae's low moan, Vivie said, "Excuse me," and turned back to the cot. "What is it, kis hiba? Do you need something?" Instead of her sister's response, the clip of Alice's coppery brown, suede T-strap pumps met her ears.

"How is she?" the woman asked, reaching over and cupping her hand over Mae's forehead.

"Better than she has been," Vivie responded.

"She feels a little warm. A slight fever, perhaps."

"It comes and goes."

Alice reached over and squeezed Vivie's hand. "Well, no worry. We're going to take care of everything."

Her brow raised. Had she misunderstood? Was Mae going to America, too? She wanted to ask but did not. And what about Poppa?

With Alice attending to her sister, Vivie drifted over to the window. Outside, the brown mackerel tabby crouched atop the trash can, seemingly intent on some unseen prey below. A moment later, the cat sat upright and licked his paw, then reached up and began grooming his ears. When he leapt down, the tabby backed up against the metal can, raised his tail and, with a shake, released a stream of spray.

He was probably one of the fathers of Mirabelle's kittens. Mirabelle was the name Vivie had given to the slight calico. In the last couple of weeks, she had noted the young queen's burgeoning form. *I won't be here to care for the kittens.* She winced at the thought.

When the tabby tom trotted out of the alleyway, Vivie's focus was drawn to a man in black standing at the entrance. Her eyes focused on his militaristic uniform. While the cap and distance obscured his features, Vivie *could* tell one thing—he was watching their shack. Was he one of those people Mama had cautioned her about? She turned to warn her father, hesitating at the mention of her name.

"And as for her," Oswald stated, "I'll make the necessary arrangements and have my attorney take care of the paperwork, Lofo. We'll get Vivie a passport and get Mae admitted to a private hospital where she'll receive the care she needs."

Passport? Hospital? Vivie's brain short-circuited at the words, the stranger forgotten.

"But it's such short notice, Oswald."

"Don't worry, Lofo. Money has a way of opening doors."

Her father nodded.

Alice rose and approached the two men.

"Os?" She touched her husband's shoulder. "Vivie's going to need clothes before we leave. While you and Lofo finalize the arrangements, I'll take her shopping. That is," Alice hesitated, "if it's okay with you, Lofo?"

He lowered his head.

Oswald placed his hand on his friend's shoulder. "We all go through difficult times, Lofo. Don't let pride stand in the way."

Ignored, Vivie stood silent during the exchange and watched a cockroach scuttle across the floor. She chewed the inside of her lip. No one was asking her what she wanted. Her entire future was being decided without her input.

Lofo looked up. "Go with Néni Alice, Vivie."

"But, Poppa, what about—"

"Vivie, go."

Her shoulders drooped. "Yes, Poppa." She turned and followed Alice.

Outside, Vivie's nostrils flared at the fresh pungent scent of tom cat. As they started down the alley, she halted. Up ahead stood the man in black, watching—and waiting.

CHAPTER 19

Vivie sucked in her breath, her heart pounding.

Alice turned. "Vivie? What's wrong? Did you forget something?"

Her eyes darted from Alice to the stranger. "It's him," she whispered.

"Who?"

"That man up ahead," she murmured.

"Jamison?"

"You know him?" Vivie stammered out.

"Yes. He's our chauffeur."

Not the Russians. She gave a sigh of relief at the thought. A moment later, her eyes lit on the shiny black limousine parked on the street.

Upon their approach, the tall, slender, red-haired young man rushed to open the car door for them.

Alice touched her shoulder. "Vivie, this is our chauffeur, Jamison. Jamison, this is Vivie."

He nodded. "Yes, ma'am. Nice to meet you, Miss Vivie." As Jamison assisted Alice into the limo, he asked, "Where to, ma'am?"

"The Rue de Paris shopping district, please."

• • • • •

Inside the dressing room, Vivie stiffened at the sales clerks' whispers of *petit gamine* and *enfant sale.* A knot formed in her throat. Throwing the clothes to the floor, she bolted from the changing area and headed for the door.

"Vivie? Vivie! Stop! Come back!" Alice shouted after her.

Outside she hesitated, meeting Jamison's stare, before turning and fleeing down the crowded sidewalk.

"Jamison, stop her!" Alice yelled.

At the thud of feet, Vivie glanced back. In that instant, her foot slipped on a large pile of dog feces. Losing her balance, she fell backwards onto the sidewalk. Vivie grimaced. A myriad of emotions flooded through her—pain from the fall, mortification of making a spectacle of herself, and disgust at the smear of dog poo on her leg and down her dress.

"Are you all right, Miss?" Jamison took her arm and helped her stand as a breathless Alice rushed up to them.

"Vivie? Are you all right? What happened? What's wrong? Please tell me."

She hung her head at the barrage of questions, staring at the wad of dog poo clinging to the side of her worn loafer.

Alice placed an arm around her shoulders. "Vivie? Your mother and I were close friends. I hope we will be, too. I know this is difficult for you. Won't you please tell me what happened?"

The soft fragrance of Alice's Chanel No. 5 filled her nostrils, reminding her of Mama and replacing the stench of ripe dog feces. Vivie took a deep breath, then raised her head and looked into Alice's green eyes. "It was the clerks," she said softly.

"What about them, Vivie?"

Her cheeks flooded with warmth. "They called me...a 'little street urchin' and..."—her voice broke—". . . a 'filthy child.'"

Thunder filled Alice's face. "Outrageous! I'll have Oswald speak to the shopkeeper. Come, Vivie. Let's go to the hotel and get you cleaned up. Then we'll find a different place to shop."

Walking into the lobby of the Normandie Hotel on Quai Georges V, Vivie cringed. She sensed the eyes of the hotel's guests and staff upon her. Did they also see her as a 'street urchin' and a 'filthy child?' Oh, if they only knew her secret.

Moments later, Vivie slid into a tub of bubbles. The warm water seemed to soothe away all the hurt and pain, both physical and emotional, of the last few months. She inhaled the soft lilac scent of the bubble bath. As Vivie soaked in the suds, Norsk came to mind. The beloved feline had liked to sit on the edge of the tub, swatting at the bubbles. Her throat ached at the memory. Where was Norsk? Starving in the streets? Flattened on the cobblestones? Lying dead in a ditch? A knock at the door startled her.

"Vivie?" Alice asked. "Are you okay in there?"

With her wash cloth, she hastily wiped away her tears. "Yes, ma'am."

"May I come in?"

"Yes, Néni Alice."

When she entered, Vivie's brow raised at the sight of the small stack of clothing boxes in her hands.

"These should fit," Alice said. "I got your sizes from your other clothes, then sent downstairs to the hotel's dress shop for a few things. When you finish your bath, we'll go out and get you a new wardrobe for the trip."

Vivie gave a reluctant nod, her throat tightening at the thought.

An hour later, they returned to the shopping district. Vivie stood in the dressing room, trying on a selection of clothes as Alice eased aside the curtain and entered with a frilly, cotton candy-pink, organdy dress.

"Look, Vivie! Isn't this gorgeous? It would go so well with your red hair."

"No, thank you."

"But, Vivie, give it a chance. Please try it on."

"No, thank you," she repeated.

"Why, Vivie?"

"It's not something I care to wear."

A crease appeared between Alice's eyebrows, then disappeared. "All right, then. Step out here and make another selection."

"No, ma'am. I don't care to."

"But, Vivie, you'll need a party dress."

She shook her head and sighed. "No, Néni Alice. I won't be attending any parties."

Alice gave a slight shrug, letting the matter drop.

A short time later they emerged from the shop, followed by an attendant carrying a tall stack of boxes. Vivie wore a blue plaid, A-line jumper with a white turtleneck shirt under a gray, wool, double-breasted coat. On her feet she wore bobby socks and brown penny loafers. A gray felt hat with a burgundy band and bow of grosgrain ribbon sat atop her unruly mass of auburn curls.

Jamison opened the car door. "You look very nice, Miss."

Heat filled Vivie's cheeks. She ducked her head. "Thank you."

He nodded to Alice, "Where to, ma'am?"

"We're to meet Mr. McNabb at Le Grand Large."

"Yes, ma'am."

•   •   •   •   •

Vivie looked down at the menu. Her mouth watered at the variety of choices. Salmon, duck, chicken, steak, lobster, shrimp, crab, pheasant.

"Order anything you like," Oswald said. "Anything at all."

Mae came to mind. "Do you think they have some ice cream?"

"Ice cream?" Alice reached over and touched her hand. "For lunch?"

Vivie subtly shook her head. "Not for me. For Mae. I'd like to take some back to her. It's her favorite, you know."

Oswald and Alice exchanged a glance.

Vivie's eyes darted between them. "What's wrong?"

"Well...uh, Vivie," Oswald started. "You see, uh..."

Alice shook her head. "Let me explain, Os. If you keep this up, we'll be here until next week." She turned to Vivie. "Dear, Mae's in hospital."

"The hospital?"

"Yes. Oswald and your father had her ambulanced there after we left."

"Is...is she going to be okay?" Vivie squeaked out.

Alice's eyes focused on the table. Her ruby-red fingernail traced the pattern on the knife's handle.

Oswald cleared his throat. "Physically. The doctor said Mae should be well in a couple of weeks. But she has some—other concerns—that are going to take longer to treat. And in truth, Vivie, may not be treatable at all."

"What do you mean?" she hoarsely whispered.

"Her mind, Vivie," Alice softly answered. "The trauma and stress of the last few months have taken a strain on Mae."

In that instant, time receded. Vivie was transported into the bedroom of the old farmhouse. Maigret's words, "The little one. She is weak," echoed in her head. She flashed to the old woman tapping her finger just above her ear and saying, "Not right in the head."

Back in Le Grande Large, the room seemed to spin. A wave of nausea hit. Vivie leapt up and bolted from the table. Her eyes frantically raked the restaurant seeking the restroom door. Unable to locate it, she darted outside and vomited in the street.

A second later, Alice was rubbing her back saying, "It's going to be all right, Vivie. Everything's going to be okay."

No, it isn't, she thought as she gave a dry heave. *Nothing is ever going to be okay again.*

CHAPTER 20

That evening, Vivie stood near the ocean liner's boarding ramp with Alice and Oswald. Despite the warmth of her new coat, she shivered. Her teeth chattered more from nerves than the chill air as she scanned the milling crowd for her father. According to Oswald, Lofo had promised he would see her off. Vivie fidgeted. It was almost time for the last boarding call. Where was he?

"Vivie!"

Her heart soared at his familiar voice. Maybe Poppa had come to take her back home! Never the house they all once shared, but the one they lived in now. Maybe he would say, "This is all a mistake. You don't have to go to America. You can stay here with me—and Mae." But the moment Vivie looked into his eyes, her heart plummeted.

He pulled her aside, out of the path of revelers and boarding passengers. From his ragged coat, he withdrew a flat rectangular package. It was wrapped in butcher paper and tied with twine. Poppa handed it to her. "Keep this with you always. Never let anyone see it, Vivie. It is very important that you remember this."

"Yes, Poppa."

"Be brave, Vivie. Whatever happens, always know that I love you very much."

Before she could reply, her father had disappeared into the crowd and was gone like the feral cats in the alleyway that morning. Tears stung Vivie's eyes. Poppa had said he loved her, and yet he was sending her away. Despite the milling crowd of people, Vivie, stood there all alone—now completely isolated from everyone who had ever loved her.

"Come, my dear." She looked up to see Oswald's sad smile. "It's time for us to board." With a heavy sigh, Vivie turned and walked to the ramp with him.

Alice's arm encircled her shoulders as they made their ascent. Vivie briefly stumbled at the realization that every step was taking her farther away from who she was. Everything in her life had now been stripped from her—her family, her past, her Norsk. Vivie gulped and choked back a sob, struggling to catch her breath. That day in November seemed so far away. Its series of events had altered her life forever like a chain of dominos set in motion.

Around her, bright specks of confetti swirled in the air like multicolored snowflakes. Streamers unfurled and spiraled down onto the docks below. People waved and cheered. On deck, stewards wove through the celebrating throng intoning, "All ashore that's going ashore." Vivie peered down upon the revelers. Her eyes scanned the mayhem, seeking one last glimpse of Poppa. Was he still down there watching her depart?

The ship's whistle blasted. Vivie longed to dart across the deck and down the boarding ramp, then run until she could run no more. A loud cheer rang out, snatching her attention. The gangplank had been wheeled away, the moorings lifted, and the ocean liner was easing toward the open sea. As tears clouded Vivie's eyes, the receding colors melded together like melting crayons, creating a kaleidoscopic view of the distant pier. She swallowed against the knot in her throat.

"Come, Vivie." Alice's hand grasped her elbow. "Let's head to our staterooms and freshen up before dinner."

At the captain's table that evening, the women were dressed in elegant gowns and the men in tuxedos. Clad in her blue jumper, Vivie took another spoonful of the beef bouillon. She ignored the prattle of inane conversation, lost in worry over Mae and Poppa. As her spoon aimlessly stirred the broth, a burst of laughter intruded into her thoughts.

"Well, Vivie, you are a quiet one."

Mrs. Abingdon, the overbearing woman who had dominated the dinner conversation, responded to the captain's remark. "Children should be seen and not heard. It is apparent that she was raised right."

A flame flared in Vivie's breast. "Yes, ma'am. I was." She straightened and met the woman's eyes. "My parents taught me to express my opinion and contribute to any conversation, but to always be mindful that I can substantiate what I say and to not indulge in rumor and speculation."

"W-w-well, I never—" the woman sputtered. Her eyes narrowed to slits in her reddening face. "Come, Herbert." She rose and stormed out, her husband following in her wake.

Vivie bit the inside of her lip. Maybe she had said too much. "I'm sorry," she said.

"Don't apologize, Vivie," the captain chuckled. "Mrs. Abingdon is a bit of a bore. I'm glad someone had the gumption to put her in her place for once." Those who knew the woman from previous cruises laughed and nodded in agreement.

Two hours later in her stateroom, the tears flowed. Vivie cried because she was alone. She cried because she was scared. She cried because she missed her sister—and Poppa. *He told me to be brave,* Vivie thought, wiping away her tears. "I must make him proud," she said to herself. "I must be brave for Poppa."

At the thought of her father, Vivie's hand slipped under the pillow and touched the flat package. Thoughts of what was inside began to gnaw at her gut. She eased over and locked the connecting door between her room and Alice and Oswald's. Then, she pulled out the package and untied the twine. Carefully peeling back the butcher paper, Vivie peered inside. She gasped. Poppa had entrusted her with this? But...why? What did it mean?

The doorknob rattled. "Vivie, are you okay in there?" Alice called.

She fought to control her breathing. "Yes, ma'am. Just a minute." Vivie yanked back her bedcovers and stuffed the package and its wrappings under them.

"Is everything okay?" Alice asked, when she opened the door.

"Yes, ma'am. I was just changing into my pajamas."

"Are you sure, Vivie? You look a little flushed." Alice's hand reached out and cupped Vivie's forehead.

"Yes, ma'am. I'm fine. Really I am."

Alice slowly nodded. "Well, all right. If you need anything tonight, Vivie, anything at all, just knock. We're right here."

"Yes, ma'am. I will."

"Well...okay. Goodnight."

"Goodnight, Néni Alice."

When the door closed, Vivie fell across the bed, her breath whooshing out. She looked over and watched the clock. The enormity of what Poppa had entrusted her with now weighed on her thoughts. Five minutes passed, then ten. After fifteen minutes, she eased the packet from under the bedcovers, rewrapped it, and stuck it under her pillow. Tomorrow, she would find a safer place to keep it.

CHAPTER 21

By the time Néni Alice called Vivie for breakfast, the butcher-paper-wrapped packet was safely hidden. As Oswald guided them down the corridor and into the dining area, Vivie's jaw tightened at the thought of another encounter with Mrs. Abingdon. Her eyes scanned the room as they approached the buffet bar. A sigh of relief escaped her at the realization that the opinionated woman was not there.

After breakfast, Vivie explored the ocean liner. Art deco furnishings filled the plush accommodations and lounges. She passed a theatre, several gift shops, and a café-grill. The abundance of available food was overwhelming to Vivie. What she and her family would have given for just a bite of this when they were starving in Switzerland.

There was an area for table tennis and shuffleboard on one level of the ship. On another, several people braved the chilly weather, swimming in the heated outdoor pool. She passed a gymnasium filled with exercise equipment, stopping to watch a man lift weights and another do repetitions on a rowing machine.

Vivie headed down a narrow corridor and opened a frosted glass-partition door. A cacophony of female voices greeted her like the hens clucking in Maigret's chicken coop. The beauty parlor's heavy perfumed scent assaulted her nostrils—closing her throat, almost choking her like the church's ceremonial incense. Vivie scanned the small salon. Beyond the women getting manicures were those being shampooed. One smiled and waved. It was Alice, motioning to her. As she started to approach, Vivie glanced over at the line of women sitting under the hair dryers. All except one had their noses buried in movie and gossip magazines. Mrs. Abingdon sat with a copy of *True Confessions* clutched in her fist, staring daggers at her. Vivie blew a kiss to Néni Alice and hastened out the door.

Back up on deck, Vivie watched the rise and fall of the waves. Gray clouds were forming on the western horizon. In the distance swam a pod of whales.

Turning to head back to her stateroom, Vivie spied a book lying beside one of the deck chairs. She picked it up and read the title, *The Three Musketeers.* One of Mama's favorites. A lump formed in her throat. Wondering who the book belonged to, she opened the cover and saw a library stamp: American Presidential Lines.

Vivie walked over to the purser. "Excuse me, sir?"

"Yes, miss?"

"Is there, by chance, a library on board?"

"Yes, there is."

•   •   •   •   •

Following the purser's directions, Vivie headed for the stairway. At the top of the steps, she stopped short. Her eyes riveted on the slender black tail, slowly waltzing back and forth at the corner. Vivie's heart skipped a beat at the sight. As she eased toward it, the tail disappeared. Vivie dashed forward and followed. Rounding the corner, she spied a black and white tuxedo cat, sauntering down the corridor. Without realizing it, she followed the feline into the library where it leapt onto an over-stuffed club chair and began to groom.

Vivie approached the librarian. "Here," she said absently, her eyes never leaving the cat, now curled in the sun-drenched chair. "I found this book on deck."

"Thank you." The young man pushed his round-framed spectacles back up on his nose. "I see you have an eye for Simon."

"Simon?"

"The ship's cat."

"I like cats," Vivie said.

"Do you have one?"

"Yes," she started to say, but stopped herself. "Well...I used to have one. Norsk."

"I know how that is. I had a dandy ginger tabby once. Marty. Got run over by a car."

"I'm sorry," she managed to strangle out.

As a young woman entered to request a title, Vivie wandered over and sat down on the floor next to Simon's chair. The cat observed her through slitted eyes. She gave him a long slow blink, then turned her head away. A moment later, his paw rested on her shoulder.

After that encounter, Vivie spent the remainder of her two weeks at sea reading in the library with Simon curled in her lap.

•   •   •   •   •

"Come, Vivie!" Alice called. "We need to get to the rail. Oswald's waiting. You must see this."

"Yes, ma'am." Vivie donned her coat and followed her through the corridor.

Alice linked her arm through hers as they emerged on deck and eased their way through the crowd. She cringed as the woman's mink stole brushed against her skin. Its head flopped up and down on Alice's shoulder. When Vivie's blue eyes met the black, beady, glass eyes of the dead mink, she shuddered.

At the rail, Oswald turned. "There you are! I thought my girls were going to miss the most beautiful sight in the world! Look there, Vivie."

Her eyes followed the point of his finger. There, in all her glory, stood 'Lady Liberty,' enlightening the world. Vivie studied the statue, Libertas, the Roman goddess, France's gift to the United States. The sun's rays illuminated the spikes of her crown. A knot formed in Vivie's throat upon seeing the wave of the statue's hair and its impassioned face. So much like Mama's. They watched for several minutes, then Oswald turned. "Come on girls. Let's get ready to disembark." As they made their way through the crowd, she gave a final glance back at the Statue of Liberty.

•   •   •   •   •

Vivie's mouth fell open as Jamison greeted them at the foot of the gangplank.

"Here, let me take that for you, Miss." He reached for the butcher-paper-wrapped packet.

"NO!" she burst out and turned away.

Jamison stepped back, his eyes widening.

Oswald gave a slight shake of his head.

Vivie's cheeks grew warm. "I'm sorry," she stammered out. "I can carry it myself."

"Yes, Miss." He turned to Oswald. "The car's ready, sir. I've made arrangements for the luggage to be delivered to the Algonquin like you cabled."

"Thank you, Jamison. Ladies?" Oswald waved Alice and Vivie into the limousine and slipped in behind them.

"How did Jamison get here before us?" Vivie asked as they settled in their seats.

A hearty laugh burst from Oswald. "I sent him back in a company plane, Vivie. I had some business I needed him to attend to before our arrival."

"Oh."

The limo eased out into the New York City traffic. Jamison masterfully guided the long black vehicle through the busy streets. Vivie's eyes widened. Chaos reigned. Cars, buses, trucks, and yellow cabs crept bumper to bumper. Bicycle messengers darted in and out. Traffic lights changed from amber to red to green. Pedestrians filled the sidewalks. Horns honked, people yelled, and brakes screeched.

Massive skyscrapers and buildings towered overhead, lining the crowded sidewalks. It was almost claustrophobic. To Vivie, it seemed as though she had been swallowed up and was plunging downward inside a stone, metal, and glass ogre. She had never experienced anything like it. *Wait till I tell, Mae,* Vivie thought, then her shoulders sagged. She could not tell her sister. With Mae in Europe, it was unlikely she would ever see her again. Vivie sank back against the seat, lost in a sea of sadness, no longer interested in her new surroundings.

A short time later they stopped in front of an elegant off-white edifice with forest green awnings above the windows. Emblazoned across the marquee-like front entrance in large white script were the words, "The Algonquin." Large, potted, ornamental trees book-ended the entrance. As

Jamison opened the limo door, Oswald cocked his head and looked at Vivie. "You know, my dear, we generally stay at the Plaza when we're in town, but Alice thought you'd prefer staying here."

Her eyes narrowed. Tucking the packet under her arm, she exited the vehicle and stared up at the Beaux-Arts inspired building. Rising above its off-white edifice was a red brick and limestone façade. Below the twelfth floor's cornice, six terra cotta lions' heads ornamented the building, their mouths open in a roar. Vivie tightened her grip on the package as Alice took her arm.

A doorman greeted them at the entrance. They were then ushered into the hotel's oak-paneled foyer where the aged dark wood of the floor-to-ceiling pillars gleamed with a rich luster. Oswald nodded. "Nice. *Very* nice, indeed."

As he and Alice proceeded to the registration desk, Vivie roamed about the plush lobby, taking it all in. Jewel-toned high-backed sofas and overstuffed Edwardian and wingback chairs were clustered in intimate groupings. Chinese porcelain lamps rested on the nearby end tables, their light reflecting off the small brass bells that summoned the hotel's inconspicuous wait staff. Diminutive tables and writing desks were interspersed throughout the seating area.

Vivie gravitated to the newsstand, its racks filled with an assortment of newspapers and magazines. Above was a display of popular novels. As her eyes studied the titles, the chime of a grandfather clock caused her to turn. Wandering toward the antique timepiece, her gaze was drawn to the sofa opposite. There lolled a large ginger tabby cat. At her approach, the feline jumped down, strolled over, and began to wend about her ankles. Deep, throaty purrs rumbled from his throat. Vivie dropped the packet and fell to her knees on the red, black, and gold Oriental rug. Scooping up the portly feline, she exclaimed, "Oh! You are just divine!"

As the cat bumped his head against her chin, the hotel concierge stepped forward. "Well, I've never seen Hamlet take to a newly arrived guest like he's taken to you."

She smiled, her eyes never leaving the marbled tabby. "Hamlet?"

"Yes. The previous hotel owner once took in a stray he called 'Rusty.' When the actor John Barrymore saw the cat, he supposedly remarked that it needed a name more befitting his stature and called him Hamlet. At least that's how the story's always been told. So, every cat since then has borne that name."

"Interesting," she said, scratching the feline's chin. His purrs intensified.

One of the brass bells pinged. "Excuse me," the man said, before turning to answer the call.

"Come, Vivie." Alice motioned for her. "Our suite is ready."

Reluctantly, she set the cat down, picked up her package, and followed her guardians to the elevator. As the door rumbled shut, Vivie craned her neck to get another glimpse of the cat.

•   •   •   •   •

Passing through the lobby for dinner that evening, Vivie's eyes darted about in search of Hamlet. Seeing no sign of him, her shoulders sagged.

At the entrance to the Rose Room, a maitre d' stood behind a lectern. When Oswald gave his name, they were ushered into the dining area. White, mirrored panels lined its red damask-papered walls and ornate dentil crown molding accented the room's pillars and ceiling.

They were then shown to a table with oak chairs upholstered in rose-red velvet. In the center of the white linen tablecloth set a bud vase holding a single red rose. Once they were seated, Thomas the headwaiter appeared— his jacket a pristine white. "Good evening," he said. "Are you ready to order? Or do you need a moment to look over the menu?"

"This is our first stay here," Oswald volunteered. "What would you recommend?"

"Our specialty of the house, sir. The chicken tetrazinni." With a nod toward Vivie, he added, "And for dessert our chocolate cake."

"Vivie?" Alice asked. "Does that sound okay to you? Or would you prefer something else?"

"What?" she responded, straining to see out into the lobby for a glimpse of Hamlet.

"What would you care to have for dinner, dear?" Alice repeated.

"Oh, anything," she answered distractedly. "Anything at all is fine."

Oswald and Alice's eyes met. He gave a subtle flick of his head and she nodded. Oswald reached into his pocket, pulled out a five-dollar bill, and handed it to Vivie. "Here, my dear. Run out to the newsstand and find yourself something to read. Perhaps you can find that cat to hang out with."

"Really?" Vivie could hardly believe her luck. "What about dinner?"

"We'll have room service send you up something later. Now, go."

It took every ounce of control not to bolt out of the dining room. Vivie circled through the lobby. She stopped by the wooden phone booths, thinking Hamlet might be hiding inside, but the cat was not in either one. Her eyes scanned the lobby. Not a sign of him anywhere. As she wandered about, she found herself in front of an oak-paneled door between the guest elevator and the service elevator. Vivie looked down to see a cat-sized door marked "Rusty" inserted into one of the lower panels. Its flap gently swung back and forth.

Before she could explore, a movement to her right caught her attention. Vivie turned. Hamlet proudly marched through the lobby with something squirmy hanging out of his mouth. The cat stopped and dropped the tiny creature on the marble floor. "A mouse!" Vivie whispered. As it fled across the room, Hamlet took off in hot pursuit. She hastily joined them.

A couple of women shrieked as the tiny rodent streaked past—followed by Hamlet and then Vivie. "Excuse me. Excuse me," she muttered to the guests as the trio made the rounds of the lobby. When the mouse took refuge in a corner behind a large potted palm, the feline pounced. So did Vivie. She scruffed the cat just as a bell boy scurried forward, his face milk white.

"Here," Vivie commanded. "Scruff him." As the young man fumbled to exchange her grip on the cat with his, she added, "Now, hold him firmly, so he thinks you're his Mama." The bell boy's eyes widened.

With her hands free, Vivie reached up and placed her thumb and forefinger around the feline's head, applying gentle pressure to Hamlet's jaws until his mouth opened. Upon extracting the damp mouse, she headed for the entrance. A smattering of light applause broke out.

After depositing the tiny creature outside in one of the planters, Vivie returned to the now quiet lobby. The bell boy stood where she had left him, the cat still in his grip. "You can let him go now," she said as the concierge approached, a frown on his face.

"Is there a problem, miss?" he asked as the young man placed Hamlet on the rug. Vivie turned and smiled. "A problem? Why, no. No problem at all."

His eyes narrowed. A bell pinged. "Atkins, please attend to that."

"Excuse me," Vivie said to him as the bell boy rushed away. "I need to find something to read." She walked off, leaving the concierge with a confused look on his face.

After carefully studying the selections, Vivie chose a copy of Agatha Christie's *Hickory Dickory Dock,* then retreated to the sofa across from the grandfather clock. She settled back into its pillowy depths as Hamlet approached. The cat sat down in front of her, then gave her a baleful stare. "Sorry to have taken away your 'play toy,'" she remarked. Vivie opened her book and began to read.

The feline leapt up onto the sofa and stalked to its other end. He sat and extended a rear leg into the air, then began to wash.

Vivie ignored him. Moments later, Hamlet climbed into her lap and began to knead. At his rumbly purr, a fleeting smile crossed her face. How many times had she and Norsk sat like this? She missed her so...and Poppa and Mae, but especially Mama. Brushing away a stray tear, Vivie tried to concentrate on the Hercule Poirot mystery, but thoughts of her family kept intruding. If she had only heeded her mother's instructions, things would be so different now. If only...

CHAPTER 22

A resounding slap echoed through the woods, silencing Csaky's screams. The man's thickset hands tore at her clothes, then flung her to the ground. A second later, he was on top of her—rutting. Csaky's whimpers drifted through the night air. Moments later, the man's fat fingers wrapped around her throat, slowly squeezing the life out of her. She grappled at his hands, her face flushing pink, then slowly darkening to a deep red as she fought to breathe. Csaky's gasps became fewer and farther between. Her struggles weakened. A moment later, her eyes rolled back in her head and she collapsed. Only the hands clenched around Csaky's slender neck held her head upright. Gradually, those stubby fingers slimmed and softened. The hands shrunk in size. They were no longer those of a forty-year-old man, but those of a twelve-year-old girl. Her hands! Her fingers!

"NOOOOOO! NOOOOO! NOOOOO!" Vivie's panicked shrieks pierced the night.

"Vivie! Vivie!" The overhead light banished the darkness as Néni Alice rushed to her bedside.

"No! No! No!" Vivie squinted in the light's harsh glare, sobbing—tears streaming down her cheeks.

"Is everything okay?" Bácsi Oswald, his paisley silk robe tied at the waist, stood in the doorway. A look of concern filled his kind face.

Vivie dropped her head in her hands and continued to sob.

Alice pulled the trembling girl to her. "She's had a nightmare, Os. Go on to bed."

He nodded and headed back into the sitting area as a knock sounded on the suite's door.

Voices drifted into the bedroom. "No, everything's fine," Oswald reassured the concierge. "The child had a bad dream." Their voices grew indistinct.

A flush of warmth filled Vivie's cheeks as she straightened and pushed away from Alice. "I'm sorry to have disturbed everyone." She hung her head. "You can go back to bed. I'm fine now." Despite her words of reassurance, Vivie could feel the woman's eyes upon her.

"I don't—" Alice hesitated. She looked down, then gave the girl a side glance. "Vivie, this isn't the first time you've had this nightmare, is it?"

With a sharp intake of breath, she softly responded, "No, ma'am."

"Do you want to tell me about it?"

She picked at the hangnail on her thumb, not wanting to share something so personal. Vivie was at a loss. She had not talked with her mother, could not talk with her father. Maigret had encouraged her, but still Vivie could not—

"Is it about what happened to your mother?"

Vivie stiffened. How did she know? Her pulse raced, and her heart pounded like a cornered animal's, ready to bolt. Then her shoulders sagged, and tears once again filled her eyes.

Alice's hand reached out and grasped hers. "I know it's a difficult thing to discuss, Vivie. If it helps any, your father told Oswald and me what happened."

She jerked back and gasped.

Alice reached over and pulled a tissue from the box on the nightstand, handing it to her.

In the silence, the metal alarm clock's loud mechanical ticks seemed to rhythmically say, "Tell her. Tell her. Tell her. Tell her."

Vivie studied her hands. Maigret's words echoed in her head: *Something's gnawing at your soul. You must conquer it. Else, it will eat you alive.* "It was all my fault," she began softly. "If only I had minded..."

Over the next thirty minutes, Vivie's words sometimes stumbled and other times flowed as she poured out her guilt. How she had caused the events that led to her mother's rape and her eventual death. Head down, Vivie peeked at Alice's reactions through teary eyes. The woman listened and nodded—occasionally offering words of comfort and encouragement, emboldening Vivie to continue. ". . . and Poppa hated me for it."

"What makes you think that, Vivie?"

"He was so cold. So aloof. Like he didn't"—she gulped—"even want me around."

A pained look crossed Alice's face. "I'm sorry you felt that way, Vivie." She reached over and clasped her hand. "Sometimes people have difficulty expressing themselves because they're hurting deep inside. I think your father probably withdrew from you to help ease your transition into our care." Alice reached up and brushed back Vivie's curls. "It's important that you realize you weren't responsible for anything that happened. None of it was your fault. And hatred for you? Vivie, that is the furthest thing your father feels towards you. Why, if he didn't love you and Mae, he wouldn't have worked so hard to keep the two of you safe."

She's right, Vivie thought, remembering two abandoned children she had once seen begging on the streets of Budapest.

When Alice left, she wept for the first time over the loss of her mother— her guilt now eased. She nestled back down into bed, her heart lighter. Vivie now well understood why this woman and her mother had been such good friends.

A gentle knock sounded at her door. "Come in."

The light from the sitting area backlit Oswald. "Are you okay, Vivie?"

"Yes, sir."

"The concierge sent up someone he thought might help ease your dreams." As Bácsi Oswald strode into the room something leapt from his arms and onto the bed.

"Hamlet," Vivie murmured. "Thank you, Bácsi Oswald."

"You're welcome, dear." He started to the door, then turned. "If you need anything, anything at all, Vivie, let me know."

"Thank you."

"Pleasant dreams."

As the bedroom door closed, she settled down under the covers, her hand stroking Hamlet's back. The cat padded and kneaded next to her, then curled up and purred her to sleep.

When Vivie awoke the next morning, the suite was silent but for Hamlet's rumbling purr. With last night's conversation still fresh in her head, she had a need—a pressing urge—to connect with her mother. Vivie eased out of bed and retrieved the packet from its hiding place. She unwrapped it and quickly flipped through its now familiar contents. Over the last two weeks, Vivie had found it comforting to sit alone and explore the package. It made her feel closer to her family. Occasionally a tear slid down her cheek, but then she would recall her father's words: *Be brave, Vivie.*

She again shuffled through the contents. *Where is it?* Vivie thought, conscious of Hamlet's investigation of the butcher paper and twine. He pawed at the piece of string, then pounced. *It's got to be here...unless I was careless.* She gulped and pushed the thought away.

One by one, Vivie carefully spread the papers out on the bedcovers. Hamlet padded onto the butcher paper, kneading it into a bed. *It's not here. It's NOT here!* The girl's throat tightened. Her stomach lurched. A wave of nausea hit. She closed her eyes and took a deep breath, gradually letting it out in an attempt to slow her breathing. Vivie opened her eyes. She took another deep breath before giving the documents a closer look. With trembling hands, she began picking up each paper—carefully examining it, front to back.

As she reached for the fourth one, an unmistakable guttural hacking sound met her ears. She glanced over to see Hamlet crouched over the documents, his body heaving as he began to retch up a hairball. "NO!" Vivie screeched, reaching across and unceremoniously sweeping the cat off the bed and onto the floor. As documents followed, she scrambled after them. A split second later, her bedroom door swung open. Alice and Oswald rushed in just as Hamlet darted out.

On her knees, Vivie glanced from her guardians to her precious documents, now strewn across the bed and floor for all to see. Her eyes widened. The one thing she had been looking for was now lying at Oswald's feet. As he reached down and picked it up, Vivie's head dropped in shame. *Oh, Poppa! I've let you down.*

Alice stooped and began to collect the papers as Vivie sat almost immobile, not quite sure what to do since she had exposed the family secret. Oswald cleared his throat, "Vivie, I've been meaning to talk to you about these documents."

She sucked in her breath.

"I think it might be better if we stored them in a safety deposit box at the bank. Not only are they provenance regarding your heritage, but there are many that have great value."

She stiffened at his words, not knowing what to say.

"Yes, Vivie," Alice agreed as she returned the documents to the butcher paper.

Breath rushed from Vivie's lungs as the realization hit: *They know who I am. They know what I am.* She subtly shook her head. How could she have been so naïve? Of course they knew. Alice grew up with Mama in boarding school.

Vivie finally found her voice. "If you don't mind," she hesitated. "I'd really like to keep them with me. I like"—she choked out—"having them near." Tears welled as her eyes drifted down to her hands clasped in her lap. "And," she softly added, her voice breaking, "it's what Poppa told me to do." She glanced up into Oswald's concerned face. Vivie could tell he was struggling with her decision.

"Very well, Vivie. We'll do it your way."

"Well," Alice clapped her hands, "now that that's settled, let's get you something to eat. We've got a big day ahead of us. Lots to see and do."

$$\bullet \qquad \bullet \qquad \bullet \qquad \bullet \qquad \bullet$$

Vivie sat front row center in the Grand Tier at the Metropolitan Opera House, flanked by Oswald and Alice. She glanced below at the milling crowd—men in tuxedos and women in gowns and furs, their hair stylishly coiffed. Not so different from formal events in Budapest.

Her throat tightened at a memory of Mama and Poppa headed to the opera, she in her seafoam gown and him in his white tie and tails. Vivie gulped, pushing the recollection away, and turned her thoughts to the last few weeks. With Oswald and Alice as her guides, Vivie had visited the city's iconic landmarks. Places she had read about but thought she would never see. Her one disappointment being the Central Park Zoo. The caged animals had restlessly paced, circled or lethargically lay on the unrelenting concrete pads of their enclosures. She grimaced, finding the mere thought of their conditions disturbing.

As the lights dimmed, a hush fell over the auditorium, broken only by the opening strains of the orchestra. Vivie turned at the slight pressure on her arm.

Alice leaned in and whispered, "I think you're going to love *Carmen*, Vivie."

She nodded in acknowledgement and settled back in her seat. When Risë Stevens appeared and began to sing, Vivie gasped. She knew that voice. That song! Poppa had had that phonograph record.

"Are you okay?" Oswald softly asked.

"Yes," she whispered back, her eyes riveted on the stage.

•　　•　　•　　•　　•

The opera's heavy, deliberate beat lingered, throbbing within her, long after the performance ended. Vivie tossed and turned in her bed, the mezzo-soprano's performance continuing to replay in her head. She donned her robe, grabbed her book, and slipped out of the quiet suite.

In the lobby, Vivie curled up on the couch across from the grandfather clock. As she began to read, Hamlet soon joined her. It was how she spent most evenings, sometimes becoming so engrossed in her book she forgot where she was. Returning to reality was always a little disorienting—finding she was not in Poppa's study with Norsk, but in the hotel lobby with Hamlet instead. Thoughts of her beloved cat had grown fewer and farther between. Vivie's heart still ached for her, but the sharpness had dulled somewhat.

As she began to nod, the faint hint of Chanel No. 5 filled her nostrils. *Mama?*

"Vivie?" Alice softly said. "Come. Let's get you to bed."

•　　•　　•　　•　　•

Vivie stood outside of the New York City Public Library. Out of all the places she had visited, it was her favorite. As she again admired the massive marble lion sculptures that guarded its entrance, a cultured, low-toned voice drawled, "Beautiful, aren't they?"

The girl turned to see an old man. He was slight, his shoulders stooped.

"Patience and Fortitude," the stranger continued. "Edward Clark Potter was the sculptor. He did these after he sculpted a couple of lionesses for the Morgan Museum's McKim Building. Have you seen them?"

"Yes," she nodded, enchanted by his voice that was almost lyrical, much slower and drawn out than the fast-paced, sharp ones here in the city.

"That's Patience on the south side there," he pointed with his cane. "And Fortitude on the north."

"You seem to know a lot about them."

"I should. The marble started out in my hometown. Knoxville, Tennessee. At Candoro Marble Company where my father worked." He proceeded to tell her the history of the lions, ending with, "And that's not just any marble, mind you. It's pink marble, one thing Knoxville is known for."

"Pink marble? It doesn't look pink."

"Take a look at it on a rainy day. That's when it's most evident." A horn sounded. He turned. "Well, that's my ride."

As the man toddled toward the car, Vivie waved and called after him, "It was nice talking with you." She turned back toward the lions, her eyes narrowing.

·   ·   ·   ·   ·

A week later, Vivie stood at the window and watched the rain pepper down on the 44th Street traffic.

"What time is it?" Alice asked. She reclined on the chaise lounge, flipping through the latest copy of *Vogue.*

Before Vivie could respond, Oswald stormed into the suite, his face ashen and a paper clutched in his fist.

"Os?" Alice immediately rose and started toward him. "What's wrong?"

At the alarm on his face, all Vivie could think was, *Poppa?*

CHAPTER 23

Abilene, Texas, April 1957

As the plane taxied to a stop, Vivie studied the tarmac. *So small,* she thought, comparing the airport to New York's Idlewild.

Oswald stretched. "Going to be good to get back to the ranch."

"See?" Alice patted his arm. "Aren't you glad you talked to the hospital?"

He nodded. "Yes. Mother has always had a tendency to exaggerate." Indigestion. Not a heart attack. Still, the telegram's scare had resulted in this trip to Texas.

Stepping off the plane, a dry, dusty gust of wind whipped Vivie's hair about her face.

"Welcome to Abilene, Vivie." Oswald waved his arm across the expanse.

She took a step back as a bevy of reporters rushed the private plane shouting, "Mr. McNabb! Mr. McNabb! May I get an interview?"

"Are you here for business or pleasure, Mr. McNabb?"

"Mr. McNabb? How long will you be in Abilene?"

Oswald smoothed his tie, seeming to preen under the attention.

"Is Bácsi Oswald famous here?" Vivie whispered to Alice.

"Oh, just the story of 'local boy does good.' It's always the same every time we fly in." She glanced down at Vivie. "And perhaps while we're here, it would be best to call us Uncle Oswald and Aunt Alice." She shook her head. "Calling us Bácsi and Néni might confuse the locals."

"Okay, Aunt Alice." The words felt odd as they rolled off Vivie's tongue. Her attention turned back to Oswald.

"We'll be visiting with family, and then heading out to the ranch," he told the reporters. "Maybe even line up a barbecue or two." Oswald signaled a nearby hot dog vendor. "Here, fellas. Let me buy you some dogs and a round of root beers."

Vivie's eyes widened.

Oswald turned. "Vivie? You want one?"

"No!" She stepped back.

"Come on. Try one," he urged.

Alice stepped forward and took the offered frankfurter. "They're not half bad, Vivie, especially with mustard, onion, and chili." She gave a little laugh. "I'll tell you a secret. When I first came to America, I thought they were actually made from dogs."

Vivie's eyes narrowed. "What *are* they made from?"

"Mostly pork scraps. They're a little like sausages, but not near as spicy. Here. Try a bite of mine." She pinched off a portion and handed it to Vivie.

The girl tentatively nibbled at it. "You're right," she nodded. "Not too bad."

"Do you want one?"

"No. Not right now, Aunt Alice. Thank you."

The small crowd of reporters parted as Jamison drove up in a light green Cadillac convertible. "Wow! Would you look at that beauty!"

"Never seen one of these before."

Oswald grinned. "It's a 1957 Cadillac Eldorado Biarritz. One of a kind."

"Can we get a picture?"

"Certainly!"

Flashbulbs popped as Oswald posed beside the car and answered more of the reporters' questions. Jamison loaded their luggage into the trunk, then opened the door for Alice and Vivie. Oswald followed. As he waved to the reporters, Jamison pulled out of the airport.

Ten minutes later, the car stopped in front of a stately brick house on South Sixth Street. On the columned wrap-around porch sat an older man, bearing a strong resemblance to Oswald. By his side stood a slight gray-haired woman, her hand resting on his shoulder.

"Vivie?" Oswald said as they approached. "These are my parents, Joseph and Ruby."

"A pleasure to meet you, Mr. and Mrs. McNabb." Vivie shook their hands as Oswald continued.

"Mother? Father? This is my ward, Vivie."

"Nicely mannered child," Mrs. McNabb stated as they proceeded into the house.

While the family visited, Vivie wandered over to a photograph-filled table. The portraits and casual photos of special events reminded her of home. Her throat tightened. All those physical memories of her past were gone—forever. All except the most important one. Hidden away in the packet inside her luggage.

• • • • •

"Well, here we are, Vivie! Lytle Lake ranch," Oswald announced.

Her eyes scouted out the spread as she emerged from the car. Cattle grazed in the distance. A white, two-story farmhouse, its wrap-around porch lined with rockers, sat to her left. To her right was a massive barn and a corral where two horses paced. Vivie immediately gravitated to the heavily pregnant cat lying in the shade of a stand of privet. As she eased toward her, a short wiry man emerged from the barn. "Ah, Señor McNabb!" he called out.

"Raoul!" Oswald responded. He walked over and slapped him on the back. The two men grabbed each other's hands and shook them, large grins filling their faces. "Vivie? Come here and meet one of my oldest and dearest friends. We grew up together. Now, Raoul watches over the ranch for me when I'm away. His wife, Maria, manages the house and cooks."

"Nice to meet you, sir." She held out her hand.

"Raoul? This is Vivie, my ward."

"Nice to meet you, miss. I hope you'll enjoy your stay here."

"What's her name?" Vivie nodded toward the pale-colored feline.

"Doesn't have one," he responded. "She's just a barn cat."

Vivie cringed internally at the slight. *So demeaning,* she wanted to say. Instead, she bit back the words and said, "I think I'll call her Lilac."

"Lilac it is," Oswald said.

"Indeed," Raoul agreed.

Three days later, Vivie burst into the ranch office. "They're here! They're here!" she exclaimed.

"Who?" Raoul looked up from his desk.

"The kittens! There's a black one, one that's lilac-colored, and a tiny gray runt."

"Don't get too attached," he warned. "Runts usually don't make it."

"Oh, but I *know* he will!" Vivie replied. "I'll make sure of it."

•　　•　　•　　•　　•

Vivie lay curled up in the stall beside the feline family reading *Archy and Mehitabel.* She had discovered the battered volume about the friendship between a cockroach and an alley cat in the den's bookcase. Turning the page, Vivie glanced down and smiled at the two-days-old kittens.

"Who are you, and what are you doing here?" an unfamiliar voice barked out.

She flinched and gawked up at a strange man blocking the stall door. "I'm Vivie," she managed to stammer out. "I'm taking care of Lilac and her kittens." The girl cringed under his scowl, her eyes darting about for a means of escape.

"Kittens!" the cowboy spat. "Just what we need around here. More damned cats!" He shook his head in disgust. "Got too many as it is."

"Why would you say that?" Intrigued, Vivie momentarily forgot her fear.

Before he could respond, Raoul walked into the barn. "Tom, you're back!"

Vivie's shoulders sagged with relief.

"How did the roundup go?" Raoul continued.

"Good. Who's the kid?" The man flicked his head in her direction.

A prickly sensation crept up the back of Vivie's neck.

"She's Señor McNabb's ward."

"So the old—"

"Tom," Raoul interrupted. "Why don't you get washed up. Maria's made tamale soup for dinner."

"C'mon, Sam. Let's go." Vivie then noticed another man standing off to the side in the shadows. He turned and followed Tom toward the bunkhouse.

Raoul glanced over at her. "Don't let him worry you, Vivie. His bark is worse than his bite."

I'm not so sure, she thought, a sense of unease creeping up her spine.

CHAPTER 24

A week later, Vivie tucked the tail of her red gingham shirt into her blue jeans. Today, they were going to a barbecue at an adjacent ranch. It was the last thing she wanted to do after yesterday. Vivie stooped down and dug in the closet for her black and white saddle oxfords, her mind replaying the previous day's events.

At the rodeo grounds, they had made their way through the milling crowd and settled into the McNabb family box. Raoul was already there. He stood at the front talking with a couple of other ranchers. Oswald excused himself and returned with popcorn and sodas. Vivie nibbled at the cardboard-like pieces of fluff, salty but flavorless. Nothing like the popcorn Mama used to make in the fireplace. Vivie gazed at the puff of corn, remembering Norsk stalking and batting stray kernels across the floor.

A voice over the loudspeaker intoned the beginning of the events: the recitation of the Pledge of Allegiance, followed by an off-key rendition of the national anthem, and concluding with a prayer for the country and the safety of the day's participants. The first announced event was barrel racing.

Vivie scrutinized the rodeo ring where large casks were intermittently spaced. Near the gate stood a gray-haired cowboy with a stop watch clutched in his hand. His brows were drawn down in seemingly serious concentration. At the crack of a gunshot, Vivie's eyes darted about, assessing her best avenue of escape. Then she realized everyone else was focused on the ring where a rider had emerged and was tightly circling the series of barrels. "Fifteen seconds for Dean on Serendipity, folks," came over the intercom. Vivie eased back against her seat, trying to control her breathing. By the third round, she was prepared for the starter pistol, turning her attention to the competition. She watched breathlessly as rider after rider took to the course, each urging and guiding their mounts around the colorful drums in the shortest amount of time.

After a brief intermission, the announcer said, "Next up, folks, is the calf roping event." At the starter pistol's shot, Vivie leaned forward in expectation. Across the ring, two chutes popped open. A rider on a roan gelding, his lasso swinging, galloped out of one. From the other, a rust-colored calf erupted. A second later, the cowboy's lariat snaked out and snagged the young bovine's neck, jerking him to a stop. Vivie gasped, then cringed when the wrangler leapt from his horse, slammed the calf to the ground, then nimbly tied its feet together as it bawled and struggled to rise. "Ten seconds," the rodeo judge stated. "That's the record to beat." When the crowd cheered, Vivie was mortified. As the same scenario happened again and again, waves of nausea assailed her. Just when she thought she could not endure another minute, intermission was called.

"Exciting! Isn't it?" Raoul hollered over the cacophony of the crowd.

Vivie managed a weak nod, swallowing down her nausea. Telling herself, maybe the next event would not be as bad. But to her horror, it was—as was each event that followed. She had thought the afternoon would never end.

BOOM! Vivie was snatched back into the present. She leapt up, grabbed her shoes, and bolted for the door—thoughts of that day in Buda spurring her forward. In the hall, she ran into Oswald.

"Whoa, there, Vivie!" He took hold of her arms. "Where you going in such an all-fired rush?"

She gulped and stammered out, "The shotgun blast!"—her heart thudding as though it would burst from her chest.

"Is that all? Probably just Raoul scaring off some critter around the hen house."

Vivie nodded, her breath whooshing out. "Okay, okay." Bácsi Oswald. Here, she was seeing a different side of the man. Less cultured and refined 'down on the farm.'

"I was just coming to get you, Vivie. We're about ready to go."

"Okay. Just let me slip on my shoes."

"Do you want to ride with Alice and me in the car? Or would you prefer to ride in the back of the pickup truck with some of the ranch hands?"

Vivie flinched as the rattly black truck in Switzerland came to mind. Her throat tightened. "The car's fine," she squeaked out.

"Are you okay, Vivie? You look a little pale."

She drew in a slow breath and let it ease out. "I'm fine, Uncle Oswald."

"Well, let's go. Alice is waiting in the car."

Her eyes widened upon seeing Jamison. His standard chauffeur uniform had been replaced with western garb.

"Howdy do, Miss Vivie," he said as he opened her door.

"Howdy," she reluctantly responded, dreading the day ahead. As she settled back into her seat, Tom strode out of the barn with a burlap sack. Vivie's eyes narrowed as the cowhand tossed it to Sam in the bed of the pickup.

A moment later, he climbed inside the truck cab, started the vehicle, and pulled out of the driveway. Jamison followed. They drove down the dusty road lined with grazing cattle. Oil derrick pumps bobbed in the distance like hens pecking corn.

As they approached the river bridge, the pickup slowed to a stop. Jamison pulled up behind the truck. Vivie leaned forward for a better view. "Why are we stopping here?"

"I don't know," Oswald replied.

Sam jumped from the bed of the pickup, grabbed the burlap sack, and strode toward the bridge rail. "What's he—" Vivie's stomach clenched. Bolting from the car, she raced after him. As he sailed the weighted sack into the air, piercing high-pitched cries filled her ears. Vivie seized Sam's arm. "What was in that sack?"

He shrugged. "Just those kittens Tom wanted to get shed of."

"Kittens?" Vivie screeched. She reached down and tore off her saddle oxfords, then scaled the rail.

"No, Vivie!" Oswald yelled.

"Jamison!" Alice pleaded. "Go after her."

While plunging downward, everything Poppa taught her about swimming and diving flooded through Vivie's head. As the water washed over her, she flashed back to her mother jumping into the river to save Mae.

Vivie blinked in the murky depths. Her eyes darted about in search of the burlap sack. She needed to hurry. It would not take much time for Lilac's babies to drown. They were so young.

Her lungs began to burn. She was going to have to surface for air soon. Then, Vivie saw it. She grabbed the sack and headed toward the surface. As her head broke the water, Vivie noticed Jamison swimming toward her. She nodded, and they headed for the bank.

On shore, Vivie shrugged off his help as her trembling fingers frantically struggled to unknot the piece of twine. She fought back the urge to weep, concentrating on the tight knot.

"Here."

Vivie glanced up. Jamison held out a pocket knife. "T-t-thanks." Her hand shook as she reached for it.

"Let me." He squatted beside her and grasped a section of the burlap. A second later the knife blade ripped through the fabric. Jamison peeled back the material, revealing three, tiny, motionless forms.

"No!" Vivie gasped. As the others made their way down to the bank, she picked up the black kitten and shoved it into Jamison's hands. "Quick!" Vivie ordered. "Do exactly what I do." She scooped up the lilac one. Holding her upside down, Vivie shook the kitten. Then, she flicked her finger five times against its chest.

Jamison upended the black one and did the same.

Next, Vivie righted the kitten. "Do this." She gently blew into its nose in five-second intervals. As Jamison did too, she laid the miniature feline in the palm of her hand and used an index finger to massage the small chest. Vivie picked her up and blew again. No response. She glanced over at Jamison. It was apparent he was not having any luck reviving his kitten either. *C'mon, little one. Please. Please, Saint Gertrude. Please,* she silently pled as they continued to repeat the motions.

Five minutes later, Vivie studied the still form. "It's no use." She burst into tears, laying down the lilac kitten and picking up the runt. "We were too late," Vivie wailed. She looked down at the gray kitten, so much smaller than his littermates. Her fingers wrapped around him. He was so tiny he fit in Vivie's closed fist. She brought her hand to her lips and whispered inside, "I'm so sorry, az én kis cica. I'm so, so very sorry."

Vivie's stomach churned. Three lives needlessly ended. She glowered at Tom, her eyes spitting fire. "Why?"

Before she even realized what she was doing, Vivie leapt up and charged the man. Her fists flailed against his chest as she screamed, "You're despicable! Vile! Cruel! Heartless! I hate you—" Jamison and Oswald rushed forward and tried to pull her off him as she continued her tirade and fought to push them away.

Then, Vivie gasped and stepped back as her fist seemed to explode. She opened her hand and looked down. A little pink mouth gaped open and emitted a squeak. "You're alive!" Vivie cried. "I thought you were dead." She dropped to her knees, clutching the kitten to her chest, and sobbed.

Oswald squatted down beside her, rubbing her back. "Such an itty-bitty little thing." His finger reached down and stroked its tiny head as Alice draped a blanket over Vivie's shoulders.

"Yes," she sniffed. "We need to get him back to his mother." Her eyes drilled into Tom. The man took a step back and looked away. Vivie's blood ran cold. She stood up, again advancing toward him. "That was you, wasn't it?"

He took another step back, avoiding her eyes.

"You killed Lilac. Didn't you?" Her voice rose. "That was the gunshot before we left the house. Wasn't it?"

Oswald stepped forward. "Answer her, Tom."

He shook his head. "She's just a kid, Mr. McNabb."

"She's not 'just a kid,' Tom. As far as I'm concerned, Vivie is my daughter, and if you have disrespected her, then you've disrespected me. You can head on back to the ranch and collect your things. Consider yourself fired."

Vivie laid her hand on Oswald's arm, then stood on tiptoe. When he leaned toward her, she whispered in his ear.

"Oh, and one more thing before you go," Oswald said to Tom. "What did you do with Lilac?"

"*You* find the damned cat," he spat.

"We need to find her!" Vivie's voice cracked. "I want to bury her with her kittens."

"We will," he reassured her, patting her hand. "If we have to cover every acre. We'll find her."

A murmur of conversation broke out among the hands as Tom stalked off in the direction of the ranch.

"Uncle Oswald?"

"Yes, Vivie?"

"Ever since I came to stay with you, you've always asked me what I wanted." She gulped, then continued. "What you could do for me."

"Yes, Vivie?"

"Well...now I know." Her voice broke. "I know what I want."

"What is it, Vivie?"

"I never want something like this to happen again. I want the cats and dogs at the ranch spayed and neutered."

"That's just stupid," Sam muttered.

Oswald's head snapped up. He scowled at the ranch hands standing about. "What I said to Tom goes for all of you. From now on, this ranch will be run responsibly. And if you have problems with that, get your things and go." His thumb jerked back toward the ranch. Oswald turned to Raoul as Sam and another cowhand headed down the road after Tom. "When we get back to the house, call Doc Butler out here to see about getting those animals fixed."

· · · · ·

That evening, Alice came into Vivie's room. "Is Little River doing okay?"

"Yes, ma'am." She held up the nursing bottle showing how much milk the kitten had taken. Then, Vivie placed him on her hand and began stroking his back.

"What are you doing?" Alice asked.

"I'm burping him."

"Burping him?"

Vivie nodded. "They have to be burped just like babies."

"I didn't know that. Of course, I didn't grow up around animals."

"Here. Hold him a minute." Vivie rose and headed into her bathroom. A moment later she returned with a cup of warm water, a cotton ball, and a wash cloth. She took the kitten from Alice and laid him across the terrycloth square, then dipped the wad of cotton in the water and rubbed it gently under his tail.

A look of confusion crossed Alice's face. "What on earth are you doing, Vivie?"

"Helping him eliminate. If Lilac were alive, she would stimulate his bottom by licking it. It's how kittens learn to go to the bathroom. Since he doesn't have a mama, we have to do it this way."

The woman shook her head. "Vivie, you constantly amaze me with all you know."

She shrugged. "I just read."

•   •   •   •   •

Later, Vivie approached Oswald in the den. "I'm sorry for today."

"Sorry? Why, whatever for?"

"For ruining the barbecue. For losing control and hitting Tom. For saying all those bad things to him. I was taught better."

"Vivie, it's okay to lose your temper. Everybody does once in a while."

True, she thought, but knew her mother would be mortified.

"There's something I've been meaning to talk to you about, Vivie." He gripped his newspaper, leaning forward. "I meant what I said today. Alice and I've come to think of you as our daughter. We're too old to ever have children of our own and would like to adopt you."

"But...Poppa—" she choked out.

"I know, Vivie. But this is something that your father and I discussed that day in France. He gave his permission but said the decision would be left entirely up to you."

Poppa had given his permission for her to be someone else's child. It was as though she had been slapped. Her eyes drifted to the floor as the magnitude of this news engulfed her.

"I don't need or expect an answer now, Vivie. You think on it. Take all the time you need. And if and when you are agreeable to it, you can let me know." He rose and kissed her on the forehead. "Well, I'm off to bed."

Upstairs, Vivie plodded into her bedroom. She checked on Little River, snuggled in his fur-lined bedding kept warm by a hot water bottle. Her finger reached out and gently stroked the orphaned kitten. "We're so much alike," she whispered. "You've lost your family, and I've"—Vivie hiccupped—"lost mine."

She glanced over at the clock. "Thirty minutes until you need to be fed again. Might as well stay up." Vivie retrieved the butcher-paper-wrapped packet from its hiding place, sat down on the bed, and opened it. She then pulled out the photograph, her finger tracing the familiar faces of her family. When Vivie came to her father's, tears spilled down her cheeks. "Why, Poppa? Why?"

CHAPTER 25

"What are you doing?" Vivie screeched.

Oswald stood in her room with another man. Her butcher-paper-wrapped packet lay open before them, exposing her closely guarded secret.

She charged them like a lioness protecting her cubs. Venomous words spewed from her lips as she scooped up the butcher paper and its contents, then fled to the barn loft.

'Treachery' was the one word that screamed in Vivie's head as she sat reassembling the package. She swiped at the tears of anger streaming down her cheeks. Poppa had trusted Oswald. His betrayal was like a gut punch—to both of them. And to think, less than a week ago, the man had said he wanted to adopt her!

At the creak of the ladder's rungs, Vivie turned—expecting to see 'the traitor.' Instead, it was Alice. She crossed the loft and sat down beside her. "I understand you're upset."

Vivie did not respond.

"You know, Oswald is only trying to help."

"Help?" Vivie's voice rose. "How? By exposing who I am?"

"It's nothing like that, Vivie." Alice reached out for her, but she pulled away. "Oswald believes your documents need to have notarized translations. It's for your own protection. That's why Ben—Mr. Vargas—is here. He's Oswald's attorney."

"That doesn't matter, Alice!"

"Yes, it does, Vivie. See, Benedek is originally from Szombothely and...he knew your mother."

"He knew Mama?" she whispered.

"Yes, Vivie. He did."

She remained silent, not knowing what to say. The clucks of a banty hen in the barnyard filled the silence as Alice's words swirled in her head. Then distant voices drew her attention to the open loft doors. Below, Oswald and Mr. Vargas stood talking beside a black sedan.

Alice rose. "Well, I better head back to the house." As she reached the ladder, Alice turned. "The decision is ultimately yours, Vivie. Oswald won't force the issue. And I've told him, he should have discussed the matter with you before invading your privacy. It won't happen again."

As the woman descended the ladder, Vivie stood and stared out the loft opening. She watched Alice approach the two men. They talked for a moment, then the attorney got into his car and drove away. Vivie ducked back as Oswald glanced toward the loft. For the next hour, she sat with the packet clutched to her chest, wrestling with her decision.

•   •   •   •   •

"Vivie, start packing. We're going to Egypt." Alice headed into the girl's closet and began examining her wardrobe. "Hmm. Just as I thought," her muffled voice said. "When we stop over in New York, we'll need to do some shopping."

The girl sat cross-legged on the bed, playing with Little River. A month had passed since his rescue. Vivie's brow furrowed. "But I thought we were spending the summer here."

"Well, those *were* the plans," Alice continued, stepping outside the closet. "But Oswald received word last night about some banking matters that need to be addressed. Have you ever been to Egypt?"

"No, ma'am." Her thoughts momentarily drifted back to Hungary and that day in the van with Andrew and Martin.

Alice sat down beside her on the bed. She scooped up Little River. "He's grown, hasn't he?"

"Yes, he has." Vivie gazed at the kitten, a pang of concern stirring within her. "But who'll look after him while we're gone?"

"Maria. You know how she dotes on him, preparing him puréed chicken livers."

She nodded, her throat tightening at the thought of again being parted from someone she loved.

"Oh, Vivie! You'll love Cairo and Giza. There's so much to see. The Pyramids, the Sphinx, the Antiquities Museum..."

•   •   •   •   •

Alice was right. Vivie had loved Egypt, her one disappointment being that no temples or shrines remained of the cat goddess Bastet. En route to Luxembourg, she gazed out the plane's window. Cloud formations seemed to glow in the sunlight. The landscape below resembled the quilted coverlet that once draped her grandmother's bed.

"Here, Vivie." Oswald held out a tiny box.

She opened it and gasped. "Oh! Bácsi Oswald!" Vivie held up a miniature figurine of Bastet, marveling at its intricacy. "It's lovely."

He nodded. "Alice thought you'd like it to remember Egypt by, rather than a piece of jewelry."

Vivie gave a little shiver of delight. "Yes. Thank you so much." They were beginning to really know her—her likes and dislikes. She smiled at the thought, despite the heaviness she harbored in her heart. A 'dark aura' Maigret would have said. Whether to let Oswald and Alice adopt her constantly lurked at the edge of Vivie's thoughts, wearing at her like a terrier with a bone. She had lain awake again last night, tossing and turning about the decision, wishing she had Norsk to confide in—or even Little River.

As the plane banked, Vivie glanced down at her watch. Soon they would be landing. At the thought of seeing Mae, her stomach jittered as though a hundred hoppy bugs leapt about. It had been five months. The sanitarium had recommended this visit in hopes that Vivie's presence might stir Mae's memory.

Vivie's fingers caressed the tiny cat sculpture as she thought back to Le Havre and the last time she had seen her sister. Tears pricked her eyes, remembering how she had not gotten to say goodbye. But she would make up for that today.

•   •   •   •   •

Jamison met the plane in Luxembourg and chauffeured them to the McNabb's penthouse apartment. An hour later, they arrived at the hospital where Vivie was shown into a small room. Her sister sat in a chair, gazing off into space. "Hello, Mae."

The girl made no response.

Vivie sat down across from her, placing a hand on Mae's arm.

Her sister slapped it away and ran screaming to the nurse. As Vivie tried to approach, Mae's cries intensified. Tears of terror coursed down her cheeks. She grappled at the nurse, trying to climb her as though she were a tree.

"I'll tell you a story, Mae," Vivie's voice wavered. "Your favorite one."

Still, the child shrieked and sobbed, refusing to let Vivie near.

•　　•　　•　　•　　•

"Are you okay?" Alice stood in the doorway of her bedroom.

Vivie nodded, too numb to make a verbal response.

"I know today was upsetting." Alice walked over and sat beside her on the window seat. "Oswald's talked to the doctor. He's arranging for some specialists to treat her."

"Do you think it will help?"

"Honestly? I don't know, but it can't hurt." She reached up and tucked a stray curl behind Vivie's ear. "All we can do is try. And Oswald will do *everything* he can for her."

The girl sighed and watched the traffic below—compartmentalizing the deadness that engulfed her, much as she had done when her mother died.

CHAPTER 26

Greenfield Massachusetts, October 1957

Vivie entered her dorm room to find her desk drawer open and Roslind flipping through her passport.

"Gosh! Where *haven't* you been?"

For a split second, she could not breathe. Blood rushed through her veins. Vivie's sight clouded, then cleared. Her eyes darted to the bookcase. Safe. She breathed a sigh of relief.

"You okay, Viv? You don't look so hot."

"I'm fine." She swallowed and managed a tight smile as she walked over and retrieved her passport. That was the one thing she loathed about boarding school. No privacy. Girls coming and going at all times. Sometimes knocking, sometimes not. Nosing about closets and drawers. 'Borrowing' clothes and make-up. Thankfully, she did not have anything they were interested in.

Roslind plopped down on Vivie's bed and cocked her head. "It must be so wonderful to be able to travel."

"Yes, my unc—" Vivie stopped and corrected herself. "My father's an international banker. We travel a lot as part of his work." While not a lie, it certainly seemed like it. Oswald was now legally her father.

She had reasoned to herself that it made sense. Having the last name of McNabb instead of Degirdro distanced Vivie from her true identity. Also, there would be no more complicated explanations of how she called Oswald uncle, when he really was not. No more trying to explain away her parents' absence. Mama's was simple. She was dead. But Poppa's? That was extremely complicated...and she never really knew what to say.

Poppa had said that he loved her, but did he really? After all, he had abandoned her on a dock in Le Havre like a kitten dumped at a roadside park. Then there were the arrangements he had made for Vivie to be someone else's child, never sharing that information with her. It was the antithesis of everything he had taught Vivie: Communicate. Discuss. Question. Express concerns and feelings. He had done none of that with her.

Roslind sat looking expectantly at Vivie.

"I have a photo album of our trips, if you'd care to see."

"Sure."

Vivie walked over to her bookcase, surreptitiously glancing at its side to assure herself that the butcher-paper-wrapped package was well-hidden. Heaven knew, it was one of the safest places in the dorm. She subtly shook her head. Most of these girls were only focused on boys. They could care less about books or studying. An imperceptible smile crossed her lips as Anders's remark about young men came to mind. How they turned one's thoughts to marriage, cooking, and babies. Not hers, though!

"What do you want to see first, Roslind? Egypt? Tanzania?" Vivie continued to rattle off exotic locales as she walked back over to the bed.

"Hey, Vivie!" Nicole shouted from the hall. "Phone."

"Coming." She handed Roslind the album. "Be right back."

"Vivie?" Oswald asked when she answered. "I've got business in Switzerland next week. Would you like to go along? Perhaps visit your mother's grave?"

Her stomach clenched as a wave of memories washed over her: the guilt she had felt back then—even though Vivie had known since her arrival in the United States that she was not to blame for the circumstances. How helpless she had felt after her mother's death, but how she had had to be strong for Mae. She was not ready to go back.

"I've got exams coming up," Vivie managed to stammer out. "I probably need to stay here and study. Maybe next time." Not *exactly* a lie, since she *would* have exams coming up—eventually.

"Very well. Another time, then."

Why didn't I tell him the truth? she thought as she hung up the phone. *He would have understood. He always does.*

As she started back to her dorm room, Nicole and Roslind rushed up to her.

"Quick! Get a jacket, Vivie," Nicole said. "Ginger's taking us hiking to collect samples for our biology project."

"No, thanks."

"Ah, c'mon, Viv," Roslind pleaded. "Ginger says she's a trained guide. It should be fun."

Vivie sighed. "Well...okay."

•   •   •   •   •

Two years later, Vivie lay on her back looking up at the stars. Orion. Ursa Major and Minor. Canus. Poppa had taught her to identify the constellations. Under the night sky, her parents seemed so near. Vivie closed her eyes and listened to her classmates murmuring in their tents. She could almost believe it was the soft hum of Mama and Poppa talking in the distance.

Vivie thought back to their escape from Hungary. While it was an arduous journey, filled with fear and starvation, they were together. They were a family. Now, all she had left was bittersweet memories. Vivie never thought she would enjoy hiking and camping after what they had experienced, but she did.

She smiled, recalling that afternoon Roslind and Nicole had talked her into collecting biology samples. Ginger, their group leader, was not as experienced as she had pretended to be and soon they were lost. As panic set in, Vivie stepped forward. "Calm down, girls. Everything will be okay." She checked the position of the sun, searched for spiderwebs and moss around the trees, sought out trail blazes and cairns—all skills honed while escaping Hungary. Forty minutes later Vivie had guided them back to 'civilization,' where she was hailed a hero—and eventually became their unofficial nature guide.

A shooting star caught her eye. Vivie watched until it vanished into the night, then scanned the sky for more.

As sleep engulfed the voices in the tents, she concentrated on the natural night sounds: the hoot of an owl, the croak of frogs, the raspy buzz of cicadas, the churr of a raccoon. The latter triggered Vivie's memory of that night by the campfire, her father's love for her shining in his hazel eyes. *Poppa,* she thought, *Where are you? Did something happen? Are you—dead?*

• • • • •

At the close of her senior year, Vivie sat at the dining room table surrounded by books. She paused in her writing and stared across the room. Her mind wandered. It had been two months and she still had heard nothing about her college application. Vivie had submitted only one. What was it Maigret would have said? Something about 'putting all her eggs in one basket?'

She opened her folder and pulled out her copy of the application. With a four-point grade average, she should be a shoo-in, but one never knew. Vivie glanced over her list of extracurricular activities: President of the Honor Society. Captain of the Debate Team. French Club President. Equestrian team captain. Outing Club President. Literary Society Vice-President. Head Math Club Tutor. Drama Club member. She then scanned her list of interests: art, dance, literature, music, theater, foreign languages.

Vivie shrugged. If she did not get in, she could always travel with Alice and Oswald. Maybe go to Luxembourg and spend some time with Mae, then apply again next term.

She tucked the copy back in her folder, then glanced down at what she had written. Vivie scrunched her nose, wadded up the sheet of paper, and started over.

Oswald walked into the room. "What are you working on, Vivie?" He peered over her shoulder.

"My valedictory speech." A deep sigh escaped her.

"Hmm. Maybe I can help. What's your topic?"

"Robert Frost's 'The Road Not Taken.'"

"Ah, yes." He cleared his throat and began to recite. "Two roads diverged—"

"Vivie! Vivie!" Alice charged into the room like a school girl, an envelope in hand.

She froze. *Poppa?*

CHAPTER 27

Alice shoved the piece of mail into her hand. "Open it, Vivie! Open it."

She gaped at the blue and gold crest, her hands shaking. Vivie's stomach clenched as her adoptive parents' eyes bored into her. She swallowed past the knot forming in her throat and broke the seal. Pulling out the folded piece of paper, Vivie opened it and glanced down. A gasp escaped her. "I got in! I got in!" She ran into Oswald's outstretched arms.

"Graduating a year early! *And* getting into the Sorbonne!" His arms engulfed her in a tight hug. "I'm proud of you, Vivie. Your parents would be proud, too."

Mama and Poppa. The thought of them dampened her excitement. She wished they were there to see.

Alice picked up the letter that had fallen to the floor. "Well, I think this calls for a celebration!"

The Sorbonne. Vivie subtly shook her head in disbelief.

• • • • •

Three months later, Vivie, Alice, and Oswald stood in the furnished Parisian apartment within walking distance of the university.

"Are you sure this is the one you want?" Oswald asked. "Because we can get you a larger one."

"And redecorate," Alice added.

"It's perfect just as it is," Vivie replied.

"Are you sure?" Alice asked. "It *is* rather small for entertaining."

"Entertaining?"

"I think she means socializing," Oswald clarified. "After all, you're going to want to have friends over."

"I hardly think so," Vivie responded.

"Why, that's part of what college life is," Oswald said. "Meeting new people and making friends."

"Maybe even a nice young man?" Alice hinted.

"Not for me, it isn't." Vivie glanced from Alice to Oswald. "I came here to study. To learn. To get an education and make something of myself. Not to meet people and make friends." Her brow raised. "Nor find a husband," she added.

"But you can do all of it, Vivie. Study some. Play some. The two are not mutually exclusive," Oswald said. "It's a balance. A compromise."

"I understand," she replied. "But I've seen what happens when dreams are destroyed. And I don't want that to happen in *my* life."

Vivie then told them about Guta—and the regret and longing she had seen in the old woman's eyes. "I don't want that to be me," she said. "I don't want to be in my sixties thinking, 'I wish I had done this or that.'"

•　　　•　　　•　　　•　　　•

At the Sorbonne, Vivie continued to excel in her studies, completing her bachelor's degree in three years. Looking forward to graduation, she sat in the campus lounge pouring over the master's degree course offerings.

Yvette interrupted her. "What are you doing over the break?"

"Nothing special," she shrugged. "I have some personal matters I need to attend to."

"Personal matters? Oh, like what—"

"Yvette? Come on!"

"Thank goodness," Vivie whispered to herself as her nosy classmate's boyfriend summoned Yvette away before she could ask anything more.

A week later, Vivie was in Switzerland, standing over her mother's unmarked grave. She had finally decided it was time to confront her past. Chase away the ghosts that still haunted her at times. Lay things to rest so she could move on with her life.

"Hello, Mama," Vivie said softly. "I'm sorry it's taken me so long to come see you, but I just wasn't ready." A lump formed in her throat. "I've missed you every day. There were so many things over the years that I've wanted to tell you. First...I want to say I'm sorry."

Vivie's voice broke. Her breath quickened, and her pulse began to skip as that old childhood guilt struggled to assert itself. She gulped and closed her eyes for a moment. Taking slow measured breaths, she reflected upon Alice's words of reassurance that night at the Algonquin. *It's important that you realize you weren't responsible for anything that happened. None of it was your fault.*

In control once more, Vivie continued. "For so many weeks after you died, I felt responsible and so guilty about that day on the road. I believed I caused everything." She reached up and wiped at the tears trickling down her face. "But...Alice helped me understand that it was not my fault. She's such a good woman, Mama. I can see why you were such close friends. She and Oswald...they've taken such good care of me. Even adopted me. At first, it hurt—knowing I would be Vivie McNabb instead of Vivie Degirdro, but then I realized it's a level of protection for who I really am." She dropped her head. "I've kept our secret all these years. No one knows except for Néni Alice and Bácsi Oswald." *And Mr. Vargas,* she thought but did not say.

Vivie looked up. The angelic statue stood in the distance, clutching her stone doll. "I wish I could say that Mae is fine, but...she...her mind never recovered. She's in the sanitarium in Luxembourg. I try and visit whenever I can. Sometimes she knows me..." Vivie sighed and shook her head. "And sometimes she doesn't. Oswald always makes sure she has everything she needs."

Her throat tightened. "And...Poppa." Vivie shook her head, staring out across the small cemetery. "I don't know what to tell you about him." She shrugged. "It's like he completely vanished. Poppa hasn't been seen or heard from since we left Le Havre in 1957. I think Oswald even hired a detective to try and find him, but...he had no luck."

She gazed down at the grave. "I graduated from the Sorbonne, Mama, with a dual degree in French language and literature. In a few weeks, I'll start grad school. And I've applied to teach at one of the collèges. I hope you're proud."

Vivie glanced back at the church. It seemed so much smaller now. Her eyes returned to the graveyard. "Bácsi Oswald said he'd move you to the cemetery in Luxembourg if I want, but I don't know. Is it right? Would you want to go somewhere else? Or are you happy here? Maigret and Josef are over there in the corner by the stone fence, so the caretaker says. Their graves are unmarked as well. They took good care of us, Mama. Maigret was so kind with Mae."

Her thoughts slipped back to the red-cheeked child running in from the barnyard spouting, *"Do you know eggs come from a chicken's butt?"* An imperceptible smile curved her lips. "Sometimes, I think Mae might have been better off if we had left her with them." Tears filled her eyes. "I don't know, Mama. I just don't know." At the approach of footsteps, Vivie wiped her cheeks.

"Good afternoon." An old man of medium height wearing a clerical collar stood beside her.

"Good afternoon."

He nodded toward her mother's grave. "She never gets visitors. Sometimes, I come out here and talk with her. With some of the others as well." The minister waved his arm out across the cemetery. "I practice my Sunday sermons on them." He looked back at Vivie. "Did you know her?"

"Yes. She was my mother."

A crease formed above the man's brow. His eyes narrowed. He adjusted his glasses and peered at her. "Ah, yes. Let me think a minute...Violet? No. Victoria?" He shook his head.

"It's Vi—"

"It's Vivie!" he finished. "You probably don't remember me. Reverend Montcliff."

"Oh, yes," she said. "You were so kind and generous."

"Not me, child. I only do the Lord's work, Vivie. I supply the hands. HE tells me what to do."

She smiled and nodded.

"I'll tell you what. When you finish visiting with your mother, step inside for a cup of tea, and we'll catch up."

"That would be nice. I'd like that. You go ahead, Reverend. I'll be right there."

As he walked back to the church, Vivie looked down at her mother. "Maybe you are fine right here with Reverend Montcliff. Perhaps, I'll just ask Oswald for a marker." She kissed her fingers, then stooped down and pressed them against her mother's grave. "I love you, Mama," she whispered, before turning and walking away.

CHAPTER 28

Le Havre, France, Spring 1964

A week later, Vivie took a deep breath and slowly let it out before stepping into the alleyway. It had been seven years since she had left. Things looked so much smaller now. The shack she had shared with Poppa and Mae was gone. Nothing stood in its place. She had held out a faint degree of hope that maybe, just possibly, there might be some trace of her father here. Instead, all she found was an empty, garbage-strewn lot.

"Meow."

Vivie eased toward the overturned trash can. At her approach, a skinny calico appeared. A tortoiseshell kitten circled and rubbed against the cat's side.

"Mirabelle," Vivie murmured, then shook her head. Too many years had passed. One of her grown kittens? Or a grandkitten?

The feline's pitiful cries pierced her heart. Poor thing. Starving from the looks of her. Vivie rummaged in her jacket pocket and pulled out a small package of cheese kisses. The cat's cries intensified as she opened the wrappers, the kitten skittering away at the rattle of cellophane. Vivie stooped and crumbled the cheese on a discarded newspaper. The calico crept forward, gobbling it down.

When Vivie reached over and stroked her bony back, Norsk padded into her thoughts. Despite the passage of time, her throat tightened, and her eyes moistened at the memory of her beloved cat.

Blinking away the tears, Vivie stood and watched the kitten creep toward its mother. "I'll be back in a bit," she said.

Fifteen minutes later, Vivie returned and loaded the two felines into a carrier. After delivering them to a vet to be spayed and adopted out, she found herself having dinner at Le Grand Large. As she ate, Vivie reflected on the day she was there with Oswald and Alice. A skinny, half-starved twelve-year-old. Completely overwhelmed, her world upturned. Without her parents' dearest friends, there's no telling what would have happened to her—and Mae.

•   •   •   •   •

Two years later, Vivie, Alice, and Oswald dined on the Champs-Élysées.

"Ah! Spring in Paris," her adopted mother sighed. "There's nothing to compare."

"I can't remember the last time we were here," Oswald said.

"For my graduation," Vivie reminded him. "When I got my bachelor's degree."

"And here you are completing your master's." He shook his head. "I don't know how you do it. All that coursework in addition to teaching."

Vivie shrugged. "It's what I love. What I thrive on."

"So, how *was* teaching this year?" Alice asked.

She grimaced. "Extremely frustrating."

Oswald frowned. "How so?"

"Unlike the children at the collège last year, only a handful of the lycée students seemed genuinely interested in learning. The others?" Vivie sighed. "I seemed to spend more time on discipline and character lessons than actual instructional knowledge."

Alice shook her head. "That's a shame." She reached over and squeezed Vivie's arm. "Maybe things will be better next term."

"Oh, definitely."

"How can you be so sure?" Oswald inquired.

"Because while I'm working on my doctorate, I'll be teaching at the Sorbonne!" She grinned.

"Oh, Vivie! That's wonderful!" Alice cried.

"Indeed!" Oswald agreed.

•   •   •   •   •

"Good evening, François." Vivie greeted the cemetery attendant as he opened the gate for her.

"Full moon tonight, Mademoiselle," he nodded.

"You're right. I probably won't be needing a flashlight." Vivie carried the humane capture traps and her backpack inside the cemetery.

"Seen two new ones."

"What do they look like?"

"A long-haired tortoiseshell and a silver tabby. Torti looks pregnant."

"Figures." Vivie shook her head and sighed. "Thanks. I'll keep an eye out."

She set off down the now familiar path. It had been three months ago that she had made the thirty-minute drive to the Montmartre cemetery to work on a lesson plan for her graduate students. Vivie remembered that day as though it were yesterday. She had crossed the blue wrought iron bridge on the Rue Caulaincourt, then parked and made her way down to 20 Avenue Rachel. Upon entering the cemetery gate, Vivie had stopped at the conservation center and picked up a map. She had scanned through the listings: Georges Feydeau, Émilie Zola, Théophile Gautier, Stendal...and Alexandre Dumas, Mama's favorite. So many famous writers were buried here.

Vivie had admired the leafy canopy that seemed to cradle areas of the secluded graveyard. Getting her bearings, she set off to explore. Twenty minutes later, Vivie had made her way through the seemingly wall-to-wall tombs and mausoleums and neared the far end of the blue bridge. When she approached a cobweb-covered mausoleum, a skinny tabby had skittered from its doorway and hied across the grounds.

As Vivie ventured farther, her eyes caught furtive movements here and there. At first, she had thought it was only leafy shadows stirred by the faint breeze; then realization hit. Dozens of feral cats inhabited this graveyard. She inched her way into the more secluded areas, where felines quietly sunned themselves on the marble tombstones. In that moment, Norsk had come to mind. Vivie knew then she needed to help these cats.

Now here she was, a regular sight, traipsing through the cemetery with her traps and teaching the staff how to responsibly manage the feral cat colony. Reaching the far end of the bridge, Vivie baited and set the traps. A short distance away, she settled back into the recessed entry of a mausoleum and waited. As the evening passed, the steady overhead drone of traffic became more intermittent. She stifled a yawn, reviewing tomorrow's full schedule in her head: A meeting with her advisor. Grading student exams. Finishing up next week's lesson plans. Researching her dissertation.

"SNAP! SNAP!" rang out into the night.

Vivie's head jerked up. Seconds later she was headed for the traps. "A three-fer!" she crowed with delight. In one sat the pregnant torti and her companion; in the other, what appeared to be a six-months-old calico. Vivie glanced down at her watch. "Let's get you to the vet, then I can head back to the library and study."

•　　•　　•　　•　　•

"How's Mae?" Reverend Montcliff asked.

For the last four years, Vivie had visited her mother's grave on school breaks—always sharing her news. Afterwards, she enjoyed spending time with the reverend. Vivie shook her head and stirred her tea. "There's been no change in her condition. Oswald moved her to a private hospital last month. He believed it would be better for her."

"We will keep her in our thoughts and prayers."

"Thank you," she nodded. Changing the subject, Vivie added, "I received my doctorate." She was proud of her accomplishment. Vivie had chosen to do her dissertation on Alexandre Dumas as a tribute to her mother. She gave a soft laugh and shook her head. "I can't believe I'm now *Dr.* Vivie McNabb."

"Congratulations!" Reverend Montcliff reached out and patted her hand. "Your parents would have been so proud."

At his words, a pang shot through her heart. Swallowing past the lump in her throat, she managed to say, "I hope so." Blinking back tears, Vivie volunteered, "There's more news."

"Well, let's hear." He freshened her cup of tea.

She took a deep breath and stared out the window at the bouquet of flowers on her mother's distant grave. The words she had uttered to Csaky earlier rang in her head. "Mama, I've come to say goodbye for a while." Her voice had broken. "You see...I have a teaching position in the United States..."

"A college in Middlebury, Vermont," Reverend Montcliff repeated.

Vivie had been so focused on her thoughts, she was unaware of telling him the news.

"That's wonderful, Vivie."

CHAPTER 29

Middlebury, Vermont, September 1968

At the reception for the new faculty, Vivie stood in the buffet line, evaluating the selections. Her eyes riveted on the cheese ball. "Excuse me," she said, quickly exiting the line and heading for the door.

Outside, Vivie stood against the building, trying to slow her breathing. As she stared out across the campus, she swallowed at the nausea rising in her throat. *'Too much excitement.'* Vivie recalled her mother's words from that long-ago day. Maybe they were more applicable here. It *had* been a stressful week—getting settled in her new apartment, visiting second-hand shops for furniture, becoming familiar with the town and college campus. More importantly, safeguarding her ever-present butcher-paper-wrapped package—the only proof of her true identity. The secret her parents had urged her to keep. Her only tangible link to the past.

"Are you okay?"

"W-what?" Vivie turned to see one of the college deans, regarding her with concern. "Oh, yes." How to tell him the chopped nuts on that cheese ball reminded her of those maggots on that severed hand in Győr. The flashback had unnerved her. "I just needed to get some air."

"Yes. It is a little stuffy in there...in more ways than one," he added with a smile.

She gave a weak laugh.

"I hope you'll like teaching here at Middlebury, Dr. McNabb."

"I'm sure I will....Oh, Dean Reynolds," she called after him as he started back inside.

The man turned.

"I couldn't help but overhear your earlier conversation about computer integrated circuitry. It's a topic that interests me. I'd like to audit some of your classes."

Discussing the possibility, they headed back inside the building.

•　　•　　•　　•　　•

Second semester, Vivie sat in the campus library, reviewing her notes on computer logarithms. Last fall, she had followed up her discussion with Dean Reynolds and registered for two of his computer classes that did not conflict with her teaching schedule. This term, she was enrolled in two more.

Vivie rubbed her forehead. Something was definitely wrong with this formula's equation, but what?

"Hey, Dr. McNabb! Fancy seeing you here."

She looked up to see Amelia and two more of her French 101 students.

"Planning tomorrow's assignment?" Nathan squeaked out. He gulped, his Adam's apple giving a leap as though trying to escape his throat. There was a hint of panic in his eyes like that of a trapped feral cat.

"Relax, Nathan," she reassured him. "I'm working on my computer assignment."

"Your assignment?" Patti frowned. "As in homework?"

"Exactly," Vivie replied.

Amelia's eyes widened. "You're taking classes, too?"

Ah! The naiveté of freshmen. "Yes, even us 'old foggie' teachers still like to learn."

"But you're not like *that*," Patti said. "You're more like one of us."

"Thank you for the compliment," Vivie responded.

"We probably should head on," Amelia said. "We've got a physics exam in the morning."

"You go ahead," Nathan replied. "I'll catch up later." He picked up Vivie's textbook. "You're taking Dean Reynold's computer theory class?"

"Indeed, I am."

Nathan pulled out the chair opposite her and sat down. "I had that last term. Piece of cake."

"Really?"

"Made an 'A' in the course and hardly even cracked a book."

And perhaps that's why you can't conjugate French verbs, Vivie thought, trying to repress a laugh. "Hmm. I'll make a deal with you, Nathan."

"A deal?" He blanched, his voice squeaking again like a twelve-year-old experiencing puberty.

"I'll tutor you in French, if you'll help me figure out the problem with this formula."

A grin broke across the young man's face. "Gee! That'd be super."

•   •   •   •   •

"Vivie?"

Dean Reynolds stood in her office doorway.

"I've got that computer journal you wanted to borrow."

"That's great!" She grinned. "I can't wait to read it."

He sat down in the armchair opposite her desk. "And...I was wondering..." The man paused.

"Wondering?" Vivie echoed, her head tilting toward him.

Dean Reynolds cleared his throat. "Would you like to go to dinner and a movie this weekend?"

She sat back in her chair and took a deep breath. Guta's advice about not compromising her dreams surfaced and swirled in her head. Vivie slowly exhaled.

He sat waiting, expectantly.

"I'm sorry, Dean Reynolds, but I don't think it would be advisable."

"Why not, Vivie? It's not like you're actually a student. You're faculty like me. And you can call me Paul. We're not in class."

"It's not that."

A puzzled look crossed his face.

"Dean Reynolds—"

"Paul."

"Paul...while I appreciate the offer, I don't socialize. Neither professionally nor personally."

"I don't quite understand, Vivie."

"It's a personal decision I made long ago. It has nothing to do with propriety...or you."

He nodded and slowly rose. "Well...I still don't understand, but I do respect your decision." Paul started toward the door, then stopped. "If you ever change your mind, Vivie..."

She shook her head. "I won't."

"Well, okay." He nodded toward the journal. "There's a really interesting article on page eighty-five."

"Thanks," she said as the man headed out the door.

"Whew. That was awkward," Vivie said to herself. Paul Reynolds was a nice man, and they shared a common interest. Maybe in another life where things had been different, she might have considered his offer. One thing was for sure, she was embracing Guta's advice—living her life as she wanted, eschewing the complications of personal relationships.

"Uh, Vivie?"

Dean Reynolds again stood in her doorway.

"Yes, Paul?"

"I wanted to tell you that I think computer science is a field you should consider pursuing. You have a real talent for it."

Her brow raised.

"I'm not 'feeding you a line,' Vivie. I really mean it. Over the last year, you've proved you have a lot to offer."

"Seriously?"

Paul nodded. "We need people with your acumen to advance this field." He sat back down. "If you like, I'd be happy to design a coursework plan for you."

CHAPTER 30

Loretto, Pennsylvania, Fall 1974

"Who would care to expound on how the Seven Years' War influenced Voltaire's *Candide?* Arthur?" During his response, Vivie's eyes were drawn to a shadow on the door's window. She nodded in agreement as the student continued his point.

Vivie glanced down at her notes, then back up as an older, heavy-set man entered her classroom. *Hmm. Who is he?* she thought, acknowledging Diane's raised hand. As she challenged the young woman's supposition, Vivie's gaze shifted to the now-seated man. There was something so familiar about him.

Upon her students' dismissal, he rose and started toward her. "Oh!" she gasped. "I can't believe it!"

"Yes, Vivie. It's me." He reached out and grasped her hand. His blue eyes shone beneath bushy sandy blond eyebrows that resembled a couple of hairy caterpillars. A broad smile peered out from under his scrub brush of a mustache.

"You look so much like your father," she laughed.

"Yes, that's what they say."

"Oh, Theodolf. I can't believe you're here. It's been so many years."

"Hasn't it?" He stepped back, scrutinizing her. "Here you are. All grown up. You haven't changed."

Vivie laughed. "Oh, yes, I have."

"Well, taller...and older."

"Hush!" she said. "Let's not talk about ages. How in the world did you find me?"

"Through some correspondence your guardians sent to my parents."

I had no idea, Vivie thought, then remembered that fateful afternoon—Guta pressing their address into her mother's hand. Poppa must have passed it along to Oswald.

"I see you're an assistant professor of French here at St. Francis."

Theodolf's question interrupted her reflection. "Yes. That and studying computer technology. What about you?"

"I've been working with Paul Leyhausen. He's completing a book, *Verhaltensstudien an Katzen*, that will include his studies of feral cats."

"Oh, yes. Ferals. The bane of my existence."

"Mine, too." Theodolf nodded. "Let me take you to dinner."

"Sorry." Vivie shook her head. "I've got colonies to feed. And...an errant feral to trap."

Her old friend softly chuckled and took her arm. "Well, then...we better get busy and get this done if we're going to eat tonight."

"Are you serious?"

"Of course."

"Okay. I'll get my things, and we'll go."

"Do we need to stop by your place and get a trap?"

Vivie chuckled. "Just wait till you see my station wagon!"

"Wow!" Theodolf exclaimed as they approached it. "You've got everything! Traps, food, water, nets, carriers..."

"Pretty much."

As twilight slipped into dusk, the two of them sat in the darkening station wagon eating takeout. With Vivie's three managed feral colonies fed, soft conversation filled the vehicle, reminiscent of their talks at Traiskirchen. As the hours passed, their eyes remained fixated on the distant trap—watching and waiting.

•　　•　　•　　•　　•

Vivie buttoned the black shirtwaist blouse, then slipped into the matching pencil skirt. A black blazer completed the ensemble—all courtesy of the Salvation Army's thrift store at a cost of less than fifteen dollars. Eschewing style for comfort, she sat down and donned her black anklets and Reeboks—

the latter her one 'major' expense for this somber occasion since her white ones would not do.

It had been six years since she had last been to the ranch. So much had changed, and yet her room had remained the same. Vivie walked over to her dresser and fingered the photograph of Little River. She needed to pack it in her suitcase before she left. After all, this would probably be the last time she was here.

A tap sounded at the door. "Come in."

"Miss Vivie?" Jamison still ducked his head in respect after all these years. "It's time to head to the church."

She studied the chauffeur, now stooped with age, but still a consummate professional when it came to dress and duty. He had always been so kind and helpful. Thoughts of that day at the river came to mind. Jamison squatting next to her, trying to revive the drowned kittens. Her throat tightened. "Is mother ready?"

"Mrs. McNabb is already in the car, Miss. She sent me for you."

Still 'Miss.' She dropped her head so he would not see her smile. "I'll be right down."

The drive to Abilene was subdued. Alice wept quietly as Vivie reflected on Oswald's impact on her life. She recalled the day he had shown up unexpectedly at her dorm. The expression on his face had chilled her. It was sad, his eyes pained.

"Come," Oswald had said. "Let's take a walk, Vivie."

What was wrong? Questions popped in her brain like firecrackers on the Fourth of July. *Mae? Poppa? Alice?*

They walked in silence across the quad, finally sitting on the stone bench under the chestnut tree. Glancing up, Oswald began quoting Longfellow's poem. "Under the spreading chestnut tree, the mighty smithy stands..."

Vivie held her breath, trying to control her rising panic. Her adoptive father had always beaten around the bush when it came to sharing a piece of bad news. She slowly exhaled, then took another deep breath—trying to prepare herself for what was to come.

Oswald reached over and clasped her hand. "Vivie...it's Little River," he had said hoarsely.

He had traveled from Bangkok to the boarding school in Massachusetts to tell her the kitten had escaped the house and fallen prey to a hawk. Raoul had managed to kill the raptor, but Little River had not survived the fall.

Her adoptive father had not wanted her to read the news in an impersonal letter or hear it over the phone. He had cared enough to take time from his busy schedule to come to the school and tell her in person. While his actions had not relieved the sting of the news, it had meant the world to Vivie.

The small Episcopal church was packed to overflowing. Friends, family, reporters, even overseas coworkers were there to pay their last respects. Oswald's midnight blue urn sat on a pedestal at the front of the sanctuary, banked by flowers.

Vivie put her arm around Alice, drawing her near. The familiar scent of Chanel No. 5 filled her nostrils. She thought of Mama as she stole a sideways glance at Alice. Her adoptive mother had aged significantly since she had last seen her—so thin and frail, like Mama at the end.

•   •   •   •   •

Alice died a scant three months later. Now, Vivie sat in Mr. Vargas's office listening to his explanation of the will.

"Vivie? The bulk of the estate has been placed in trust for you and Mae with Oswald's bank as executor. You and your sister will receive monthly stipends to cover your expenses."

She nodded.

As the attorney droned on about the process, Vivie drifted back to the first time she had sat in his office—the butcher-paper-wrapped packet clasped tightly against her chest. Alice's explanation that day in the barn loft had helped her understand the need to have notarized translations of the packet's contents. But just because she had understood did not mean she had liked it. She had hated turning over her documents but, in the end, the man had proven he could be trusted. Now, with Oswald and Alice gone, Mr. Vargas was the only one who knew her secret.

"Here is something you need to take care of, Vivie. Oswald specifically left this for you." The attorney's words catapulted her back into the present. He held a small brown envelope in his outstretched hand.

Vivie leaned forward, reaching for it. She glanced down to see her name in Oswald's neat script. After thanking the attorney, Vivie left the office. In her rental car, she tore open the envelope and a small key with a round tag dropped into her lap. She pulled out the accompanying letter and read:

Dear Vivie,

I can't begin to tell you how much you meant to Alice and me. We were blessed to have you as our daughter. I know your parents would have been so proud of the young woman you have become and all that you have achieved.

I want you to know that I searched long and hard for your father these many years, employing several detective agencies, but never found a trace of him. I am sorry for that.

While I failed in that regard, I did succeed in another. Please take the enclosed key to the storage center address included below and you will find something I know you will cherish.

Love,
Dad

Vivie stared at the key, slowly turning it in her hand. Whatever did this mean? She pulled a map from the glove box and looked up the address. Thirty minutes later, Vivie stood outside the storage unit, the key gripped in her hand. Taking a deep breath, she inserted it into the lock, turned it, and pulled open the door.

Inside sat two large objects shrouded in giant cloths. Stepping forward, Vivie reached up and pulled the sheeting off the first one. As it slid to the floor, she gasped and took a step back, not believing what she was seeing. Her hand shook as she reached over and pulled off the second cloth sheet.

Vivie reached out and braced herself against the wall, gasping for breath as the storage space appeared to spin. "Oh, Mama," she whispered, tears pricking her eyes.

Before her sat a large armoire and dressing table. Csaky's armoire and dressing table. Or were they? Maybe they were just reproductions that Oswald had made at Alice's behest.

There was only one way to know for sure. Her breath quickened as she got down on her hands and knees and peered at the bottom of the table. Vivie's head dropped to her chest. Tears cascaded down her cheeks. She sat on the floor and wept at the blurry sight of the childish scrawl of her name and the picture of a cat that she had drawn underneath Mama's dressing table when she was five-years-old.

CHAPTER 31

Loretto, Pennsylvania, Spring 1981

Dear Theodolf,

Sorry to have been so long in responding to your last letter. So much has happened. Since Alice and Oswald's deaths, my life seems to have been consumed by probate. While Mr. Vargas has handled most of the details, the disposition of the properties has fallen to me.

All I'm keeping at this point is the apartment in Luxembourg because of its proximity to Mae. Unfortunately, there's been no improvement in her mental status. From the reports, some days are worse than others.

At least I've had my teaching, course work, and the ferals to keep me halfway sane. But now I've got a big decision to make.

Vivie sat back, her eyes drifting from the letter to the job application lying on her desk. Did she really want to do this? Leave St. Francis? Vivie picked up and paged through the SUNY catalog, studying the New York university's course offerings in computer science and math.

She reflected on her conversations with Dean Reynolds at Middlebury and the career path he had designed for her. It was hard to believe that twelve years had passed.

Her eyes again scanned the course offerings. They were pretty impressive. And it was a perfect opportunity to teach in her specialty while obtaining degrees in computer science and mathematics.

Vivie picked up and re-read the job announcement. She definitely met all their qualifications. 'Nothing ventured, nothing gained' as Maigret used to say. Vivie shrugged, pulled the unfinished letter from the typewriter, and inserted her application.

•   •   •   •   •

On stage, Vivie awaited her presentation. Her hands shook as she smoothed the muddied papers. Adrenaline coursed through her veins as she sat trying to slow her breathing.

Dean Hawkins leaned over, a look of concern on his face. "Are you nervous, Dr. McNabb?"

"No," she whispered. If he only knew. It was not nerves. She knew this material backwards and forwards. Vivie had given this presentation on computer architecture and organization multiple times.

Upon graduating from the State University of New York: Potsdam with dual masters' degrees in computer science and mathematics, she was offered a teaching position at St. Bonaventure University. The papers she had authored on computer technology over the last two years often led to lecture requests such as this one.

Usually these speaking engagements were so mundane, but not today's—all because of a puppy stranded on an interstate median. She had slammed on her brakes and pulled over onto the highway's shoulder while horns blared and vehicles whizzed past.

When Vivie stepped from the car, the young dog dashed toward her as a semi bore down on them. She darted forward, snatched the stray, and jumped back just as the truck blew past—its horn blasting. The vehicle's resulting draft whipped and pummeled her. She stumbled down onto the grass but kept the pup's scruff firmly in her grasp. Her blood raced. A few minutes later, they were in the vehicle—the puppy safely tucked into one of her carriers, but not before leaving muddy paw prints across her presentation.

A quick swing by the veterinary clinic and now here she sat. Vivie contemplated her damp, soiled skirt. Dashing across the parking lot, she had noticed the muddy paw prints and hastened into the restroom to scrub them out. Well, at least they were not as noticeable—and she would be standing behind the lectern.

Vivie took another deep breath and slowly let it out as Dean Hawkins rose and approached the podium.

"Good afternoon, students, faculty, and invited guests. We are fortunate to have Dr. Vivie McNabb from St. Bonaventure University here to speak with us today on the application of Tanenbaum's micro-architecture."

As the applause faded, Vivie rose and crossed the stage.

●　　　●　　　●　　　●　　　●

Back at home, Vivie sat with the butcher-paper-wrapped package on her lap, reminiscing. She had not visited its contents in a couple of years, but now was compelled to do so.

After the lecture, she had stopped by the veterinary clinic to check on the puppy before he was placed for adoption. The sight of a man in the reception area had stunned her. "Poppa," Vivie had whispered. It had taken her a second to catch her breath. While the resemblance was uncanny, it was not him. He was too young, and she was too old. Nevertheless, the experience had shaken her, stirring memories of long ago. Now she sat wondering what her life would have been like if they had not had to flee Hungary.

The doorbell rang.

"Just a minute." Vivie shoved the packet under the couch, then answered the door.

"A delivery for you," the postal carrier said.

"For me?" Vivie reached for the large box.

"It's pretty heavy," the man said.

She stepped aside and let him set the carton inside her apartment door. Once he left, Vivie noted the mailing labels. International mail. She studied the embossed return address: 'Sellers, Howell & Bertrand, Esquires.' Taking a pair of scissors, Vivie split the packing tape and opened the box flaps. Inside was another box with an envelope taped to the top. She gasped and stared down at the name typed on the envelope. It had been a lifetime since anyone had called her 'Vivie Degirdro.' She sat there for a moment, contemplating the possibilities. Poppa? Her hands shook as she pulled the envelope free from the tape. "Oh, no!" Vivie moaned as she read the letter.

Dear Miss Degirdro,

It is with deepest sympathy that we regret to inform you that Dr. Theodolf Anders Berlinger has passed away. It was his wish that you have his research.

Yours,
Amos Bertrand, Esquire

With trembling hands, she opened the accompanying letter.

Dear Vivie,

If you are reading this, then I have joined my parents—and so many others that have gone before me. Despite the passage of years and our sporadic contact, I've never forgotten that gawky twelve-year-old with the curly red hair and determination to feed one stray cat—even if it meant she had to starve. I was very impressed by that.

It was nice being able to spend time with you in Loretto and seemed only fitting that we spent the evening cat trapping. That's why I want you to have my research.

Maybe one day the world will be a better place for all cats, both feral and tame. One can only hope that trap-neuter-return will eventually be embraced and practiced throughout the world. In the meantime, carry on the cause.

I am blessed to have known you and shared your love for cats.

Yours,
Theodolf

Vivie clasped the letter to her breasts as tears flooded her eyes. "Oh, Theodolf. You taught me so much." She crossed herself and said a prayer. After wiping her cheeks, she extracted the inner box and opened it. Her hand gently caressed the handwritten journals. She pulled one out and began to read.

.   .   .   .   .

"Hey, Vivie!" David, one of her colleagues, stood in her office doorway. "Stumbled across this in a second-hand bookstore when I was down in DC this past week," he continued as he entered. "Thought you might like it."

Her eyes widened at the book in his outstretched hand—*Maverick Cats*. On the cover was the sketch of a feline peering out of a patch of weeds. She reached for it, immediately drawn to its subtitle: *Encounters With Feral Cats*. "Ellen Perry Berkeley? I'm not familiar with her." Vivie tingled with excitement.

Over the last month, she had poured over Theodolf's writings, re-reading them several times, then sought out the referenced books and articles on feral cats, particularly those written by Paul Leyhausen. She now knew why Theodolf had thought so highly of him. Leyhausen's research shattered so many myths, like a cat's impact on wildlife.

While David rattled on about his trip, she nodded at him—only half-listening. Vivie flipped to the back of the book and skimmed its resources. Some familiar, some not. Having discovered the dearth of information available on feral cats, new resources made her giddy. A self-satisfied smile curved her lips at the name: Paul Leyhausen.

"Later I went out to dinner with some friends," David continued.

Why was he still here telling her about his trip? He needed to go away and let her explore this new treasure!

"They were talking about these two ladies who've been trapping and releasing cats in the DC area. Sort of sounded like what you do."

Vivie's full attention instantly riveted on the man, her heart skipping a beat. "Who are they? Do you have some contact information on them?"

"No. Sorry, I don't. I didn't pursue it because the guys began joking around and started in making disparaging remarks about so-called 'cat ladies.'" His fingers placed air quotes around the term.

Vivie's jaw tightened.

"Oh, here's your mail. I picked it up while I was getting mine." David handed her the stack of catalogs.

"Thanks, I appreciate that." She held up the book as he headed out the door. "And thanks for this."

"Any time."

"Irgum-burgum!" Vivie seethed after he left, fuming over the ignorance of his dinner companions. *So easy to mock what you refuse to understand.*

She grimaced. *If people acted responsibly—spayed and neutered and didn't abandon them—these cat problems wouldn't exist.*

With a huff of disgust, Vivie set aside the book for later and reached for the collection of mail. As she sorted through it, a coursework catalog slid to the floor and fell open. Picking it up, her eyes focused on the page's bold-typed course offering: **Doctorate Degrees in Computer Intelligence.**

"Hmm. Interesting," she said to herself. "Maybe I should look into this." In scanning the listings, a name jumped out: University of Tennessee, Knoxville. She cocked her head. "Knoxville, Tennessee. Now, why does that sound familiar?"

Vivie sat back and stared out her office window. Rain poured down on the campus. Students darted about, juggling their books and umbrellas on their way to class. As her gaze drifted toward the distant stone monument, a fragmented memory began to surface and take form. She smacked her desk. "That's it! The old man outside the library. Knoxville, Tennessee. That's where he was from."

She sat back, remembering his words. A week after their conversation, in the pouring rain and over Alice's objections, Vivie had again walked the three blocks to the New York City Public Library. There sat the lions in all their glory, only now there was a distinct pinkish cast to their marble.

Vivie smiled at the memory. The old man had been right.

She reached for the phone and punched in the long-distance number. "Yes. I'm interested in your doctoral program in computer intelligence..."

CHAPTER 32

Knoxville, Tennessee, July 1992

Vivie stood inside the modest, 1945, white, two-story house on Moody Avenue, three if you counted the basement and connecting garage. She fanned herself with the realty company's prospectus. It was definitely cooler inside than out. After walking the property's boundaries, beads of sweat continued to trickle down her back. The empty house echoed with the realtor's voice—nattering on about her other listings of newer homes and their amenities on the east, west, and north sides of the city. Vivie had traveled those areas with other realtors and was not impressed. They were too urban and congested for her taste. But here? There was just something about the south side that appealed to her, probably the proximity of woods and nature. Plus, it still had a rural, small-town feel to it.

"Shall we look at some other houses?" the realtor asked.

"I think not. Let me sleep on this and get back to you."

Early the next morning, Vivie again drove her rental car across the Henley Bridge into South Knoxville. With the windows down, she noticed a distinct drop in temperature as she crossed the expanse. No doubt attributable to the tree-covered hillsides and the ubiquitous kudzu that covered many undeveloped areas. To some degree, the green space reminded her of being up north in Vermont.

At the stop light, she glanced down at the map. There was a particular destination that intrigued her. Turning off Chapman Highway, she eventually found herself on a two-lane road. A short distance later, a large, marble sign appeared: Ijams Nature Center. Vivie turned down the heavily wooded lane and parked. It was hard to believe that this natural area was so close to the city and her house. Her house? Did that mean she had made the decision to buy her first home? Was she finally creating a permanent place for herself and her belongings? Settling down? With these thoughts in mind, Vivie exited the car and spent the next two hours exploring some of the trails.

On the way back to her hotel, she noticed a small directional sign: Fort Dickerson. Vivie signaled and slowed to a stop, turning left when the traffic allowed. At the top of the curvy hill, she got out and explored the earthen fortress, reading its Civil War history and that of the adjacent Fort Stanley. As she started back down to the highway, Vivie noticed parking for an overlook area she had missed on her ascent. She pulled in and exited the car. At the overlook, Vivie gasped. Down below was one of the most beautiful pristine lakes she had ever seen. Chills of delight raced up and down her spine. The view reminded her of Austria and its breathtaking bodies of water. "This is it," Vivie said to herself. "This is home."

• • • • •

With her furniture in place, Vivie reached into her satchel and removed the butcher-paper-wrapped packet. Where to hide it was her first order of business. She walked from room to room before finally settling on her bedroom, behind Mama's armoire. It should be safe there. Vivie pulled out the stool from the mahogany dressing table and sat down. Untying the packet's twine, she pulled back the paper and sorted through the familiar contents, lovingly caressing the enclosed photograph. Mama, Poppa, Mae, and a twelve-year-old Vivie. She remembered the day as though it were yesterday. Saint Stephen's Day 1956, just a couple of months before they had to flee. Despite the fact that the Communists banned the celebration in 1945, her family had secretly continued the August 20th tradition.

Vivie sighed. She really should put this packet in a safety deposit box at the bank like Oswald and Alice had always urged. But Poppa's words continued to hold sway, even after all these years, *'Keep this with you always. Never let anyone see it, Vivie. It is very important that you remember this.'* She slowly shook her head. So many memories, so many years. Vivie continued to reminisce as she restored the packet and slipped it behind the armoire.

• • • • •

"Irgum-burgum!" Vivie muttered, dropping her head. "Not again." Her shoulders sagged. At dusk, she watched the feral cats ease out across the manicured lawn and head for the dumpster on the Hill at the University of Tennessee. Vivie stood there, lamenting the fact that too often students turned their cats loose when they left campus in the ignorant belief that the felines could survive on their own.

How many times had she trapped and rehabilitated these abandoned cats over the years? How many thousands of dollars had she spent on their veterinary care? Their food? Their litter? Re-homing them? It was not that she begrudged the expense. It was that she resented having to take on the shirked responsibility of others.

The small colony bolted at her audible sigh.

Back at home, Vivie flipped through the phone book's yellow pages. Her finger traced down the veterinary listings and stopped at Central Veterinary Hospital on Clinch Avenue. A block away from campus. That was convenient. She picked up the phone and punched in the number.

Three weeks later, the colony was under control, and she had managed to socialize and adopt out the kittens through the veterinary hospital. Every evening before heading to the library to study, she fed the small colony— trapping any new arrivals and transporting them to the clinic before it closed.

• • • • •

Vivie adjusted her mask as she drove down Neubert Springs Road. She had only been in Knoxville for a month when she had been diagnosed with pollen and mold allergies. Vivie shook her head, recalling the exchange with the physician.

"But I've traveled and hiked extensively. All over the world, in fact. And I've never been plagued by allergies."

Dr. Gregory shook his head. "You know, Vivie, there's a saying in these parts. 'If you live in East Tennessee long enough, you're bound to get them.'"

"Well...I could understand, possibly, if I had been here several years. But one month?"

The memory vanished at the sight of a motionless gray feline on the shoulder of the road up ahead. She slowed.

Vivie signaled, then pulled over and stopped. Shivering in the bleak February cold, she retrieved a newspaper and towels from the back of the hatchback. Vivie then walked over and stooped down to wrap the body for disposal at the vet. *Dead at least a day...if not two,* she thought, studying it.

As Vivie draped a towel over the dead feline, a strident mew drew her attention to the brush. She gently turned the cat on its back, then closed her eyes and grimaced. A nursing mama. Vivie's blood pulsated with rage.

After loading the dead feline into the back of the vehicle, she followed the plaintive cries. Scouring the nearby brush, Vivie discovered the black kitten—now orphaned by a negligent driver. The baby's eyes were matted shut. Despite the cold, fleas coursed through its fur like a raging river. "Oh, you poor thing!"

Vivie scooped up the kitten and carried it to the nearby creek. She immediately dunked it into the icy water in an attempt to displace the fleas. Several leapt onto her. She would have to strip down before going into the house tonight.

As the kitten shivered and jerked, Vivie gently rubbed its small body to increase its circulation and prevent hypothermia. When the trembling eased, she lifted the kitten's tail and took a peek. Female. "Okay, Carmen," Vivie said as she pulled open the neck of her shirt and tucked the kitten into her bra. "Let's get you to the vet, before I head on to campus."

·   ·   ·   ·   ·

Vivie sat in her office, scrolling through the auction site listings. She had been diligently searching for a particular item for months, even submitting a detailed request on several 'want' lists without fruition. Maybe it was just a waste of time. What were the odds she could find one after all these years? Vivie chuckled to herself. With her mathematics degree, she could probably figure that out! Giving a shrug, Vivie continued her search. She glanced at the computer's clock. *One more page. I have time for one more page.*

She moved the cursor down and clicked 'Next.' When the page loaded, her eyes scanned the small images to the left. Vivie blinked and leaned forward. Was she seeing what she thought she was seeing? Her heart began to race, her breath coming in short, rapid gasps. Could it be? Vivie's fingers fumbled with the mouse. She clicked on the auction listing, holding her breath as the page loaded. Vivie sat there for a moment, studying the image—drinking it in. She could not believe it. After all this time! She scrolled down and read the object's description, then the auction details. Bids closed in three days. Vivie moved the cursor to the auction box and clicked. Determined to win, she typed in an exorbitant amount and pressed 'Enter.'

"Congratulations! Your bid has been accepted," appeared on the screen.

Vivie clicked back on the image. Memories of Budapest and her family's escape flooded through her head.

A rap on the door interrupted her. "Dr. McNabb?" Gillian, her teaching assistant, stuck her head in and tapped on her watch. "You're late for class."

CHAPTER 33

Luxembourg, Spring 1993

A month later, Vivie parked the airport rental and gazed out across the pristine lawn. The grass resembled a plush carpet, seemingly not a blade out of place. Seasonal flowers bloomed in the well-tended beds of the facility.

Emerging from the car, Vivie grabbed the cloth tote and headed for the private hospital's entrance. Several years ago, Oswald had spared no expense finding this perfect place for Mae.

"Good afternoon, Dr. McNabb." Pieter, one of the receptionists, said. "How was your trip?"

"Pleasant," she replied, pushing the flight's turbulence, the screaming child, and the rude smelly man from her thoughts. "How is Mae?"

"About the same."

She nodded. Vivie always asked, but the answer never changed. She continued to hold on to that one ounce of hope that someday, just maybe... "Well, at least she's not worse," Vivie responded. "And that's always a good thing."

"Yes, ma'am."

She headed down the corridor to her sister's suite. Vivie eased the door open and stepped inside. Mae sat in a cushioned chair, staring off into space.

Vivie studied her sister. The chestnut curls, by necessity—and age—were long gone, replaced by soft waves. Her hair was short, neatly kept. Vivie recalled the popular pixie-cut style of the late 1950s, similar to the actress Shirley Maclaine's in Hitchcock's *The Trouble With Harry*. Mae's streaks of gray gleamed in the sunlight like Poppa's that long-ago day in the cemetery. Vivie's throat tightened at the flash of memory. The woman-child was heavier than the last time she saw her, but that was to be expected since Mae refused to participate in any of the facility's activities. At least the physical therapist tried to interact with her daily.

"Hello, Mae," she said softly.

Her sister's head turned, the hazel eyes appearing to slowly focus. "Where have you *been*, Vivie? I've been looking for you *all* over. You *said* you were going to tell me a story." The fifty-year-old remained trapped in the mind of a petulant four-year-old.

"A story, Mae? Which one would you like?"

"'The Enchanted Cat.'"

Vivie's heart skipped a beat as she recalled the last time she offered to tell her that tale. Csaky's voice echoed in her head, *I don't think that's an appropriate story at this moment. Please tell something else.* "Perhaps another—"

"NO!" Mae's face flushed red. "'The Enchanted Cat,'" she demanded.

Familiar with the determined set of her jaw, Vivie knew there would be no reasoning with her. "All right, Mae." Vivie pulled a chair near, sat down, and began. She did not want to tell the tale. Not just because its hanging evoked the memory of the charred AVH officers, their bodies dangling from the large oak like macabre moth cocoons. It was the attempted drowning of the cat. As memories of that awful Texas afternoon came seeping back, Vivie gulped and continued on—finally making it through the tale.

She had no sooner finished when Mae demanded, "Tell me another."

Vivie reached out and grasped her sister's hand. "In a minute, Mae. I have a surprise for you."

The woman-child's eyes brightened. A smile broke across her face. "A surprise, Vivie? A surprise just for me? Is it my birthday? Can I have ice cream and cake?"

"No, Mae. It's not your birthday. But...I think we could probably find you some ice cream and cake."

Her sister clapped her hands as Vivie reached into the tote and pulled out the brightly wrapped package. *I hope I'm doing the right thing,* she thought, laying the product of her long search and recent winning bid in Mae's lap. She watched her sister tear off the present's paper and pull open the box.

"Where have you *been*, Dodo?" Mae wailed, bursting into tears. "I've been looking for you all over." She sobbed, clutching the antique replacement of her long-lost doll to her breast.

As Mae rocked back and forth with her Dodo, Vivie blinked back tears and stepped out of the room in search of some ice cream and cake.

CHAPTER 34

Knoxville, Tennessee, November 1997

Vivie methodically opened the back of the hatchback and hauled out the humane capture trap, along with a can of Fancy Feast—the shrimp, crab, and sardine variety. At the edge of the woods, she pulled the can's tab, opened the trap, and dumped the fishy contents on top of the spring bar. Hooking the cage door open, Vivie picked up the can and lid, then retreated to the warmth of the car.

In the shadowy interior, she gathered the stack of student papers and began to read. The assignment had been "Voltaire—Misogynist or Not?" Her red pen flew across the pages, critiquing the arguments for and against.

Fifteen minutes passed. She glanced up at the distant trap. Was that movement nearby it? No. Just the brush's evening shadows stirring in the faint breeze. She opened the plaid thermos and poured herself a mug of steaming coffee. Vivie settled back in the driver's seat and continued her grading.

Ten minutes later an unmistakable 'SNAP!' rang out into the night air.

Grabbing her flashlight and a towel, Vivie hastened toward the occupied trap. No scent. At least she had not trapped a skunk. In the dusk, it appeared to be either a possum or a small raccoon. *Not again.* Vivie focused the flashlight's high-beam on her catch. A grin replaced her grimace. "Got you," she said as the Maine coon mix hissed and spit, writhing and spinning in the cage.

Once she draped the towel across the wire trap, the cat quieted and hunkered down into the far corner. After loading it into the hatchback, Vivie glanced at her watch. "Ah! Thirty minutes until the vet closes." She started her car and headed for the clinic.

•   •   •   •   •

"Hi, Dr. McNabb." Curry greeted Vivie as she walked through the doorway. "Another feral?"

"How did you guess?"

The receptionist shrugged. "The usual?"

"Please. And have Dr. Ferrell check the right rear leg. There's some favoring of it."

"Will do. Male, female, or don't know?"

"Take a whiff."

Curry's head drew back. "Unmistakably male." She entered the information into the veterinary hospital's database. "Do you have a name for him?"

"D'Artagnan."

The receptionist shook her head. "You and Mrs. Ruthers certainly come up with some interesting names for your rescues. Where did this one come from?"

"Student apartments," she said with disgust.

"No," Curry said. "I meant the name."

Mama's favorite book was her first thought. "*The Three Musketeers.*"

"Right. I knew that name sounded familiar."

The clinic door opened. A woman walked up to the desk and signed in.

"That's a new hairstyle on you, isn't it, Curry?" Vivie adjusted her mask.

"Yes, it is," she responded.

For the next couple of minutes, the two exchanged opinions on the subject.

"Ahem."

Curry looked up. "Oh, hey, Mrs. Ruthers. We were talking about you earlier."

The woman nodded.

Vivie noticed her strained face.

"Let me call a tech up front for D'Artagnan, and I'll be right with you." Curry picked up the two-way radio. "Can someone come up front to take a cat back?"

Mrs. Ruthers walked over to the window and peered out.

Curry marked the sign-in sheet, then entered information into the database. "I'll call for them to bring up Prairie, Mrs. Ruthers. It looks like it was $125. Cash or credit?"

"Credit."

Vivie wandered over to the cat food aisle and eyed the shelves.

"Looks like there's not an available attendant to collect Prairie," Curry said. "I'll go get her. Did she have a carrier?"

"Yes. The funky painted one," Mrs. Ruthers replied. "You know, Jason's favorite."

Curry gave a laugh and exited the reception area.

Vivie walked back over to the desk, a thirty-pound bag of Science Diet under her arm. "Curry mentioned that you do rescue."

"Some. Ferals mostly. Primarily black ones since they're usually the first slated for kill at the shelters."

Vivie nodded. "I know."

"The most challenging to date is one that Jane, the office manager here, finally twisted my arm into adopting. She was a particularly obstreperous feral they had had in the back for several months. Her name was Satan."

Vivie's eyes widened. "Satan? Satan? Why Satan was one of mine!" Glee filled her heart, finally getting to meet the woman who had adopted this special feral cat. "How's she coming along?"

"Slowly. For the first two weeks she hid in a box and wouldn't come out. So, I renamed her Pandora."

Vivie chuckled with delight. "I love it!" As a vet attendant approached with her empty trap, she reached into her checkbook and tore out a deposit slip. "If you need anything. Anything at all," she stressed, "give me a call. Here. This has my info on it." She shoved the slip of paper into Mrs. Ruthers's hand.

Curry reappeared. "Sorry it took so long. Someone had moved the carrier to the basement."

"May I see?" Vivie inquired, stooping down. "She's beautiful. A little on the skinny side."

"Yes. Dr. Martin's prescribed some nutritional supplements. She was on her third litter when I trapped her. They"—the woman nodded her head to Curry—"tamed her four kittens and adopted them out."

"That's wonderful," Vivie said. "Make sure you keep in touch," she called after her as Mrs. Ruthers exited the building.

"Anything else for you?" Curry asked.

"Just add this bag of food to my bill."

"Yes, ma'am. Have a good evening."

Vivie failed to respond as she exited, her mind still reeling from meeting the woman who had accepted the challenge of her Satan.

•   •   •   •   •

"Hello. Is this Vivie McNabb?"

She clutched the phone's receiver, sucking in her breath at the unfamiliar voice. *Old habits die hard*, Vivie thought, slowly exhaling. "Yes," she replied.

"You probably don't remember me. We met at the vet about three years ago. I'm Lea Ruthers. I adopted Satan."

Her heart skipped a beat. "Yes. I remember you. How's..." she hesitated, searching her brain for the cat's name. "How's Pandora getting along?"

"Progressing. She came into the kitchen the other night while I was making lasagna and actually cried for some cheese."

A crow of laughter burst from Vivie. "It's so rewarding earning a feral's trust. Isn't it?"

"Yes. There's nothing like it." Lea continued, "Look. What I'm calling about is I saw a notice you posted about a found cat. It resembles one missing in my area."

"Where do you live?" Vivie asked.

"Colonial Village. It went missing in the vicinity of Mooreland Heights Elementary School."

"Hmm. Doubtful it would have ventured this far. You know lost cats are usually within a three-block radius of where they go missing."

"I know. But...just thought I would give it a shot. It's a male."

"Sorry. This one's a female that came from Sam Duff Field." A heavy sigh of disappointment met her ear. "But hey, Lea? I've got a cat for you."

"No, you don't, Vivie. I've got enough of my own."

"Oh, but I do. She's black. She's feral. She'll fit in with all the rest, and you'll never know she's there."

Lea chuckled. "Sure, Vivie, sure."

She ignored the hint of sarcasm and continued. "I tell you. When I spay her, she is yours."

"No, thank you, Vivie. Hey, I've got to run. I'm going to be late for work. Thanks for thinking about me in regard to the cat, but no, I can't take her."

Hmm. That's what you think. Vivie hung up the phone. "Easter?" she called out. "Get ready. You're going to have a new mama." A smile crossed her lips.

•   •   •   •   •

Three years later, Carmen sat on the counter hissing, her fur puffed out. Vivie ignored her. For the moment, she only had eyes for her latest rescue. The long-haired, black cat practically inhaled the plate of food Vivie had set down. Her bony frame showed through her scraggly fur. Poor thing. What a horrid time she had had. This stray's resemblance to Norsk was uncanny. Same face, same eyes.

For a split second, Vivie was catapulted back to 1956. Ironically, today—November 4, 2003—was the forty-seventh anniversary of the invasion. Poor Norsk. Was this how she had suffered? So many years had passed since she had thought of her beloved cat. With all the unrest in Hungary back then, it was highly unlikely Norsk ever had anyone to rescue her. She had likely died on the streets, either from starvation, poisoning, or some tragic accident. Despite the years, the thought of Norsk's suffering still brought tears to her eyes.

A strident meow broke her revery. Vivie looked down at the wedge-headed cat staring up at her, then back at the empty food dish. Overriding her better judgement, she opened another can of food and filled the plate.

Three cans later, the bedraggled cat lay stretched out across the couch on her back—front and rear legs extended. The other felines gave her a wide berth. Vivie sat in the armchair staring at the rescued stray. She sighed. "I guess I'll call you Cosette."

The next morning, she awoke to a rumbling in her belly—or at least it seemed so. Vivie opened her eyes. The new rescue nestled against her, emitting a steady purr. A smile curved Vivie's lips. She hated to disturb the cat, but she did. "Sorry," Vivie told her. "I've got a deadline to meet." As she donned her robe, Cosette sat on the floor giving her a baleful look.

Vivie fed the cats and emptied their litter boxes. Fifteen minutes later, she was showered and dressed, sitting at the upstairs computer with a toasted bagel and a cup of coffee. Books of computer theory surrounded her. She reached into her satchel for the red folder and frowned. Where was it? Vivie got up and sorted through the books. Maybe she had left it downstairs. She headed into the breakfast nook where the radio was playing Bach's "Concerto For Violin in A Minor." Not on the table or the chairs. She made a pass through the living room. Where could it be? Then, she visualized it. On her desk at work. She had had it in her hand when Ashley called and said Cosette was ready to go home. Vivie heaved a sigh of disgust. "Well, I'll just have to go get it," she muttered to herself.

Vivie grabbed her keys and her jacket and headed out the door. Backing out of the driveway, she looked both ways before easing out onto the street. Her car had just cleared the curb when a massive explosion occurred. It was the last thing Vivie remembered as she was thrown forward, then whipped back—the car spinning and splitting apart as glass shards and metal fragments filled the air.

CHAPTER 35

At the edge of consciousness, voices and sirens filled Vivie's head.

"EMT's are working on the driver in the blue car," a female officer stated.

"I'm shocked anyone survived," a gravelly voice replied. "As soon as I saw the impact, I radioed for a fatality officer."

Vivie opened her eyes, aware of the flashing lights. She tried to speak, but the words would not come.

"The driver of the beige car must have been doing near seventy," the gravel voice continued. "Didn't even brake. Just t-boned the blue car which had the right-of-way."

"How'd you get here so fast?"

"I had just pulled into Frussie's for an early lunch."

Footsteps crunched across the pavement. "My God! Would you look at this mess?" a nasally voice drawled.

"Here comes one of the EMT's now," the woman observed.

"Driver in the beige car is dead," he said. "The fellow reeks of alcohol."

"Figures. How's the woman in the blue car?" gravel voice inquired.

"Damnedest thing," the EMT replied. "For the most part, she appears to be okay. A little shaken up."

"You've got to be kidding!" gravel voice exclaimed. "Her car's split in half. How in the hell does someone survive a wreck like that?"

"Guardian angel?" the EMT posited.

"A cat guardian would be more likely," the nasal voice drawled.

"Huh?"

"Look!"

Split thirty-pound bags of cat food and busted forty-pound boxes of cat litter were spilling from the car and scattered across the highway, along with an assortment of shattered plastic cat carriers and bent metal crates and traps.

"That's what saved her life," he drawled. "All that crap absorbed the impact."

"Guess I'll never make fun of cat ladies again," gravel voice remarked.

Vivie winced at the term as the EMTs strapped her to a gurney, then loaded her into the ambulance.

In a matter of minutes, Vivie was admitted to the emergency room. As she regained her wits, she motioned to a nurse. "I need to make a call."

"You can as soon as we get some tests and x-rays and you're admitted to a room."

"No," Vivie insisted. "I need to make a call *now*." She grimaced, fumbling for the gurney straps.

"What are you doing?" The nurse rushed forward.

"I *told* you," Vivie insisted, gritting her teeth. "I *need* to make a phone call."

With an exasperated eye roll, the nurse stepped back, her hands on her hips. "All right" she huffed.

"Thank you," Vivie said, as she was wheeled to a nearby desk.

•　　　•　　　•　　　•　　　•

Two days later, Dr. Black and his wife helped Vivie up the steps and into the house.

Lea Ruthers stood at the door wringing her hands. "I'm so glad you're okay, Vivie. You gave us quite a scare. How do you feel?"

"A little sore and headachy but fine otherwise."

"Are you sure?"

"Yes. How did things go here?"

"We managed." Lea nodded to the veterinarian and his wife. "The Blacks came and helped out and so did Faye. All the cats were fed and littered."

"Well, Vivie," Dr. Black said. "Sue and I need to head on. We've got some things we need to attend to."

Tears welled in her eyes. "I thank you so much for not only bringing me home, but for helping out with the cats."

He gave a mischievous chuckle. "Well, you know what they say, they're our bread and butter." Sue gave a subtle shake of her head. "Let's have a little prayer before we go," he said.

"I'd like that," Vivie replied, crossing herself and bowing her head.

"He's a special kind of veterinarian," Lea said as the Blacks drove away.

Vivie nodded. "All the vets at the clinic are. Dr. Martin. Dr. Ferrell." Her eyes narrowed. "Okay, Lea. Out with it!"

"Out with what? What do you mean? What are you talking about?"

"You were white as a sheet when I walked inside. So, what's happened?"

"What's happened? You! You're what's happened. Do you know how incredibly frightening it was getting your call?"

•   •   •   •   •

Vivie looked from the stack of legal forms lying on her desk to her folder of notes for next term's classes, and then to the pile of automobile ads. "Thank goodness for winter break," she sighed, trying to decide what to tackle first. Glancing out the window, Vivie sighed at the light bands of snow flurries swirling about. "Guess I need to check on my feral colony caregivers." She reached for the phone.

After several calls, Vivie went into the kitchen and made a cup of tea. Carmen followed. "Probably should work some on my dissertation," she told the cat. Grabbing her notebook from the table, Vivie headed for the gabled attic. Halfway up the stairs, she stopped and sank down on a step. Vivie grimaced. *Odd to be so winded*, she thought as she tried to catch her breath. *Probably just stress.* With a shrug, Vivie rose and headed on up the stairs.

Three hours later, she huffed and puffed, struggling to lug a forty-pound box of cat litter from the basement. Vivie collapsed into an armchair. "I'm so weak. I must be coming down with something." After a brief rest, she took some aspirin and drank a glass of grape juice. Later, Vivie heated up a bowl of chicken soup, then made an early night of it—climbing into bed by 7:00 p.m. with a book in hand and Carmen at her side.

•   •   •   •   •

That February afternoon, Vivie's head rested on her office desk, her chest tightening as though she had just run an uphill marathon. She groggily raised up as the door opened, and Professor Okeke stepped inside.

"Are you okay, Vivie?" A look of concern crossed her colleague's face. "I knocked a couple of times."

She nodded. "Yes, Ada. I'm fine." Vivie sighed and straightened her allergy mask. "Just taking a cat nap before class, that's all."

"You know, Vivie..." Okeke walked over and sat down in the armchair across from Vivie's desk. "I know it's none of my business, but I think you try to do too much."

"What do you mean?"

"Let's get real, girlfriend," Ada grinned and folded her arms. "While you may dress like a college kid..." She pointed toward Vivie's t-shirt, blue jeans, and tennis shoes. "You're no longer a spring chicken."

A wry smile crossed Vivie's lips. She *would* be sixty in July. That hardly seemed possible. And yet, it could explain a lot—her lack of energy, shortness of breath, the fatigue. "You're right. I'll stop on the way home and get some vitamins."

"Well, that's a start." Ada nodded to the candy wrapper and cup of tea on her desk. "You also need to make more of a conscious effort to eat right, cut back on some of your activities, and take better care of yourself."

"I know. I know." Vivie held up her hands.

"Go on home and get some rest," Okeke said. "I'll cover your afternoon classes."

"But—"

"No arguments, Vivie. Go home!"

•   •   •   •   •

Two months later, Professor Okeke stuck her head in Vivie's office. "You need to see about that cough."

"It's nothing," she responded, adjusting her mask. "April's pollen. A little worse than usual this year."

"Still," Ada said, "the doctor might be able to give you something."

After her colleague departed, a choking cough cut off Vivie's breath. Her eyes watered as she gasped for air.

Back at home, another coughing jag hit. Once the strangling sensation eased, Vivie made her way into the kitchen and prepared a cup of tea, letting the steam fill her head. As memories of her mother's coughing spells came to mind, she retrieved the packet from behind the armoire and carried it to the couch. Upon sitting down, Carmen leapt into her lap and began to knead. "Ah—my sweet—girl," she choked out.

•   •   •   •   •

Vivie sat in the doctor's office three weeks later, awaiting test results. After a brief knock, Dr. Maxwell entered—her chart in hand. Flipping through the pages, he asked, "How are you feeling today, Vivie?"

"Somewhat better, but I still experience periods of coughing and wheezing. What did the tests say?"

Dr. Maxwell tucked her chart under his arm. "They show a few anomalies, Vivie. It may be nothing more than a false positive. Or your chronic allergies transitioning into something more serious like asthma. I'd like to admit you to the hospital for a few days to run more tests."

Vivie gasped, her breath catching. A coughing jag hit. As she struggled to breathe, Dr. Maxwell quickly placed an oxygen mask over her face. Vivie lay back on the exam table, a myriad of thoughts whirling in her head.

Once her breathing eased, Dr. Maxwell peered down at her. "Better, Vivie?"

She nodded.

"Are you agreeable to the hospitalization?"

"How soon?"

"After witnessing this episode, today if possible."

She shook her head. "No. Not today. I need time to make some arrangements."

Back home, Vivie flopped in the armchair. Carmen leapt into her lap. "So many things to do—" she murmured to herself, her hand absently stroking the cat's fur. "I'll need to call Lea and tell her what's going on. See if she'll oversee the cats..." Vivie thought of her father, recalling his words, *Be brave, Vivie.* "Poppa?" she whispered, reaching for a spiral notebook. "Sometimes it's hard to be brave."

CHAPTER 36

June 24, 2004, 6:30 p.m.

Turning the page of Vivie's spiral notebook, my head drew back at the sight of the yellow post-it note adhered to the center of the next page. Scribbled across the boxy square were the words: 'To be continued...'

Not now, I immediately thought. Vivie's dead.

I glanced at the bedside clock. Two hours had passed since I had begun to read. At some point, Carmen had abandoned my lap and retreated to Vivie's pillow. From the doorway, Andromeda—a fat tortoiseshell—observed me with her luminous green eyes.

I continued to sit on the bed, stunned. Trying to absorb what I had just read. Was this fiction or fact? Despite our friendship, I knew little about Vivie—other than her passion for cats and her dedication to their rescue. And most of that was gleaned at the vet, early on—before I had even met her.

How I had resented Vivie at that first meeting, monopolizing the lone, veterinary receptionist while I was in a rush! Who would have ever thought that that awkward encounter would have developed into a lifelong friendship—now cut short.

In all those years, I had never asked her the circumstances of Pandora's rescue, nor Easter's. Well, too late now.

How could it be that a woman having tests for what presented as asthma would be diagnosed and dead a month later from lung cancer? Hell! She didn't even smoke! And why didn't the hospital see it back in November when they x-rayed her after the car wreck? It made no sense.

I scrutinized the tattered packet, now lying beside me on the bed. If this story were true, could it be the same package that Vivie's father gave her when they parted in Le Havre? Was this the packet she had safeguarded throughout her life?

My eyes then drifted to the antique armoire and dressing table that dominated the small space. I recalled my initial thought upon seeing them. How they had seemed out of place among the other furnishings. Expensive, handcrafted, and honed from quality materials rather than cheaply made and mass produced from inferior components.

Intrigued, I got down on my hands and knees and stuck my head under the table. Too dark. I pulled out my key chain flashlight. Illuminated in its beam was the childish drawing of a cat. Scrawled next to it was the name, 'Vivie.' I shook my head in disbelief.

My attention then returned to the packet. I picked it up and sat back down on the bed. As I pulled one end of the twine, the knot snapped, and a microburst of dust arose. Minuscule particles floated through the air. Carmen sneezed. Drawing back the paper, I sorted through the jumbled contents of yellowed documents with official-looking seals and fragile newspaper clippings. At first glance, all were unreadable. Then I stumbled across the notarized, attached translations, signed and initialed by Vivie. I gasped, not believing what I was reading. Wow! This was mind-boggling. My head was spinning. How had Vivie managed to keep *this* secret?

At the bottom of the pile was a small, cocoa-colored, cardboard folder. Inside, I found a photograph of Lofo, Csaky, Vivie, and Mae Degirdro dated August 1956, before their world was torn apart. If I had any doubts about the information I had just discovered, their formal dress in this old black-and-white photo dispelled them.

Still shaking my head in disbelief, I carefully slipped the papers back inside, then rewrapped the package and retied the twine. Tucking it under my arm, I made one last check on the cats and closed up the house for the night.

It was still daylight when I drove home. After feeding my cats, I sat outside on the porch in the fading light—still stunned about who Vivie actually was. The day's stress finally broke my resolve. Sobs wracked my body for what I had lost. For what Vivie had lost. For what the cats had lost.

Tears streamed down my face unchecked until a faint mew drew my attention.

I stilled, holding my breath. No furry faces peered out the window. Maybe I was just imagining things.

As my thoughts returned to Vivie, the shrill cry sounded again, then again. Where was it coming from? As the persistent mews intensified and increased in frequency, I tracked them to the side of the house behind the rhododendron bush. Beneath it, in the fading light, sat a tiny bundle of black fluff the size of a tennis ball.

As I eased toward it, the kitten bolted—vanishing in the gathering dusk. I scoured the bushes and flower beds, even the ditch, with no luck. My stomach churned. Where had the little mite gone? I was clueless, and the fall of night was not helping. Hating to give up, I reluctantly returned to the porch only to again hear the plaintive cries.

Back at the rhododendron bush, an ironic hour-long game of cat and mouse ensued until I finally discovered the kitten's bolt hole—the crawl space of the vacant house next door. Securing the vent, I set a trap inside and came back home to wait.

Upon entering the house, I spied the butcher-paper-wrapped package on the table and realization hit! There I had been sitting alone on the porch grieving Vivie when out of nowhere a *Feral. Black. Kitten.* appeared on my doorstep—obliterating my sorrow!

What were the odds? Infinitesimal!

There was only one explanation: VIVIE! This smacked of her. She knew my passion for black feral cats, particularly kittens! No doubt about it. Vivie had sent this tiny feline to comfort me in my time of sorrow. She had probably laughed at my antics in pursuit of this fur baby. It would be just like her.

I looked heavenward and sighed. "You never quit, do you, Vivie?"

•   •   •   •   •

About 6:00 a.m., I shined my flashlight into the dark crawl space. Inside the trap, the miniature black cat hissed and spit. Extremely feisty to be so young. Yes! Without a doubt, this kitten was *definitely* a gift from Vivie.

At the vet clinic later that morning, everyone listened as I revealed Vivie's refugee past and her closely guarded secret. They exclaimed over the gift of this feral kitten and asked, "What are you going to name it?"

Without hesitation, I answered, "Vivie."

EPILOGUE

June 28, 2004

"I was in a rush when I walked into the vet clinic that November evening in 1997 and found this tall, slender masked woman with curly, red hair monopolizing the one receptionist on duty with a conversation about hairstyles."

That Monday morning, I stood at the lectern of the Holy Ghost Catholic Church sharing my memories of Vivie at her memorial service. Four days had passed since her death. The church's sanctuary held a small gathering of those of us who knew and loved her, veterinary staff and their families, some university faculty and students, a few cat rescuers and colony caregivers, and a smattering of the curious.

Two days earlier, Vivie's obituary had appeared in *The Knoxville News Sentinel,* along with an accompanying article that revealed her closely guarded secret. The secret her Mama and Poppa had urged her to keep. The secret that had been hidden for all those years in a nondescript butcher-paper-wrapped packet. The secret that I learned the day Vivie died.

Beneath an old photograph of a man, woman, and two young girls in formal, royal dress was the following article:

HUNGARIAN COUNTESS DIES AT 60

Vivie Gabrielle Degirdro McNabb was born in Szombothely, Hungary, on July 12, 1944, to Countess Csaky and Count Lofo Degirdro. Hungary's communist occupation and the 1956 uprising forced the family to flee their homeland. Their escape led them through Austria, Switzerland and France where they faced fear, illness, starvation, and death. Eventually, Vivie was placed in the care of, and later adopted by, close family friends—Oswald McNabb, an international banker from Abilene, Texas, and his Viennese wife, Alice. While living with the McNabbs, Vivie traveled extensively. With doctorates in French Literature and Language from the Sorbonne, Vivie was working toward a doctorate in computer intelligence at the University of Tennessee, Knoxville when she passed away on June 24, 2004. Because her greatest passion was cat rescue, Vivie's fortune has been left in trust to care and find homes for her sixty remaining rescue cats. She was, and always will be, an inspiration to those who knew and loved her.

AUTHOR'S NOTE

Vivie's Secret is a fictionalized account loosely based on my friend Vivie Babb's 'secret life.' Originally, I wrote it as a picture storybook, but those who read the manuscript insisted that her story be told in this format. I resisted until the author Marissa Moss read it and concurred. Thus began my journey to craft Vivie's story with the few facts I had. I like to think that she guided me through the process since the majority of the novel was written as I sat in one of Vivie's chairs at her computer work station.

I encountered this incredible woman at Central Veterinary Hospital in the fall of 1997 when I learned I had adopted her rescue cat Satan, whom I renamed Pandora. Over the years, Vivie and I became friends and shared our rescue experiences. She entrusted me with her rescue cat Easter whom I renamed Lucrezia. Despite our friendship, it was not until the day she died that I learned that Vivie was a Hungarian refugee of the 1956 Uprising—and a wealthy countess.

Four hours after she passed away, I was sobbing on my porch when a black feral kitten appeared under my rhododendron bush. To this day, I firmly believe that Vivie sent her to me to assuage my grief. I named the kitten after her. A few days later, I adopted Vivie's favorite cat, Carmen.

I feel very blessed to have known this remarkable woman and to have shared her passion for feral cats and cat rescue. As her fictional obituary and her actual one aptly stated: Vivie was, and always will be, an inspiration to those who knew and loved her.

For information on TNR (Trap, Neuter, Release) and feral cats, please visit Alley Cat Allies: https://www.alleycat.org

REFERENCES

"ABC's of Feline CPR." The Cat Practice. Accessed: May 5, 2015.
http://www.thecatpracticepc.com/Guides/CPR.pdf

Aldridge, Leslie. "Famous Bars: No. 5: The Algonquin's Sedate Sitting Room," *Holiday*, April
1969, p. 110-111.

Barber, Noel. *Seven Days of Freedom: The Hungarian Uprising 1956.* New York: Stein and
Day, 1974.

Berkley, Ellen Perry. *Maverick Cats: Encounters With Feral Cats.* Shelburne, VT: New
England Press, 1987.

Berkeley, Ellen Perry. *TNR: Past, Present and Future: A History of the Trap-Neuter-Return
Movement.* Bethesda: MD: Alley Cat Allies, 2003.

Conard, Robert. "I Never Met A Hungarian Who Didn't Want to Learn—Memories of the
Traiskirchen Refugee Camp of 1956." *Hungarian Review,* November 28, 2013. György
Granasztoi. Accessed: November 14, 2015. *http://www.hungarianreview.com*

"CPR and Artificial Respiration for Kittens." PetMed, LLC. Accessed: May 5, 2015.
https://www.petmd.com/cat/emergency/common-
emergencies/e_ct_respiration_cpr_for_kittens

"East European Shepherd." *Russian Dog: Russian Dogs and World Dog Breeds.* Russian
Dog, 2015. Accessed March 21, 2015. http://www.russiandog.net/russian-german-
shepherd.html

"English Translation of 'Esti Dal', Kodály, Zoltán." *Musica.* The Virtual Choir Library: Music
International. Musica International. Accessed: April 30, 2015.
http://www.musicanet.org/en/texts/00/00043en.htm

*56 Stories: Personal Recollections of the 1956 Hungarian Revolution, A Hungarian
American Perspective.* Andrea Lauer and Edith K. Lauer, editors. Budapest: Kortárs, 2006.

Gadney, Reg. *Cry Hungary! Uprising 1956.* New York: Atheneum, 1956.

Gémes, Andreas. "Destruction of a Myth? Austria and the Hungarian Refugees of 1956-57." Institute for Human Sciences, 2013. Accessed: November 14, 2015. http://www.iwm.at

"The History and Traditions of the Algonquin Hotel." Accessed: April 16, 2015. http://www.algonquinhotel.com/newsroom/article/history-and-traditions-algonquin-hotel.

Korda, Michael. *Journey to a Revolution: A Personal Memoir and History of the Hungarian Revolution of 1956.* New York: Harper, 2006.

Leyhausen, Paul. *Cat Behavior: The Predatory and Social Behavior of Domestic and Wild Cats.* Shrewbury, MA: Garland Press, 1979.

"Montmartre Cemetery." Atlas Obscura, 2016. Accessed: March 9, 2016. http://www.atlasobscura.com/places/montmartre-cemetery

"Near Drowning in Cats." PetMed, LLC. Accessed: May 5, 2015. https://m.petmd.com/cat/emergency/accidents-injuries/e_ct_near_drowning

Orczy, Baroness. *Old Hungarian Fairy Tales.* The Baldwin Project: Bringing Yesterday's Classics to Today's Children. Yesterday's Classics, LLC. 2000-2015. Accessed May 6, 2015. http://www.mainlesson.com/display.php?author=orczy&book=hungarian&story=_contents&PHPSESSID=1db571bf1ea40e52fa26528a66da737f

"Pistol, Semi-Automatic-Russian Pistol M33 Tokarev 7.62mm SN# A133." *Springfield Armory Museum-Collection Record.* Accessed March 21, 2015. http://ww2.rediscov.com/spring/VFPCGI.exe?IDCFile=/spring/DETAILS.IDC, SPECIFIC=9693, DATABASE=objects,

Pryce-Jones, David. *The Hungarian Revolution.* New York: Horizon Press, 1970.

Russack, Thomas. "The Lions Still Roar at the Algonquin." January 17, 2013. *Better Buildings Blog.* Rand Engineering and Architecture, DPC. Accessed: April 16, 2015. https://randpc.com/blog/the-lions-still-roar-at-the-algonquin/

ACKNOWLEDGEMENTS

I would like to thank the following people who made *Vivie's Secret* a reality—

My master of research Richard Holt for unearthing information about Vivie's adoptive parents.

Alan May, Kevin Mallory, and April White with the Knox County Public Library System for acquiring my interlibrary loan requests.

Alice De almeida, Executive Assistant of the Algonquin Hotel, for information on their 1957 resident cat.

My writers' critique group who read the early drafts: Rhonda Rucker, Dick Willey, and Ann Schwartz. With an extra thank you to Dick who, when he read *Vivie's Secret* in its original picture book format, constantly nagged me to explore her story as a young adult novel.

Francine Fuqua and Jim Reca for their editorial consults.

My dear friend Debra Hutcheson and former Central Veterinary Hospital manager Jane Hogg for hoodwinking me into adopting Vivie's feral cat, Satan, which invariably led to my friendship with this incredible woman.

The Central Veterinary staff and doctors who worked with my rescue cats—and Vivie's—over the years, particularly Dr. Robert 'Bob' Black, Dr. Benny Ferrell, and Dr. Bill Martin.

And finally to my late friend and fellow cat rescuer Vivie Babb (1944-2004) without whom there would have been no secret and, therefore, no story to tell.

ABOUT THE AUTHOR

Born and raised in Knoxville, Tennessee, Terry Lee Caruthers is a special projects librarian with the Knox County Library System. She grew up surrounded by strong, female role models who nurtured her imagination and imbued her with a love of reading, writing, and storytelling. Terry continues to reside in South Knoxville where she shares her life with four rescue cats. *Vivie's Secret* is her first novel. She may be reached at: terry@terryleecaruthers-author.com

NOTE FROM THE AUTHOR

Word-of-mouth is crucial for any author to succeed. If you enjoyed *Vivie's Secret*, please leave a review online—anywhere you are able. Even if it's just a sentence or two. It would make all the difference and would be very much appreciated.

Thanks!
Terry

Thank you so much for reading one of our
Young Adult Fiction novels.
If you enjoyed our book, please check out our recommendation
for your next great read!

What the Valley Knows by Heather Christie

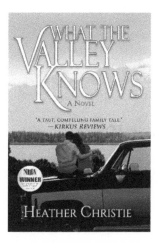

"A taut, compelling family tale."
-Kirkus Reviews

National Indie Excellence Awards- Young Adult Winner
Readers' Favorite Gold Medal Young Adult - Coming of Age
Maxy Awards Young Adult Winner

View other Black Rose Writing titles at
www.blackrosewriting.com/books and use promo code
PRINT to receive a **20% discount** when purchasing.

AUG 2020

CPSIA information can be obtained
at www.ICGtesting.com
Printed in the USA
LVHW011617090820
662758LV00003B/384